Sea Dreams

Aruda Hanna-Wilson

DEER HAWK ENTERPRISES
FLORIDA

SEA DREAMS

Cover design by:
Ray Polizzi

Layout by:
Aurelia Sands

Published by:
Deer Hawk Enterprises
www.deerhawkpublications.com
Library of Congress Control Number:
2007925038

Printed in the United States of America

Acknowledgement

Thanks must go to all my friends for their unwavering support and encouragement over all the years I worked on this book: Susan, Gail, Debbie and Bobbe, and the ladies of her reading group.

Special thanks to Aurelia Sands of Deer Hawk Enterprises, who gave me the final push to finish the darn thing.

In all things there is a beginning, a middle, and an end. For every ending, there is also a beginning. So the circle continues.

This is a story of change, a middle, an ending and a beginning:

An end to a thousand-year conflict;

An end to three hundred years of guardianship;

An end to a hundred years of betrayal by old allies;

A beginning of a new guardian;

A beginning of trust with new allies;

A beginning of a new friendship.

In the middle is the change. The middle is the story, and so, the circle continues.

Carta, like the Royal Family, is an illusion created by the singers of Lantia to deal with the leaders of their neighbors. The senior singers of each House spend six months a year in Carta. The strongest singer and her/his Family act as leader of the people. Thus, the Royal Family changes every five to ten years.

Johann Merchant (Scholar; House Merchant)

Chapter 1

Arianne, there are strangers in town. The mental message came from a tiny, curvaceous brunette with large, golden eyes.

The two young women lay on their backs staring blankly at the ceiling.

Arianne blinked twice slowly, stretched and stood up. *Patria, we are supposed to be studying.* Arianne thought back to her sister. *Stop listening to the gossip circulating in town or you will become as bad a snoop as our little sister.* Arianne pushed a lock of molten-silver hair back from her face. *Now concentrate on what you are supposed to be doing.*

But...

Patria, if it is something we need to know, our parents will notify us. Now, stop eavesdropping on other people's thoughts. You will get into trouble if Mother hears you snooping. I want you to accept the power I offer and move the painting on the wall.

Oh Arianne, come on, aren't you just the tiniest bit curious? Patria rolled to her side and watched her older sister.

Arianne stood straight, her silver eyes stern, and peered down her nose at Patria. “I am the A-Kiyama, Second Heir of the nation of Lantia. I am above such vulgar curiosity.”

She mimicked their tutor’s prim, nasal tones exactly. Patria shot her a quick glance and both young women laughed as Arianne dropped back on the large, four-poster bed that dominated the small sleeping chamber.

Patria sighed and began to concentrate. A slight humming broke the silence. The large picture of swirling blue and gold spirals on the far wall, tilted slightly.

Arianne smiled. *Very good, little sister. That took a lot of control. Mother will be pleased with you.*

What are you talking about? The darned thing barely moved. Patria objected.

Patria, why do you try so hard to deny your strength? One day, Lantia will need all her singers, and you have the potential to be one of our best. Arianne sighed. *The weakest singer among us could knock that picture off the wall. That is undisciplined power. You readjusted it slightly, that takes a tremendous amount of control and a delicate touch.*

I don’t care. I am tired of living my life training to fight a myth. Patria sent a sulky thought in reply to Arianne’s praise.

“Patria that is enough,” Arianne spoke aloud, closing her mind to her sister. “I wonder what our visitors want?” Arianne rolled onto her back and stared at the plain, undressed stone above her head.

"I thought we were above such vulgar curiosity." Patria teased from her position on the bed.

"Nobody ever comes into town through that gate. It makes this place look uglier than it is." Arianne wrinkled her nose and sat up.

"Arianne, nothing could make this place look uglier than it is. Carta is the epitome of ugliness; it proves to the whole world that Lantians are mad. Only corpses and mad men would live in a place like this voluntarily." Patria slid off the bed and walked across the naked stone floor toward the door, "At least Mother could have allowed us to have rugs in the bedrooms."

"Patria," Arianne's voice stopped the younger woman in the doorway.

"What?"

"We have the gardens. That is all we need. Carta is a place of labor and learning. It is not a place to relax."

"It's a museum, a place of penance. We have been on this world almost a thousand years. You think we would have forgiven ourselves one mistake made in anger and fear." Bitterness wove through Patria's words.

Arianne smiled, "We can't afford to forget because of what we are. We may never again act without thinking."

"Stop being so bloody perfect. This is me you are talking to, and I know better. You hate this whole charade our people play even more than I do." Patria leaned against the open door, "Ah

Arianne, it is true, isn't it? Our race is cursed with madness."

Arianne walked over and hugged her sister, "Go to your room and get ready for the rest of your lessons. Discuss what you feel with Teacher, it is something we all go through before we can become adults and accept the burden of being Lantian."

Arianne stared at the door long after her sister left, then, with a small sigh, she turned away to begin dressing for her official duties. *Accept the burden of being Lantian,* she thought sadly, *how hypocritical I have become. I tell my young sister to accept that which I cannot.*

*****

Two weeks later, Arianne stormed furiously into her mother's office. "No! Whatever it is, I'm not going to do it! All morning, I've been playing A-Kiyama for the public. I would like to have a little time for myself."

Since she couldn't slam the door, (two hundred pounds of stone and metal didn't slam well) or stamp her feet, (she knew from experience how much the stone floor would hurt), she settled for scowling at the two people in the room.

"Sit." Senior Singer Ilona of House Royale, and present leader of Lantia, was, as usual, groomed to perfection. Long, curly black hair slid neatly down her back. It, like everything around her, was under her total mental control. Ilona did not look up from the papers on the shiny, metal desk in front of her.

Arianne glanced in disgust at the only empty chair in the room. Like the other two, it was massive and carved from a solid block of stone.

"Mother--" Arianne objected.

"No." Ilona interrupted. "This is business. Your forbidden walk to the sea can wait."

Arianne, her eyes wide, sat. "How did you know?"

"I know everything that goes on in my realm," Ilona replied grimly. "Arianne, you know that our people have good reasons to distrust those who dwell in the oceans, yet still you insist on communing with them."

"Part of the fault was ours." Arianne objected.

"Through our greed for knowledge, we created a nightmare of hate and terror that came from the sea. It destroyed our home world and millions of our people. We accept the responsibility for that." Ilona agreed. "Yet, in this world, the sea dwellers, whom we trusted, stole our most precious possession: the Life Stone of our people."

"Why?"

Ilona lifted her head, her dark, gold eyes showing her surprise. "Why what?"

"Why did the Feltan steal our Life Stone?"

"Nobody has ever asked that question." Ilona sighed. "It doesn't matter why they stole the stone. What does matter is that you are jeopardizing your family by spending so much time down by the sea."

"I have always been careful. Most of the time, I just enjoy sitting by the water. I have never spoken to a sea dweller and I didn't think anyone knew." Arianne whispered.

Ilona raised one perfectly arched eyebrow, "Secrets cannot be kept long in Lantia. What would you do if I commanded you to stop?"

Arianne kept silent. She felt a shiver run down her spine as she glared at her mother.

"That's what I thought," Ilona said softly. "You couldn't stop going down to the shore. One day without visiting that place and you feel suffocated. Three days would drive you mad." She sighed. "Am I right?"

"No!" Arianne objected. "I've been on training maneuvers with the Home Guard for much longer than a week. I miss it, but not to the extent you just described."

Ilona studied her eldest daughter for a long moment. "Arianne, do you think your sister Patria would make a good A-Kiyama?"

Arianne took a deep breath, trying to quell the pain deep in the pit of her stomach. *How could Mother do this to me?* She wondered, as she struggled for the composure to answer her mother's question.

"Have I failed in my duties?" she asked. *This is not happening. It is a bad dream and soon I will awaken from it.*

"No. You would do well as senior singer for our house if anything ever happened to Rolto. However, we have one major problem. How long do you think our house would exist if your love for the ocean became common knowledge?"

Arianne frowned, biting her lower lip to contain her tears. “Patria will be almost useless as Commander of the Home Guard. It will take years to train her,” Arianne ignored the tiny voice of her conscience. “She does not have the self-confidence for the job.” As a sop to her protesting conscience, Arianne reluctantly added. “She does have a fine sense of justice and fair-play. So I suppose she would serve our brother, Bri-Kiyama Rolto, the first heir, and the people well. Are you sending me away?”

“Yes.” Ilona glanced at her husband, Arthur. His long, thin face was solemn, and his silver eyes were angry. “Your father disagrees with my decision. We have argued over our options for days, but I am senior singer and I have to do what is best for the people. I cannot allow my personal feelings to interfere with my duty to Lantia.”

Ilona nodded and leaned back in her chair. “Two weeks ago, delegates from a country called Alsia arrived in Carta. They are looking for a wife for their prince. We have given them no answer yet. I hoped that your father, using his resources as head of our nation’s security, could find out something about them.”

“Father, what did you discover?” While Arianne had no respect for the way her parents treated their marriage, she did respect the way they performed their duties to Lantia.

Ilona answered before Arthur could say a word. “Nothing. All of your father’s contacts swear they have never heard of Alsia.”

Arianne ignored her mother and spoke directly to her father, “Father, did you consult the Icina?”

Running his fingers through his thinning black hair, Arthur smiled sadly. “The spirit of this land had little she could tell me. She only knew that trouble was brewing in Alsia. She said, without a wife both the prince and the land would die.” Arthur frowned.

“When I asked her where Alsia was and why we had never heard of it before, the Icina laughed. She thinks you would be the perfect bride for the young prince.”

Ilona leaned forward. “Arianne, something is wrong with this entire situation. Lady Colsa has very strong mind blocks, and while she is a guest in the palace, I won’t try to break through them.”

“Lantian honor can be such a burden at times,” Arianne interrupted dryly.

“Do not say such a thing, even in jest,” Ilona admonished her. “As A-Kiyama, you know very well that one day Lantian honor will be all that stands between this world and destruction. I sense something is very wrong in the land of Alsia, and the Icina verifies it. Lady Colsa cares only that the young woman is of royal blood and that she is docile.” Ilona smiled at her daughter.

“Me!” Arianne laughed incredulously. Both of her parents smiled.

“Well, they know even less of us than we do of them.” Ilona shrugged carelessly. “Anyone who comes to Lantia looking for a docile woman is either mad or ignorant of our people. This woman is not mad, at least not in any way that I can sense."

Ilona leaned forward, her golden eyes were almost brown with emotion, "I need someone in Alsia whom I can trust to do what is best for Lantia. I want to know about this mysterious country and how they heard of us in the first place. You are the only one I can trust to find out what threat, if any, they hold for Lantia."

Arianne smiled bitterly. "It also solves the problem of my dangerous tendencies becoming a threat to House Royale."

Ilona nodded. "As I said earlier, it solves all of our problems."

"What if the Alsians object to me once they discover that I'm not the docile young miss they expected?"

"By the time they find out your true character, it should be too late for them to do anything at all. I have confidence in you. After all, you have survived the games played in Lantia for twenty years."

Ilona absently brushed her hair back from her face, "Arianne, I know how you feel about my marriage to your father. Remember that most of our houses have arranged marriages, especially between singers. Once you have fulfilled your duty to produce heirs, you will have the freedom to do as you wish."

Arianne shook her head. "I take promises seriously. If I make a vow to marry this unknown prince, I will keep it."

"As you will." Ilona shrugged, glanced at the papers on her desk, then looked up at her daughter. "I will notify the Alsian delegate today. You will meet them at dinner, then we will name Patria as A-Kiyama, Second Heir, in your stead." Ilona bit her lip, and smiled sadly, "Thank you."

"I am not doing this for you, Mother, but for my brother, my House, and my people," Arianne replied bitterly as she left the room.

Arianne smiled at the two young guards who saluted as she passed through Carta's front gates. Returning their salutes, she walked with long, unhurried strides. In her hands, she carried a small herb basket. If anyone asked her destination, she would tell them she was heading for the groves to collect fresh herbs and wildflowers. The guards did not stop her. They were used to their commander's daily trips.

Once in the small stand of trees growing near Carta, she quickly filled her basket, paying no attention to the peaceful beauty of the place or to what plants she picked.

You are in a hurry today. The soft whisper brushed Arianne's mind.

Greetings, Icina, Arianne set her basket under the large tree growing in the middle of the glade.

Why do you hurry so, Little One? Can you take no time to speak with me? The Icina asked.

My parents are sending me away. Arianne leaned against the tree where the spirit of the land resided.

A small branch bent and brushed her cheek. *This bothers you.* It was a statement; the Icina of Lantia knew Arianne better than Ilona did. *Listen to me well. I told your father to send you to Alsia. It is a land far away from here where the style of life is very different from yours. However, if you are strong and faithful to your word, you will find great joy in Alsia.*

“I will miss you and the sea.” Arianne whispered.

I will set my song in your mind. My people will call you Wind Speaker. Whenever you wish to speak with me, sing my song into the wind and I will answer. No matter where you go, I will always be a part of you.

Arianne closed her eyes while she listened to the small breezes that whispered in and around the glade. *Icina, what do you know about Alsia?*

Are not all the spirits of this world but one part of the Whole? This is what your people taught us when they first came to our part of the world. They sang, we listened, joined, and found peace. Now, it is time that you take the same song to the spirits of Alsia.

The breeze echoed the tree’s sigh. Y*our father asked me if you would be safe. I will tell you what I told him. The spirits of that land are troubled. They have filled their songs with pain. Whatever ails Alsia may be too great for your power to heal, but you must try or our world will suffer.*

What do you know about the people who live in that place? Arianne asked, stroking the tree gently.

I know nothing of humans, the Icina answered haughtily.

Arianne chuckled. *You know everything about the Lantians*.

Well, yes, but only because they tell me. Not all humans are as friendly to my kind as the Lantians.

After lingering another moment in the comforting shadow of the large tree, Arianne moved away to continue her journey.

No one would recognize her as the A-Kiyama if they saw her now: Her hair was completely covered and her eyes were solemn. She wore a look of resignation on her long, dark face. She was free for now. This would be her last visit to the one place in all of Lantia she felt at home. When she reached the cliffs, she stood for a moment looking at the small beach below. She removed her dress, hitched up the skirt of her short shift, and started the descent to the beach. It saddened her to think this might be her last trip.

I am going to miss this, Arianne thought.

Bending her knees to absorb the shock of her landing, she closed her eyes and jumped the last foot to the soft, white sand. Catching her breath and waiting to see if anyone had followed her, Arianne knelt close to the cliff's face. When she was sure she was alone, she relaxed and faced the ocean.

Soon, she would be leaving her homeland and this beach. Now, she just wanted to spend time enjoying the peace it brought to her. This was her favorite place to relax and escape from the pressures of court life. Here, she could shed the many costumes she wore: the elaborate gowns and headdresses the Elder Houses expected of a royal princess; the battle armor of the House Guards who served the queen; and the coarse, white robe she wore when she acted as mediator among the common people of Lantia.

In this spot, she could be just Arianne with the same hopes and dreams of any other woman her age. She could forget that she was a daughter of House Royale, and the A-Kiyama, the second strongest singer of her generation. Here, she could sit in the warm sand, watch the ever-changing rhythm of the ocean, feel the moist breeze on her skin, and listen to the voice of the waves.

Arianne smiled, her eyes filled with wonder at the scene before her. *How could my people fear this wonderful enchantment?*

"My mother has signed a marriage contract for me." Arianne said to the waves. She always talked to them; they always listened. Sometimes they brought her gossip from places where the rivers flowed. Today, however, the waves just chuckled. Arianne waited a few minutes, but they said nothing more.

"It's all very well for you to laugh," she grumbled. "Your parents aren't selling you for a few pieces of lumber to some savage prince who has never even been to the palace."

She slowly walked along the hard packed sand where water and land met. The warm ocean waves caressed her feet and ankles, as if in sympathy.

Arianne smiled softly. “How I will miss you, I am probably going to some inland kingdom where I will never see you again. Is this prince handsome? Is he cruel or kind? Is he old, and fat?” She tilted her head, listening for an answer. “So you have nothing to say? Surely you must have some gossip from the rivers that wander through the area?”

The waves made no reply. “I don’t want to go, but I am a singer, and my duty is to my people and this world. I have no say in my future. My Lady Mother has decreed that it is my duty, and I must do whatever the senior singer commands.

“My wishes have no bearing in the matter. This prince is most likely old, fat, and smelly. They are asking me to give up everything and offering nothing in return. My father gave up his House to bed a senior singer for a few years. Soon, I too will have no House; I will be the king’s wife.”

Arianne listened to the silence. Her tears caressed her checks as softly as the waves stroked her feet.

“I am in no mood to play with you today,” she snarled, kicking at the sand. Throwing back her head she cried at the horizon, “I wish you to witness what I now swear; I will not play my parents’ game, I will rule beside this unknown king, or neither of us will rule. I am a warrior and a leader, I could be the leader of this land, yet my mother wishes me to play the demure maiden.”

The waves continued chuckling, and after a long moment, Arianne joined in with a brief, sad laugh. "You are right. It will be amusing and challenging to see how long I can keep up the pretense."

With a small sigh, Arianne decided that she would not ruin her last day here with useless worries. She removed her shift, and lay naked on the soft, warm sand. The gentle sounds around her calmed Arianne's mind and relaxed her body.

Some days she could almost hear the deep ocean voice, could almost understand what it said. Today was one of those frustrating days. Why, she wondered idly, could she understand the chatter of the surface waves so clearly, and not the speech of the deep ocean?

It was almost dark when she put her shift back on and started the dangerous climb from the beach. Arianne looked out on the ocean for a moment, then picked up her basket, and ran back to the palace. She slipped in through a side door, and walked slowly up the stairs to her room.

The minute she walked into the small sitting room she shared with her sisters, Helen, her youngest sister, started talking. "Aren't you excited, Arianne? The agents of the forest prince will be at dinner tonight for the formal betrothal ceremonies. Not their prince, though, I hear he never leaves Alsia."

Arianne glanced about the small sparsely furnished room and sighed. *I could strangle Helen, or maybe rip her tongue out and throw it out the window.* She thought, as she picked up a book. *No, I am supposed to have more control than that.*

Arianne sat in one of the large, stone chairs. Its thin cushion did little to protect her from hardness of the seat. Helen, with her winsome smile, her chubby cheeks, her innocent brown eyes, and her perfectly-groomed straight, black hair, always knew what was going on in the palace. Helen, the little sneak, was always listening at keyholes, hiding in shadows, and prying into people's deep thoughts whenever she thought she could get away with it. Arianne suspected it was Helen who told their mother about her frequent trips to the beach.

Helen glanced around the room and gave Arianne a phony smile, "Our mother says the woods are the hardest and most fragrant she has ever seen. The Alsians claim that many rare medicinal plants grow wild in their land," Helen paused, and watched Arianne through narrowed eyes.

"Where are these forests?" Tiny Patria, the middle sister and peacemaker, asked.

"Nobody knows; we don't even know if they really exist," Helen added spitefully, "You are commanding an exceptional dowry, sister."

"Helen, don't tease Arianne. At least she is getting away from here. Soon, she will have her own land to rule," Patria interrupted, then softly added, "You are lucky, Arianne."

Arianne slammed her book shut, and frowned. "Lucky compared to whom?" She stood up, "I wish we knew more about this prince and his forests. Rolto should be home instead of out playing games on the border."

Helen giggled. "Rolto can't help you. He is only the heir. Mother has decided that we need the trade your marriage will bring. Who knows? Maybe the trees will talk to you," she shuddered theatrically, "The way you claim that disgusting body of water out there does."

Patria glanced in horror at her two sisters, "Helen, shut up! You have gone too far. How dare you accuse Arianne of such disgusting behavior? You are a rotten little sneak and a troublemaker."

Helen shot Patria a glance of pure malice, "You think Arianne is sooo perfect, don't you? Well, she isn't. I'm not the only sneak in this family, only you are too stupid to see that."

"Helen that's enough out of you!" Arianne turned to Patria and added, "Patria, you know Helen's spitefulness. Be careful of her, and guard your back whenever she is in the same room."

Helen's golden cheeks flushed as she stared at her two older sisters, "You both hate me, well that's fine, 'cause I hate both of you! I'm glad Mother found out what you were hiding, Arianne. I'm glad she is sending you away. Now, I won't have to live with your fake holier-than-everyone-else, I'm-the-adult-and-you-are-the-child, attitude any longer. You call me a sneak, but we both know who the real sneak in this family is."

Arianne smiled grimly. "So, it was you who told Mother about me. It's gained you nothing. Mother knows what you are and she doesn't trust you. The next marriage she arranges will be yours."

"Arianne, what did you tell Mother about me?" Helen cried.

"I didn't have to tell Mother anything. Everyone in the palace is willing to tell her what a spiteful little cat you are."

"You are only saying that because you are angry about leaving home. It's not my fault that Mother chose you to go." Helen objected.

Arianne ignored her youngest sister and stared out the window. She wished at least one window in the palace overlooked the cliffs, but the people of Lantia chose to ignore the mighty ocean that pounded on their doorstep. They owned no fishing fleet, no merchant Navy, and traded with no country whose people sailed the waters, which was probably why Ilona was so eager for her eldest daughter to leave home. Arianne, aware that she was being unfair to her mother, sighed softly and walked back to her chair.

"My Ladies, it is time for the evening meal," a page outside the door, announced.

Arianne opened the door, and smiled at the boy. His father was one of the queen's most trusted advisors. All of the young people who worked Carta were students or the children of government officials stationed in the town. No Lantian lived in Carta unless forced by duty to the country.

The three young women walked slowly down the massive stone stairs and across a wide hall. The large, drafty room where her parents held council meetings doubled as the dining hall while there were guests present. Arianne hid a small smile as she glanced at the shivering representatives of Alsia's prince.

The queen, her husband, and the elders of the twelve Houses of Lantia glanced up from the papers they were studying and smiled in greeting when the young page announced the sisters' arrival. The page stared at the paper in his hand; then, with a frown, announced, "The A-Kiyama, Patria, the Royal Princess, Arianne, the Royal Princess, Helen."

Arianne was very pleased at the look of disappointment that flashed across Helen's face.

Patria, tears in her eyes, turned to Arianne. "I'm sorry," she whispered. "I don't want to be A-Kiyama."

Arianne took her arm. "Yes, you do. Not only that, but you will make a very good A-Kiyama. I told our mother so, and you know that I am never wrong."

I can do this, Arianne whispered in her heart. *I can pretend that it doesn't matter. I can support Patria before outsiders, and the elders of the other Houses. Smoke and fire, why does it have to hurt so much?*

As the three princesses stepped into the room, Patria covered her mouth with her hand to hide her grin and Arianne smiled gently, her eyes lowered to hide the tears she refused to shed.

The representatives of the forest prince stood at the head of the long table. They were tall, with complexions ranging from light to dark olive green. Their slanted eyes were the color of emeralds, and their long, narrow faces were framed with short, greenish-black hair. The men and the women both wore dark green breeches with long, belted tunics of a lighter green. They bowed to Arianne as she walked past and she gave them a small smile. The Alsians were an attractive group of people, and though they looked nothing like the Lantians, Arianne liked the way they dressed. It was much more sensible than the clothes she wore.

The massive stone conference table was piled high with fruits, raw vegetables, and freshly-baked bread. Arianne grinned inwardly. Her mother was going all out to impress the strangers: She was playing the not-too-bright, but unthreatening savage, very well. If these people bought that, well, she had a meek, gentle daughter to sell them. Arianne's grin slid off her face and she slammed her mental defenses into place more firmly than usual. The elders were staring at her, avidly trying to catch any stray thought she might let drift to the surface of her mind. They all knew better than using a mental probe in Ilona's presence.

Arianne didn't pay much attention to the food, she was much too busy listening to the strangers' words and answering questions the elders of her own people were asking.

The elder of House Gemi directed his question to Arianne, "Why send you, instead of Patria or Helen?"

"Patria, gentle soul that she is, would die away from home. Helen would cause a war in a week." Arianne smiled gently. She noticed the alert silence of the visitors as she answered. "That leaves me."

When pressed for more information, she shook her head slightly. The elders knew better than to discuss Lantian business before strangers. “Ask my mother. If she wishes you to know any more of the details, she will tell you.” Mentally she sent a swift, terse warning to her people.

Ilona smiled at Arianne, then passed the stack of papers down the table for her to read.

A tall woman raised an eyebrow at Ilona, “You allow your daughter to read her marriage contract?” Her smile did not reach her eyes.

Ilona helped herself to one of the large platters on the table before her, “Her marriage, and her contract. I wish her to see what her worth to your people is.” Ilona waved at the guests’ empty plates. “Please help yourselves. We are not very formal here.”

The woman tightened her mouth, “I noticed. It took you over a week to even acknowledge our presence in your town.”

Ilona raised her perfect eyebrows, “Really? Have you been here that long? I didn’t realize. If you had notified us that your party was going to visit, I would have set aside a block of time to see you.” She gave a delicate shrug, “As it is, I think we have agreed to deal with you quite quickly. My people really do dislike quick decisions.”

In unison, the elders either took a drink of water or hid their faces in their salad bowls. Patria and Helen sat with wide-eyed innocence that made Arianne proud, while Arianne hid her smile.

“I dislike sending my eldest daughter off with no knowledge of where she is going. Could you give us more detail about where your country is?" Arianne's father spoke in his deep, quiet voice.

The leader of the Alsian delegate smiled spitefully, "Really? Maybe we can add a few more tons of that medicinal herb you were so impressed with, a few extra acres of trees, and some spices. Do you think that will help you overcome your distaste?"

There was a moment of stunned silence.

Shield! The terse order came from Ilona.

The Lantians at the table felt the mental shield Ilona threw around the visitors and the blast that Arthur sent toward the tall strangers. Six of the eight paintings in the hallway fell to the floor.

Arianne laid the papers she was reading on the table before her. *Father, I am impressed.*

Arthur shrugged and smiled, his anger gone as quickly as it appeared. *This is why I am not the senior singer. I lack proper control of my emotions.*

"Is it a long journey to your home?" Ilona took a delicate bite of one of the fruits at the table, then studied it carefully.

"What does that have to do with the point being discussed?" The tall woman sneered.

Ilona smiled and nodded to Arthur. He grinned as the woman's plate slid off the table into her lap. The young page, struggling to contain his mirth, rushed over to the woman and tried to help her clean up the mess. His clumsy attempts were more hindrance than help.

"I do apologize, er...Lady Calsid, this land is very unstable. Both people and things around here have a tendency to fall unexpectedly." Arthur's voice was sympathetic.

"My name is Colsa," The woman snarled, "If this area is so unstable, why don't you move somewhere else?"

Ilona opened her golden eyes wide, "This is our home. It may not suit some people, but it is ours. Material things are not important to us, nor are outward shows of opulence. We enjoy a simple life."

Lady Colsa smiled. "Be careful. If your land is this unstable, you may lose it."

Ilona looked at her and laughed. Even Arianne smiled. The elders grinned with looks of pure delight on their faces.

When she caught her breath, Ilona said briskly. "Do not make statements that could be construed as threats. You really don't want to anger us. Now, sit down and enjoy your meal."

The meal passed quitely after that. When they were through eating, the spokeswoman for the Alsians stood. "Queen Ilona, we would request Princess Arianne be ready to accompany us back to Alsian's forest in three days."

Ilona glanced up, "What is the rush, Lady Colsa? My eldest child and heir will be returning to Carta in a month. He will want to bid his sister farewell. We also have to create Arianne's wardrobe. We will not send our daughter naked to your prince's court."

"Lady, our way is not yours. We will supply the princess with the proper clothes. The styles you wear would not be suitable to the forests." Colsa smiled. "As for waiting a month, I am afraid that is impossible. We have already spent longer here than we planned."

Queen Ilona frowned. "Two weeks. You will grant that, or you will leave empty-handed."

Lady Colsa stared at the queen, and Arianne felt the woman's tension. "Queen Ilona, we will leave in ten days with or without your daughter."

Ilona slowly nodded, a smile hidden deep in her eyes. "It will be as you request." Arianne looked at her mother in surprise, then stared bitterly at the far wall, ignoring her youngest sister's snicker.

Arianne knew then that Ilona had not been totally honest with her. Yes, her fascination with the sea was a factor in her mother's decision but it was not the entire reason. What was the queen up to?

Arianne caught her mother's eye just as Lady Colsa, a smug smile on her face, exited the dining area. Ilona smiled and winked at Arianne before she too, left. Under the table Arianne stamped her foot in frustration, then winced in pain.

Mother gives me more credit than I deserve, she thought, ignoring the surprised questions that assaulted her mind from the elders. She merely strengthened her mental shields. *I don't have the first clue what she is planning. Why did Mother specify that the marriage conform to ancient Lantian rituals, as well as Alsian laws? Has Mother explained to the Alsians exactly what those rituals are? According to the agreement I have just signed, I will be officially married as soon as I step on Alsian territory. What is my mother up to? I need some fresh air to clear my senses, a short walk in the garden so that I can think.*

Arianne bowed to the elders still sitting at the table and walked briskly outside to the castle's garden. She took a deep breath of the fresh night air, then sent a swift message to her people, letting them know she was not available for conversation tonight. She walked to one of the many benches scattered throughout the area, and smiled as she studied the haphazard way everything grew. No one thought about nice neat rows. Those were for farms and farmers. When you were stationed in Carta, you needed the soothing effect of natural growth; of wildness; of no restraints.

She lay on her back in the tall grass and stared at the stars. Which of them, she wondered, was the home world?

"Princess Arianne, I am Colsa, High Priestess of Alsian's groves." Arianne jumped slightly and scowled.

W*hy did this woman follow me out here?*

Lady Colsa sat primly on the bench closest to where Arianne lay and continued speaking "I wish to welcome you as our prince's chosen. I also wish to reassure you. You have nothing to fear: You will be honored in our lord's realm."

Arianne stared at the sky, *How did this creature find me here?*

"Lady Colsa, I've no choice. I must do as my mother commands. Madam, where is your realm? What does your prince look like, and how is it that no one has ever heard of the Alsian forest before now?"

Lady Colsa smiled, “So many questions.” She murmured. “Come to us in the morning. We will outfit you for the trip to Alsia. Soon, you will have the answers to all your questions.”

“Wait, Lady Colsa. How did your prince know about us? I mean, why did he offer for one of us?”

“Ahh, but stories of the beautiful Lantian princesses have surely traveled the length and breadth of the land, Princess,” Colsa said softly.

Arianne glanced quickly at the woman, suspecting mockery. When she saw none, she snorted inelegantly. “What beauty?”

The other woman looked seriously at the young princess.

“My people will see beauty in you, child, even if you are unaware of it.”

Arianne stood as Colsa walked away to join the others. *Why*, she wondered, *did the woman lie to answer such a simple question?*

Nobody outside Lantia had ever seen any of Ilona’s daughters. They did not deal with the few merchants who passed through Carta, and none of them had ever ridden to battle at their brother’s side. How then, could Colsa’s prince have heard about them? Arianne walked slowly through the castle, ignoring all those she passed on the way. When she reached her room, she locked the door behind her and sat on her bed to think.

She had never been considered a beauty; she didn’t have the golden skin and black hair so highly prized in Lantia. She was taller than most of Lantia’s men. Her skin was the color of old bronze and she had more muscles than curves. Next to her petite, curvaceous mother and sisters, Arianne felt like a skinny giant.

Her old nurse used to tell her that she and Rolto were throwbacks to their Feltan ancestors, who helped her people at first, then betrayed them. The Feltan had silver hair, dark skin, and eyes of clear crystal that reflected all the colors of the rainbow. When they were angry, their eyes turned dark and cloudy.

Other bronze-colored people lived in Lantia, especially in the Elder Houses, but she and her father were the only ones with the strange, silver eyes. Most Lantians had eye colors ranging from pure black to a brownish-yellow. Arianne learned early that the color of her hair and eyes set her apart. Her brother, Rolto, had the same color hair that she did, but he kept his head shaved. She smiled and admitted that was not an option for her. What would the Lady Colsa have to say, Arianne wondered, when she saw the knee length mop of bright silver that adorned her head?

The next morning, Arianne, silver hair flowing freely around her, walked into the sewing room. She glanced around curiously. The Alsians had made this room their own in the short time they were here. They scattered brightly-colored rugs across the floor like leaves in the Icina's grove. Vivid bolts of cloth lay piled carelessly in one corner. Their sewing materials were neatly set on the small, stone table in the middle of the room. Arianne touched the soft materials in wonder. She was accustomed to the stiff brocades of court wear or the coarse material that was everyday wear. She had never felt anything like the supple cloth the Alsians wore.

Six hours later, when the two seamstresses set her free, Arianne was tired, hungry, and frustrated. No matter how casual and comfortable the Alsian's clothes looked, getting them made was just as exhausting as the most formal court outfit. She liked the way her new clothes looked and felt. The breeches gave her a sense of freedom. Climbing the cliffs in those clothes would be easy. Arianne smiled and relaxed. Maybe everything was going to be all right. If nothing else, she would be comfortable.

Now, if only the prince was acceptable, young, and handsome, she thought dreamily and almost laughed aloud at her fantasies. What did it matter? She must prepare herself to accept whatever the future brought.

With a sigh of relief, Arianne hurried to the door before someone decided to measure her for something else.

Lady Colsa's voice stopped Arianne at the door. "Did you think to shock us, Princess?"

"I wanted you to see exactly what you were getting in me. I'm not beautiful," Arianne said quietly, with downcast eyes. She was not yet ready to reveal the true color of her eyes, nor the power they held. Arianne distrusted Lady Colsa's smiles.

"I see," the older woman nodded.

Arianne suddenly understood that Lady Colsa thought her downcast eyes were a sign of modesty.

"Little One, all sorts of beauty are in the world. What one person might find terrifying, another might find beautiful. Do you not agree?" Lady Colsa smiled. "I know all about your people," she said softly. "I know they fear the sea, and I know why."

Arianne tensed as Lady Colsa led her to a chair. A warning flashed in her mind. This Colsa was no friend.

"Long ago, before your people came to this world, another race, the Feltan, lived here. These people, who divided their time between Earth and Sea." Lady Colsa smiled as she saw Arianne's start of surprise. "Lived peacefully with your people for many years, intermarrying into the noble houses, and holding positions of power.

"Soon, however, some of your people became jealous of the First Ones, and plotted to destroy them. The Feltan had many talents that your people didn't have. One of their lesser skills was the ability to see into men's hearts.

"So they learned of the plot against them, and late one night, they swam into the sea, leaving all their worldly goods behind them. As they left, they sent a terrible storm to lash the coast of the land. They killed hundreds of your people and destroyed most of the rich homes in Carta. That was another of the Feltan skills. They could control the elements. The Feltan have never returned to Lantia, or any other land. They spend all their time roaming the oceans of our world."

"You know much of our history, Lady Colsa." Arianne murmured, hiding her anger. *How dare this woman accuse my people of treachery?* "Did the Feltan tell you of our shared history?" Arianne wanted to know how this stranger had gained so much incorrect information about Lantian history.

"We of Alsia are close cousins to the Feltan and we are the second oldest nation of this world. We are not newcomers, like your people. Those of us who sail the oceans are still in contact with the Feltan. They told us most of it, we could guess at what was left unsaid.

"We have decided that it is time to deal again with the Golden People of Lantia. This marriage agreement is our first step in that direction. We don't judge by your standards. To us you are beautiful. You are the child of our cousin, the Feltan. The color of your hair and your eyes remind us of sunlight glinting on the sea, don't be afraid that we will find you strange; we won't. Now, run along and make your farewells, for in less than a week, we leave."

Arianne was thoughtful as she left the sewing room. Lady Colsa did not know as much about the Lantians as she thought. Colsa did not know that the new people, who later became the Lantians, had powerful telepathic gifts even before they met the Feltan. Nor did she know that intermarriage between the Lantians and the Feltan had strengthened those same powers.

Would Lady Colsa have come to Lantia looking for a bride if she had known that mind control and telepathy were common among the children of that land?

Arianne smiled wryly as she walked up the stairs to the Royal Family's living area. Lantians had never controlled the elements, instead, they made the spirits of the land and the air, friends and allies; a part of their family.

Privately, she thought that Lady Colsa would have profited by speaking to the enemies of the Lantians. She would have learned that, among those who had the misfortune of meeting a Lantian battle group, terms such as witch, warlock, and even demon, were commonly used. The families of Lantia, especially House Royale, studied hard to improve their heritage. Lantians worshipped no gods but knowledge. To them, knowledge was power, and power was every Lantian's goal. Arianne stopped walking and looked back down the stairs to the room she left the Alsian delegate, and smiled.

Beware, Colsa, soon your power will be mine. A feeling of peace drifted through her. *Yes, I will rule Alsia, and Lantia will have an ally when the darkness comes again.*

There was a bounce in her step as Arianne walked quickly toward her mother's rooms. She must tell the senior singer what she had learned today.

"Mother, may I enter?" Arianne whispered as stood outside her mother's door.

Ilona opened the door to her private chambers. "What bothers you, Daughter?"

Arianne entered the room and closed the door behind her. She walked to her mother's cluttered dressing table and sat on the low stone bench in front of it, her back to the mirror. Quickly, she repeated the conversation she'd had with Lady Colsa. Ilona frowned as she sat on her narrow bed and listened to her daughter. When Arianne was through, Ilona leaned back, her eyes closed.

"It is your decision, Arianne. You know why you must leave Lantia." Ilona paused. "The Lady Colsa requested a quiet, biddable, young princess. We named you and she asked no further questions. She knows nothing of your true self. If you wish, we will cancel this contract and find some other way to safeguard our people and our House. I will not send you into an evil situation if you object."

Arianne was silent for a minute. Her eyes narrowed as she studied the only decoration in her mother's austere chambers. A large painting, full of bright, swirling colors, covered the entire wall behind her mother's bed. Arianne's lips twitched upward. That picture had always given her a headache, and she could never figure out what it was supposed to represent.

She shook her head and brought her mind back to the conversation, "Lady Colsa lies," she said slowly, "However, the Icina claims Alsia needs me. Mother, Lady Colsa speaks as if she, and not the Prince, rules the land. Who is she?"

"She claims to be the high priestess of their religion, but you are right; she speaks as one with great power." Ilona smiled faintly. "We Lantians do not understand the power that religious leaders wield in other lands."

"No. It is more than that." Arianne shook her head. "I am going to Alsia, and if I find out that their prince is just a figurehead, then I will give them a ruling princess. I will take Colsa's power from her and send her whimpering back to her temple. I do not like a liar, unless, of course, it's me." Arianne grinned at her mother.

Ilona laughed softly. "So sweet and docile, I am proud of you, my daughter."

Arianne stared at her mother in surprise, then joined in her laughter.

Ilona stood and reached out to Arianne. "I agree with you, my daughter," she said seriously. "Lady Colsa has a dark core. She thinks you are unaware that the power of the Feltan runs strong in your blood. If you are not careful, she will try to use that power for her own gain. Use your mind-control and play a learning game. When the time is right, strike with deadly accuracy.

"Remember, always face your enemy so they can't take you by surprise. Gain power over Colsa and her people by learning all you can about them. If you need aid, send a call to us on the wind; the Icina has promised she will relay your messages to us promptly."

Ilona stood and walked over to where Arianne sat, "We must discuss another subject. If you are going to align yourself with this unknown prince, then you must be aware that the Alsians will probably want your marriage consummated when you reach their country." Ilona held up her hand to silence Arianne. "Wait until I am through, then you may speak. Sharing your most intimate secrets with a stranger will not be easy, so I will teach you a mind technique that will give you and your mate pleasure the first time. If you are lucky, you will only have to use this once. If not...” Ilona paused and glanced at her daughter.

Arianne bit her lower lip, then nodded. Ilona smiled.

“Come, sit on the bed beside me. Relax and open your mind while I share this with you.”

Arianne took her mother’s hand and walked back to the bed. When they were comfortable, Ilona’s voice sounded in Arianne’s mind. *Long ago, when our people were first created, we learned this technique and have used it often since then. I am going to show you how to block the thinking part of your mind so that only the instinct to procreate remains. You must do this both to your own mind and your partner’s mind.*

An hour later, Ilona sat back up, “There. I have given you all the help I can. Keep in touch, be careful, and remember all of your training.”

“Mother, when we spoke in your office earlier today, how did you know so much about the sea call?” Arianne asked hesitantly.

Ilona sighed, “It is the curse of our people. Each generation, one is born who feels the call. Never before, however, has the call come to one of our strongest singers.”

“What happened to the others?” Arianne asked.

Her mother smiled sadly. “They leave Lantia. I don’t know where they go, so don’t ask. My youngest brother, Rolto, was one who had been called. I named my first son after him. He was my favorite brother, and I loved him dearly.

"Before he left home, he promised me that the day would come when our people would again trust the sea; when we would no longer hide those who have been called, or treat them like criminals, and send them away from their homes and their loved ones.

"That day has not arrived, so I have been forced to decide what to do about you. It was a difficult decision, but it may turn out to be best for everyone."

Arianne nodded her acceptance and stood, "Thank you, Mother, I will remember all that you have taught me."

She stopped, her hands on the door, and glanced back at the picture, "What is it supposed to be?" She finally asked, years of frustration showing in her voice.

Ilona looked up at the picture, then at her daughter, "Inner peace," she said solemnly and gave a gurgle of laughter at Arianne's incredulous expression.

*****

Lady Colsa, a frown on her coldly beautiful face, watched Arianne walk away. She was silent for a moment, then spoke to the seamstress standing behind her. "Well, Khat, what do you think of this Lantian princess?"

The young woman Colsa addressed was shorter than she, and somehow made the brilliant green and black uniform of their religion, look drab.

Khat frowned, "Something about her bothers me. I fear that she may cause us trouble in the future. My Lady, let us leave this cold place, and let these strange people keep their princess. They are too eager to be rid of her."

Lady Colsa's smile did not reach her eyes, "Do you doubt my ability to control this young woman?"

Colsa glanced at the younger woman in distaste. She nodded at Khat, then turned and walked swiftly toward the room assigned to her. She did not look behind her, well aware that Khat was following.

The Lady Colsa entered her room and wrinkled her nose in disgust. "This is the most uncomfortable place I've ever been in. Even my small cell as a priestess-in-training was better than this." She sighed. "Close the door and tell me what you have discovered about our hosts."

Lady Colsa stared in the mirror on her wall and smiled at her reflection. She ran her hands over her long, thick, dark-green hair, then looked at Khat, "Well?" The anger in her voice was not reflected on her expressionless face.

Khat's frown deepened, "I have discovered very little. The servants are surprisingly reticent about the Royal Family. This town has no taverns or theaters, only endless parks and libraries. The people here hardly speak to each other. Their idea of a good time is to sit in one of those giant buildings and read, or to stroll quietly in one of their parks. Some days, you will see ten or more of them sitting on the ground and staring with blank eyes at some stupid bird. They will sit like that for hours, and you have to yell at them two or three times to get their attention."

Khat frowned, "I asked a group of young people what they did for fun. At first they looked at me blankly as if they didn't know what the word meant. Then, they told me that there were lots of private parties where they gathered with their friends and invited me to one."

"Well what did you learn?" Khat could be the most annoying young person at times.

"Nothing. They all stood around with drinks in their hands staring at those dark swirly paintings you see all over the place. Every once in a while someone would laugh out loud and all the others would turn and look at him or her and smile politely."

Khat shivered, "It was the strangest gathering I have ever been to. It made me feel like I was walking in a dream, a nightmare."

"Servants that don't gossip, a populace that reads instead of getting drunk and disorderly, and young people behaving at a party," Colsa raised one perfect eyebrow. "That is strange. I must find out how the queen manages to keep such wonderful control over her people."

"Mistress, this is not a joke. Whenever I ask about the princess, they tell me she is one of the best singers in Lantia. Though what that has to do with anything, I don't know. If I press for more information, they get a blank look on their faces and wander away."

"Oh Khat, stop being such a worrier. Just because this girl is a throwback, in looks, to her Feltan ancestors, does not mean that she has their abilities. In all the time we have spent here I have seen no evidence that any of these people have the gift of mind control."

"Neither have I." Khat agreed slowly. "Yet something is different here." Khat shook her head. "Something..." She bit her lip, "I don't know how to put it into words; A dream feeling, a sense that what we see is not real."

Colsa smiled, "Trust me, Khat. I am more powerful than any in this place, I would know if they were trying to deceive us."

The younger woman nodded. "I did find out one thing. Someone attempted to assassinate the queen a few days ago. A young man was hiding in the queen's office. They caught him just as he jumped out from behind the curtains."

Colsa smiled in delight, "So, not everyone here is happy. Good. What did the queen do?"

"That's the strange part. She hugged him, notified his family, and is planning to throw a party in his honor. Everyone is pleased that he got as far in his attempt as he did. It appears that this is a common occurrence, but he was the only one who made it into the queen's private chambers. The young man is now a national hero."

Colsa frowned, then smiled, "What a brilliant way to handle the situation. The queen has turned an enemy into a supporter. Hmm, I can see certain drawbacks to that course of action, but I do admire her style. What do her people think?"

"That's the strange part, some are quite happy about the whole thing, others act as if they were jealous of the young man's good fortune."

Lady Colsa nodded, "Yes. The queen making this young man a hero would encourage others to try their hands at the same game."

"That's it!" Khat exclaimed, "Everyone, including the queen, is treating the whole situation as if it were a big game."

Colsa smiled grimly, "A very dangerous game, but not our affair. I wish you could have spoken to this young person and found out why he wanted the queen dead. It might be something we could use in the future. Well, no matter. In six days, we will be gone and any further dealings we have with these people will be on our terms. After all, we will have one of their princesses." Colsa smiled smugly. "Relax, Khat, everything will work out just as I planned."

Khat looked doubtful, "Yes, Mistress, but I would feel a lot better if we weren't taking one of them with us."

Colsa laughed. "She is our hostage, Khat. Doesn't that make you feel happier? Now, go attend to your duties. I want everyone packed and ready to go in six days." Colsa frowned, as Khat walked away. "Is Khat right, am I making a mistake?" She whispered, then shook her head, "No, I have enough power to control anything this little Feltan look-alike could possibly do. Everything will work out perfectly, just as I have planned."

There were five thousand of us. We were genetic soldiers in twelve linked space ships. One moment, we were mentally linked to all our people, the next we were falling through space, surrounded by the shadow of our past. Our ships were out of control and eventually we crashed on this world. It was night and the terrified natives attacked us. Without thought, we struck back mentally, killing them all. This is our great shame, our loss of honor, the debt we must repay.

Excerpt from <u>*Penance*</u> *by*
Historian Ardea, House Royale

Chapter 2

Arianne felt a shiver of foreboding as she looked around. This was the part of Carta that had been destroyed at the time of the betrayal. In the distance behind them, she saw the line of trees that marked the Icina's grove. The roadside was littered with boulders and shattered columns. A small, overgrown path to the right showed signs of recent use. In the distance she heard the voice of the sea.

So, Arianne thought, *this is where they entered from, and not only them, but others as well. This is a well-traveled path;* Arianne glanced at the tall grass and shrubbery that grew around the area. *There is nothing this way, nothing but the ocean and the ruins of Carta. Oh, my people, what has your blindness to the sea let loose in our lands?*

"Careful, Princess," one of the men caught her arm as she stepped on a loose stone.

Why, she wondered, *are these Alsians going this way, and what is their other means of transport?*

"You show no fear." Lady Colsa's smile was smug, "That is good. I had many doubts about taking you back to my lands. I wondered how one of your people would adapt to Alsia. I'm pleased to see that you don't fear the sea."

Arianne glanced at the older woman. *That one smiles too much,* she thought absently. She noticed the strange expression on Lady Colsa's face. Arianne blinked, *the woman hates me*, was her first thought, then she shook her head, *No, I cannot be reading her face correctly, she has no reason to hate me. It is time I started to learn more about these people.*

Arianne reached out with her mind, *Mother can you hear me?*

Silence answered her. Her mind's voice hit a blank wall and her message dispersed into nothingness. She opened her mind, reaching out, and found only silence. The constant mental chatter that was always in the background in Carta was gone.

Briefly, she touched another mind, calm and watchful. *Withdraw, one listens.* It whispered, then it too, disappeared. She found no trace of her people. It was as though they no longer existed. Terror twisted through her. She was alone, falling into a silent spiral of fear, into the dark space deep within herself. Emptiness. Nothing. No one. Alone.

She was unprepared for the deep, heavy note that suddenly surged through her blood and into her mind. The power that note carried, overwhelmed her for a moment and she forgot how to breathe. Desperately, she tried to grasp the note and control it, to no avail. The song was stronger than she.

No, she thought, *I am a singer; I will not be controlled by a song.*

Then sing! The command echoed in her mind.

Arianne forced herself to breathe as she listened more closely to the note in her head. Now, she did not fight its power, but accepted it. Slowly and painfully, she changed her mind patterns so she and the note could become one.

Well done. Your people have not lost their skills.

Who are you?

You called me here, what do you want?

Arianne almost lost control at that instant as she realized the song she sang belonged to the deep ocean.

Who watches? She asked after a while.

Not your concern.

Arianne decided not to argue that point. She knew that it would be wasting her strength to try to force an answer from this powerful entity. This was not the light chattering of the playful waves, this was the true voice of the deep ocean.

Who listens?

One you travel with.

Which one?

A fuzzy mental picture that could be any one of the women in the group drifted in her mind.

Who is this woman? She asked and then waited patiently for her answer.

She is one with the power to hear our surface, one who cannot sing. That is all we know of her. The answer, when it came, was rich with the power of the single note.

How much has she learned of me from the little ones?

A sigh rippled across her nerve endings. *They are heedless and mean no harm, Daughter of Strange Stars. She knows that you play with them. She knows that you worry your future mate may be old and smelly. She does not know of your vow. Even the small ones are not that heedless*.

Arianne relaxed. *Does she hear us now*?

No. Her mind cannot hold my note. She does not hear me. That one is afraid of my strength and the little ones will say no more about you to her. I have warned them.

Arianne smiled. *Why have I never been able to speak with you before*?

Silent laughter came from the depths. *There was no need. Even now, you can barely hold my note. You must become stronger. My children, who swim in the waters of Alsia, tell me that the true blood no longer sings with them. Be careful, Daughter, you walk in danger*.

"Don't I always?" Arianne whispered, then gave a small start of surprise when a tall, thin woman handed her a bowl full of thick, rich soup with chunks of boiled bread floating in it. She ate the strangely-flavored meal while her mind bubbled with questions. She didn't even notice that they had stopped near the ocean and part of the group was already setting up camp.

"Lady Colsa," Arianne began hesitantly, "My silence has been most ill-mannered. Please accept my apologies for being so rude."

"It's all right. I understand that you are apprehensive about leaving your home and family." Colsa nodded approvingly.

"Will you please relay my apologies to your companions, as well?" Arianne stared at the fire. This act was not going to be easy.

"They can understand you. While we have our own language, we also all speak the common trade language."

Arianne glanced up and caught a look of scorn on the faces of the two men. The thin woman who brought her meal gave a small smile. The others continued to eat and ignored her.

"Will you introduce me to my escorts?" Arianne asked softly.

Lady Colsa shrugged. "The males are of no importance, mere sailors, low ranking officers. They came along in case we ran into violence. The females are priestesses of the temple. Their names also are not important."

"Priestesses?" Arianne asked.

"Yes, they are servants of our goddess," Lady Colsa answered. "Don't you have priests and priestesses in Lantia?"

"No."

"No? What gods do you worship in Lantia?"

"We have no gods in Lantia. My people believe that success and failure are the responsibility of the individual. We do not need gods to either thank or blame." Arianne smiled and leaned back on her arms while she waited for Lady Colsa's reaction to her statement.

"You worship nothing?" Lady Colsa stared at Arianne as if she was a new species of insect.

Arianne shrugged. "We see no need for it." She was aware that the two men studied her more closely. Their looks of scorn had changed into puzzled frowns.

"Then we will spend this trip teaching you the way of the Goddess. Once you understand her strength and her wisdom, I'm sure you will worship as eagerly at her feet as we do." Colsa smiled at Arianne.

"It would please me to learn of this Lady." Arianne smiled back. Not to worship, however, if this goddess were an Icina, she would make a strong ally.

"Tell me more of your country. What do your people do?" Arianne leaned forward and wrapped her arms around her knees.

Lady Colsa shrugged, "They do what most people do, work and die. Is that not the total of one's life?"

"Is that what your goddess teaches?"

"No, that is what I have observed. My husband was a good man. He dedicated his life to his country, and now he is dead. All his goodness and dedication didn't extend his life by one extra hour."

Arianne studied the older woman for a long moment, then yawned. Lady Colsa pointed to a small tent set apart from the others. "We have set up a tent for you. Why don't you get some sleep? We will speak of this again tomorrow."

Arianne glanced at the two men and found them watching her intently. The women had disappeared sometime during the conversation and Arianne was upset that they could leave without her noticing. She really had to stay more alert.

Later, as she lay listening to the quiet sounds of the night, she felt a light touch in her mind that she recognized as a thought probe. Arianne let her surface mind relax, and mimic sleep, while her deep senses traced the intruder. A flash of anger burned through her as she realized that one of the Alsians was trying to read her thoughts. For a moment, she wrestled with her fury, and when it was at last under control, the strange touch was gone.

Swiftly, Arianne checked her mental barriers and gave a small sigh of relief. Her secret was safe. All her mental barriers were still in place and undetected. Apparently someone, probably Lady Colsa, wanted to verify that Arianne was the sweet, demure, young princess she had requested.

She would have to be much more careful in the future. In Lantia where everyone had the power to touch the minds of others, Arianne always made sure that her barriers were secure. Tonight, with all that happened, she had not consciously set up her protective barriers. Only luck and habit saved her.

The sun had not yet risen when Lady Colsa stormed into the tent. "Good morning, young princess. You seem to have rested well, which is more than can be said for the rest of us."

Arianne, still half asleep, stared blankly at Lady Colsa.

"I was comfortable."

Lady Colsa nodded, "I only ask because I know how strange the quiet of the night away from a city can be."

It was Arianne's turn to shrug, "Lantians are not, by nature, a noisy people, Lady Colsa. We find quiet soothing: Loud noises upset us." How, she wondered uneasily, would it feel to be unable to touch her people's minds to be far away and alone? The memory of the terror she felt last night returned and a small shiver of unease wriggled up her back.

"So, during all this quiet did you hear anything last night? Any strange noises?"

Arianne blinked stupidly, "All the noises here are strange to me."

"How about screams? Or the sound of a fight?"

Arianne shook the sleep from her mind. "Fighting? No. I heard no fighting. What happened?"

Colsa stared at Arianne for a moment, "You say it was a quiet night, that your people are easily disturbed by loud noises, yet this morning we found the body of a young priestess behind your tent and you heard nothing."

"Was she dead?"

Colsa gave Arianne a look of scorn, "Of course she was dead, you young idiot. Or maybe not such an idiot." Colsa paused, a thoughtful look on her face. "Did you or one of your people do this? No, I do not believe that you did the deed, but I do believe you know who did it. Who are you protecting?"

Arianne pushed her hair out of her eyes. "Lady Colsa, my people have honor. We do not ambush others. We do not sneak around. If one of my people wanted you or yours dead, we would face you and say, you are dead." Arianne's smile was as cold as her voice. "Trust me, at that moment, you would be dead."

"You want me to believe that nothing at all disturbed your sleep last night? A young woman is murdered right outside your tent and you heard nothing?"

Arianne shrugged, "She might not have been murdered outside my tent. She may have been put there after she was already dead."

By someone she caught trying to pry into my mind? Not Colsa; she is truly upset. If not her, then who? Who else in this group actively dislikes me?

"Are you suggesting one of my people did this?" Colsa snarled.

Arianne frowned. "It could have been a wild beast."

Colsa looked puzzled, "A wild beast? What reason would there be for a beast to attack her? Why would this beast leave her body behind your tent?"

"Why do beasts need reason?" Arianne shook her head angrily. "Lady Colsa, I have no idea what happened to your priestess. I do know that my people had nothing to do with it. For one thing, no Lantian would come to this place. That leaves your own people or a wild animal. You choose."

"The men claim that we were being followed ever since we left the woods around your city. They believe that who or whatever followed us also killed Lucia." Colsa watched Arianne, her eyes narrowed. "You were aware that we were being followed?"

Arianne shrugged, "I do not know this area. I did feel uncomfortable when we first entered, but that was natural. This is a haunted place for Lantians."

"So, now you say that it was a ghost that killed my young companion?" Lady Colsa tightened her mouth, her anger showed in every line of her body. "Princess Arianne, do not take me for a fool. Wild beasts do not break necks, and neither do ghosts. This matter is far from over. If I discover that you kept information from me, I promise that you will regret it. Do you understand?"

"Lady Colsa I know nothing of this murder. If you think I am a liar, then give me leave to return to my people."

Colsa gave Arianne a cruel smile, "So, you do have spirit. No, I will not allow you to leave. You will stay with us. If you are guilty of anything in this matter, I will punish you. If you are innocent then you have nothing to fear."

Arianne sighed. "Who will be the judge of my guilt or my innocence?"

"I will." Colsa said as she walked out of the tent.

Later that day, Arianne and Colsa stood on the sand watching as the Alsians quietly went about packing and stacking their belongings by the water line. All of them tried to ignore the long package wrapped in one of the tents.

"Lady Colsa, you said yesterday that you had doubts about my suitability to act as your prince's wife. I'd like to know what they are. Do you think I'm not smart enough to learn your ways?"

"You're young, and your mother assured me that you're obedient. I wonder if you will fit in with a race of people whose second home is the ocean. I know how the Lantians feel about the sea. I wondered if bringing our prince a bride who is terrified of the water was wise."

"I have no fear of the water except during storms. I don't like storms," Arianne objected.

She sensed that Lady Colsa had again told a lie. Was the woman just incapable of telling the truth? Arianne could see no reason for either of the two lies Colsa told so far.

"Yes, I saw that last night. Don't worry about fearing storms, most intelligent people do. I promise that I will withhold judgment on your suitability. After all, you have only played in the shallows. It is a different experience to sail into the deeps where you can see no land at all."

"You expect me to be terrified. I don't know, maybe I will be. At least I am not afraid to take the chance."

Lady Colsa, her eyes narrowed, stared at Arianne. "You will have the chance. Let us see how you handle it."

"I will have a chance to sail?" Arianne could not hide the flare of emotion she felt at this prospect.

Lady Colsa gave a small smile at the excitement in the girl's voice, "Yes. We are waiting for a ship to take us to Alsia. We will spend the next ten days or more sailing on the ocean."

"Lady Colsa, do you know how to swim? Will you teach me?"

"We all know how to swim. I will discuss teaching you how, later."

Arianne, nodded, then she asked suddenly, "Lady Colsa, what is your prince's name?"

"Didn't your parents tell you the name of your betrothed?" Lady Colsa asked.

"No. They didn't tell me anything. Only that the betrothal was to take place, and that he was a wealthy and powerful forest prince."

"I see. Well, I've no time to talk to you now. Look, the boats have arrived. Once the crew has stored everything, and we're safely on board, I'll tell you what I can of your husband-to-be."

Arianne glanced up and promptly forgot everything else as she saw the six small boats coming toward the beach. Two people manned each boat, using long pieces of wood to propel them. Arianne finally remembered to breathe as the men pulled the boats up on the sand and began loading each vessel with baggage.

She swallowed hard. The prospect of spending ten days on these small wooden boats frightened her. *How brave these Alsians are*, she thought in awe as she turned to Lady Colsa. "Where do we sit?"

"They will come back for us."

"Are we to wait here three weeks until they make the return trip?" Arianne was disappointed. She wanted to get this ordeal over with before she embarrassed herself.

"What...? Oh, no, Princess, we will not be sailing on these boats. These are rowboats, and they will take us out to the larger ship," Lady Colsa explained with a smile.

"Oh." Arianne's face flushed with embarrassment and relief.

Lady Colsa's smile widened. "Don't be ashamed. Our ways are different from yours. How are you to learn if you don't ask questions? If you see or hear anything that you don't understand, just ask one of us. We will be glad to help you."

Arianne nodded. Again, Lady Colsa had lied. They would tell her only what Colsa decreed she should know. For now, she wanted to savor her growing excitement. She would work out how to get around Colsa's instructions later.

She was aware that the Alsians on the beach were watching her reaction to the water and the boats, but she didn't care. One of her most treasured dreams was about to come true. She paced the shore, impatiently waiting for the small rowboats to return, and for her adventure to begin.

Arianne was shaking with suppressed emotion by the time the rowboats finally returned. When one of the men who had traveled with her from Carta scooped her up in his arms and deposited her on the bench that ran the width of the boat, she gasped and grabbed the sides tightly.

"Relax, Little Princess," he teased her gently. "We've not lost a passenger yet."

Arianne gave him a nervous smile, "Then I'll try not to mar your perfect record," she replied, forcing her fingers to loosen their death grip on the sides of the boat. The man smiled and walked away to climb into another of the small boats.

An old sailor sitting in Arianne's boat winked at her. She smiled back at him and turned her attention to the sparkling blue-green water so tantalizingly near. Hesitantly, she dropped her hand over the side of the small boat and let her fingers trail in the cool water while Colsa and the old sailor talked.

She heard the man say, "I like this one, she has courage."

Colsa smiled back. "She has more than just courage. She has Feltan blood."

They stopped speaking the trade tongue and she could not understand anything else that was said. Curious, she watched the two: the old sailor was grinning; Colsa's mouth was a hard, straight line. Her body language showed her anger. Arianne hid a smile. She would have to discover the meaning of the sailor's words later.

Arianne leaned back and carefully studied her companions. Lady Colsa, her beautiful face cold and remote, her long hair tightly braided and pinned into a coronet around her head, sat like a carved figure across from her. Next to Colsa was a giant of a man. He reminded Arianne of the great southern mountains: Rugged, weathered and powerful. She blinked in startled amusement at his bare feet. His long, brown toes curled to grip the wooden bottom of the small boat. She glanced up to meet his clear leaf-green eyes that showed a hint of humor. Given the chance, she could like this man, Arianne decided.

Colsa gave her a small smile and Arianne forced herself to relax and watch the trail her fingers made as the boat went farther and farther out. It was as if the waves called her name, and the moist, sea breeze was welcoming her home.

Arianne smiled, took a deep breath, and closed her eyes in sheer joy and wonder. This was what she dreamed of all her life and finally, her dream was coming true. She was aware of a fine tremor running through her body. All her senses were set on hyper-awareness. The sailor looked at her and then at Colsa, a big grin on his weathered face.

"Aye, Mistress Colsa, this is the right one for our lord." He said softly.

Lady Colsa whispered back, "So it appears, Harl. To tell the truth, I still have doubts. Will she accept our prince, or do we start all over?"

Harl shook his head, "This is the one, Mistress, you've chosen wisely this time, I know it in my bones. We'll have no trouble with this one." He added in a louder voice, "Well, Little Princess, how are you liking it so far, being on the sea, I mean?"

Arianne opened her eyes. She had heard them whispering, but the words they spoke danced away in the sea breeze before her mind could grasp them. She swallowed twice before she found her voice. "It's wonderful, but my stomach feels strange." A small smile touched her lips, what banal words to describe the high point of her life.

"It's the motion. Nothing to worry about. Once your body gets used to the movement, you'll be just fine."

Arianne nodded and closed her eyes again. Her mother was correct. More was going on here than was visible on the surface. She'd have to be very careful. The sailor's gruff voice interrupted her thoughts.

"Open your eyes, Little Princess. Soon, straight ahead you will see the finest ship in our fleet. She's our flagship, and our prince's own vessel. That's where you'll be spending the next ten days."

It did not seem long before they reached their destination, and Arianne stared in shock at the huge ship looming over them. It was larger than most of the houses in Carta. Four tall spires that the old sailor called masts, reached for the sky. The Alsians had painted their ship the color of the sea around it.

"How do we get onto the ship?" She asked, surprised that her voice still worked.

"Rope ladders, Princess. Think you can climb one?" The old sailor asked slyly.

"I think I can manage." Arianne smiled wickedly at him, determined not to embarrass herself again. The old man's laughter rang out over the water.

Arianne sensed this was one of the skills she would have to exhibit if she were to gain any respect from the sailors. She had spent a lot of time climbing ropes down the sides of windy cliffs. Climbing a rope ladder up the side of a ship should not be too different. *Just get the rhythm girl*, her old teacher used to say.

"Then now is the time to show us what you can do." The old sailor pointed at the slender rope ladder hanging down the side of the larger ship. "You just grab hold and shinny on up."

Lady Colsa smiled tightly; she obviously did not approve of the old sailor's reaction to Arianne. "That's mariner talk. It means you have to climb the rope ladder."

Arianne nodded, took a deep breath, and grabbed the rope in both hands. She pulled herself upright, waited a moment, and carefully stepped onto the swinging ladder. Again, she paused, relaxed, and let her body move with the rope. Up, down. When she felt the rhythm, she cautiously climbed the ladder. Two sailors lifted her onto the ship when she reached the top and the watchers cheered.

"Welcome aboard Alsian's Pride, Princess Arianne. I'm Captain Khane, I hope you enjoy your trip." A deep, calm voice welcomed her.

"I'm sure I will." Arianne smiled graciously at the handsome man before her. He was the largest man she had ever seen. Captain Khane was tall with powerful muscles in his arms, shoulders, and chest. His dark green hair was streaked with white.

"Captain, why did everyone cheer when I reached the ship?" She asked, looking around puzzled.

"Well, Princess, you climbed that ladder as if you had been doing it all your life. Few beginners can manage to climb up that ladder. Most of them bounce off the sides a lot, some even fall off into the water," the captain explained as he led Arianne down a flight of steep steps and through a thickly-carpeted, narrow hallway to a small oval door.

"Here's your quarters. Someone will be along later to help you settle in. Tonight, we would like for you to join the ship's officers for dinner in the main lounge. Mistress Colsa will show you the way."

"Captain, why do you call the Lady Colsa 'Mistress'?" Arianne asked as the tall man turned on his heel to leave.

"The title of 'Lady' is reserved for the goddess, Princess Arianne. No human has the right to that title." The captain answered shortly without turning around.

"I see. Thank you, Captain." Arianne stepped into her cabin, closed the door, and gave in to the excitement that gripped her since last night.

She wrapped her arms around her waist. *I'm on a ship, I'm going to sail the ocean, and I'm going to learn to swim,* she sang to herself as she danced around the room.

Her delighted laughter rang across the room and she placed a hand over her mouth to quiet it. This was wonderful. She was going to spend ten days on a ship. No matter what happened when she reached Alsia, she would have this trip to sustain her. Arianne giggled. Not even an old, fat, smelly prince could take the joy of this away from her. Finally, she calmed down enough to take in her surroundings. Her cabin was almost as large as her room at home, but the floor was covered with thick, dark carpet. She found a small bath closet off to the right, and a wardrobe for her clothes at the foot of a narrow bed. The cabin even had a little window with silver curtains. She knelt on the bed to peer out, but all she could see were the legs of the sailors as they went by. She sighed in disappointment.

She was happily sitting on her bed enjoying the slight motion of the ship, when she heard a knock on her door. “Who is it?”

“Lady Colsa. I’ve brought you a young woman to act as your maid during the trip.”

Arianne sighed. There went her privacy. “Come in, Lady Colsa.”

Colsa entered, followed by the youngest of the women who had accompanied them from Carta. “Princess, this is Khat. If you need anything, just tell her and she will get it for you.”

Arianne nodded, *at last, an Alsian who’s shorter than I*, she thought sourly, her good mood beginning to dissipate. The young woman moved into the room and started unpacking. Lady Colsa looked around, then turned to Arianne.

“Well, Princess, are you going to be comfortable here?”

“I don’t see why not. Lady Colsa, I have many questions for you.”

“Not now, Princess. Why don’t you take a bath and get dressed for dinner?”

"Lady Colsa, I deserve some information about the situation into which I'm going. I'm not a child. Don't treat me like one."

Lady Colsa sighed. "Don't sulk, girl. I promise not to treat you like a child if you will stop behaving like one. Now, I will answer all the questions I am allowed after dinner. All right?"

Arianne looked hard at the older woman, "All right."

Two hours later, Khat had bathed, brushed, powdered, and dressed Arianne in her new green and silver tunic and trousers.

Arianne stared in the mirror on her wall and scowled. So much for her great adventure. Khat was bossier than any of the dressers at the palace in Carta. Every time Arianne objected, Khat shook her head and answered that Lady Colsa expected the young princess to look her best. After all, the entire crew except the duty section would be waiting to see Arianne. Khat insisted that she was only doing as Lady Colsa ordered. Arianne's already unstable emotions went from elation, to sullen, frustrated anger.

Arianne scowled at the young crewman who came to the door to escort her to the dining area. She never realized how important it made her feel to be one of the tallest people in a room. All these giant-sized Alsians were making her feel insignificant.

The young man took one look at her face and stepped back. "Are you unhappy with your accommodations, Princess Arianne?"

Arianne stared at her boots for a long second and forced herself to relax. “Everything is fine. I’m just a little nervous.” She lied and swallowed hard at the scornful look that crossed the young sailor’s face as he led her to the ship’s main lounge.

She passed three sailors standing together in the passageway. She walked slower as she realized they were discussing her.

“That the Lantian?”

“Yes, she sure don’t look like no fierce warrior.”

“She don’t look like no witch either.”

“Maybe not, but then we got one dead priestess on board. Don’t none of you forget that.”

“Oldie said none of them would do that.”

They were all silent for a moment, then the first voice asked. “What does a witch look like?”

“I don’t know, but that shy little girl don’t look like one.”

“Oldie said they were shape-changers, and we shouldn’t be fooled.”

“That mercenary? What does he know about Lantians?”

“Well, his country is a close neighbor and a friend to Lantia.”

Arianne heard no more as she and her escort moved away from the speakers.

A rustle of movement greeted them as they entered the large area. She had never seen such luxury. Heavy green and silver drapes hung at the windows. Thick carpet a shade darker than the one in her room covered the floor. Snowy white table cloths, trimmed with silver, covered every one of the tables, and real silver dinnerware with long-stemmed glassware sat before every man and woman in the room. Everyone turned to watch her walk toward the captain's table at the far end of the room. As she moved through the crowded lounge, she heard snatches of comments.

"Small, pretty, but she won't be a match for Colsa."

"Wonder what Colsa promised her to get her here?"

"Think she knows about our prince?"

"She looks kind of stupid to me. She'll be easy for Colsa to control."

"I don't know. I've heard rumors about the Lantians, and they say she killed one of Colsa's priestesses. She just stared at her and bam. The woman was dead. I think this one may be more than we see."

"I heard the priestess saw her true form so she killed her."

"Who? That little bit of girl? Naw, more like Colsa killed the priestess in a fit of temper."

"Not Colsa, that one wouldn't dirty her hands, but I wouldn't put anything past them little vipers who call themselves priestesses."

"She seems okay, a little shy though. Always staring at the ground, like she is too scared to meet your eyes."

"Harl likes her. He says she has Sea Dreams."

"Harl would like anyone that Colsa chooses."

"Don't underestimate our Harl. He is Captain Khane's man. He likes Colsa, but his loyalties belong to the sea."

By the time they seated her, Arianne's mood had gone from simple anger to bone-shaking fury. She was sure that anyone seated near her must sense the air shimmering around her. When the long-nosed, pointy-faced officer seated next to her touched her hand and said in a condescending tone, "Nothing to be afraid of, no one here will hurt you." Arianne ground her teeth.

Rodent, she thought viciously, then ran a battle sequence in her head where she blasted every member of the ship's crew into their basic elements, then scattered those elements across the world. After that, she felt better. Or she did, until the captain stood up to introduce her to his crew.

"Mistress Colsa wishes me to introduce the Princess Arianne, eldest daughter of the Lantian Ruling House…"

A loud crash at the back of the room interrupted the captain's statements. Arianne glanced up just in time to see an embarrassed young steward easing out of the room. At the table next to hers, a man laughed softly, and another whispered, "What's gotten into Oldie?"

"Who knows? Maybe he's afraid we are going to find out he's been lying about his precious Lantians."

The captain glared at the speakers and when the room was quiet again, he continued. "...and the candidate to be the Chosen of our royal prince." The captain turned to Arianne, “Would you like to say anything to the crew?”

Arianne smiled, “I would like to thank you all for the gracious welcome that I have received since entering Alsian territory.” She paused and glanced at Colsa to see if the older woman realized the import of her last three words. A frowning Colsa stared back. Arianne nodded in satisfaction and turned back to the crew.

“I am looking forward to meeting each of you during our trip to Alsia. If you have any suggestions on changes you would like to see instituted to make travel or trade easier, please don’t hesitate to let me know. Once I reach Alsia, your prince and I will consider all your suggestions.”

Arianne thought of a few more things she would like to say, however, none of them fit the image she was trying to project. Besides, she just issued a challenge and the fury on Colsa’s face showed the woman was well aware of it. The captain glanced at her with a frown on his face, sighed, and sat.

The first three courses consisted of slimy creatures served raw, and still in their shells; dried strings of sea grass; and hard, tasteless biscuits.

Arianne, aware that every eye in the room was on her, swallowed hard. She ignored the slimy stuff and chewed on the grass, which, she discovered, was as tasteless as the biscuits. Her seatmate took delight in explaining what every plate contained, and urging her to try a little bite of everything.

"Princess, this is considered a delicacy in Alsia," he whispered, picking up a slimy creature and pushing it under her nose.

"Was it once a living creature?" Arianne asked.

"Yes, it was. It lived in the sea. You should try it. They really taste a lot better than they look."

Arianne thought that wouldn't be hard at all. "Thank you, but my people eat no living creature." She lied desperately as she pushed the hand holding the fork away from her face.

The next course was a bright green salad. Her seatmate told her they made it from a plant that grew in the deep ocean. Divers harvested the plants, and their leaves were in great demand by the wealthier members of Alsian society. Arianne ate the salad thankfully. It was salty, but the leaves were crisp, and the dressing had a pleasant tang that countered the salt. When the soup arrived, Arianne closed her eyes and commanded her stomach to behave.

"We do not make it out of living creatures." Her seatmate hastened to assure her.

Arianne sent a silent thanks-for-nothing, to whatever power created this world, opened one eye and peeped at the soup again. Her second glance revealed that the soup was as revolting as it had been at first sight.

"What is it?"

"Ground sea grass, boiled in milk. Try some."

With a sigh of resignation, Arianne placed a small amount in her mouth and gagged. It tasted as bad as it looked.

"Do you normally eat like this?" Arianne asked her seat-mate.

"Oh no, Mistress Colsa planned this feast just for you. I'm sure she will be disappointed to find so many items are not to your liking."

Arianne bit her lip and reminded herself that she had a part to play. One day, she swore, Colsa would pay for this meal. Arianne spent the rest of the meal eating large amounts of green leaves and tasteless biscuits while she tried to sort out just what was going on in Alsia by listening to the bits of conversation swirling around her.

"She's not eating much, is she?"

"Maybe she's too scared."

"Scared? I don't think so. She just challenged Colsa."

"She's just too stupid to realize what she is doing. Did you see the look on Mistress Colsa's face? That little speech is going to get her in a lot of trouble."

"I don't think so. She's got some sort of plan. That one will bear close watching."

"What's Captain Khane going to do about this one?"

"It all depends on whether or not she gets accepted. There's nothing he can do until then."

"Any word on our prince?"

"Nope. No one knows where he is. It seems like he disappeared into mist."

"Think that little girl will be any help?"

"Hah! What do you think? She's Colsa's choice."

"I don't think so. Colsa might have gone for her, but the guardians surely picked her."

"We'll see. I'll make no judgment until after the acceptance."

It was some hours later when Arianne, accompanied by Lady Colsa, returned to her room. The meal had gone on for twelve endless courses. After a while, when the wine started to flow, the company became cheerful enough. Arianne had drunk sparingly, trying to keep up with all the different conversations going on around her.

The trip back to her cabin was even longer than the trip to the main lounge had been earlier. Arianne was blinded by an anger that she knew had to be controlled before she could deal with Lady Colsa, who was walking smugly beside her. Tonight was placed on Arianne's list of things that Colsa would pay for one day.

"Sit, Lady Colsa," Arianne said as she threw herself on her bed and kicked off her shoes.

A flash of anger showed in Colsa's eyes before she smiled and sat. "Did you enjoy dinner?" Colsa's voice was a husky purr.

"It was long."

Arianne stared at the far wall of her cabin, *So, Lady Colsa, you don't enjoy receiving orders? Get used to it. I will be your ruler and you will obey me.* She gave a slight smile.

"Well, we won't always eat like that. It was a special 'welcome aboard' dinner for you."

Arianne closed her eyes and her smile turned wry. “I’m sure it was.” She murmured, then sat up and tucked her feet under her. “Let’s be honest with each other, Lady Colsa. It was a chance for the crew to stare and whisper. What I’d like to know, is exactly what they were whispering about.”

“You’re the Chosen of our prince. It’s only natural for the people to be curious.”

“Lady Colsa, give me credit for some intelligence. That was more than just curiosity. I grew up in one of the most dangerous courts on this world. I think you’d better start explaining now.”

Arianne bit her lip, *go cautiously,* she warned herself, *I must not tip my hand, not yet.*

Lady Colsa frowned as she stared at the young woman facing her, “All right. However, I can’t tell you very much. Most of the information that you will need you must obtain for yourself. If you are the true bride, you will obtain this knowledge, if not...”

“If not, then what? What happens if I’m not the true bride? Do you kill me?”

“No! We are not barbarians. If you do not suit, and if you had nothing to do with the death of Lucia, then we will send you back to your people with your dowry intact and a lucrative trade agreement to sweeten the pot. That is why I thought your little speech a bit premature. You know nothing of our customs or our laws.”

“Whose fault is that?” Arianne asked, a small edge to her voice. “You’d better hope I am the true bride, because I’ve no intention of going back to Lantia," Arianne added as she ruthlessly reined in her anger.

Lady Colsa glanced at her in surprise. "Our prince is a young man. He needs a wife with certain attributes, certain skills necessary for the welfare of our people." Colsa paused.

"What attributes?"

"That's one piece of information I can't tell you."

"Wonderful. What can you tell me?"

"Our prince's name is Brian. Our country is a large island with many forests, rivers, and mountains. We are an old nation, one of the first to be formed on this world. I have told you this before. We've had very little contact with the newer nations and none with your people. The main reason for that is your people's fear and distrust of any who deal with the sea."

"How many engagements has your prince had so far?"

"So far we have brought four young women to Alsia, you are the fifth."

"What are Sea Dreams?"

Colsa's head snapped up and she narrowed her eyes, "Where did you hear that phrase?"

Arianne shrugged, "Someone mentioned it as I was going to dinner. I overheard them."

"Harl. It had to have been Harl." Colsa snarled.

Arianne frowned, "Who?"

"Harl, the old sailor you met on the way to the ship. He talks too much." Lady Colsa's face reflected her anger.

Arianne shrugged, “All right, though I didn’t see him tonight. That doesn’t answer the question: What are Sea Dreams?”

“The sea calls your name and talks to you.”

Arianne wrinkled her nose. “This is an attribute the true bride must have, isn’t it?”

“Yes.”

“That’s all, just yes?”

Lady Colsa nodded. “That’s all. I will give you no more information. Anything else you must know, I will tell you when the time is right. Good night.”

“Wait a moment, what does your prince look like?”

“Well...he isn’t old, fat or smelly.”

Arianne frowned. “Lady Colsa, are you a Sea Dreamer?”

“Yes, I am.”

“Then why don’t you marry Prince Brian?”

“I can’t. I’m the last Sea Dreamer our people have produced, and I’m Brian’s mother.”

“Smoke and fire, Lady Colsa! How young is this prince of yours?”

Lady Colsa laughed aloud. “Thank you. My son is older than you are, but not by very much. Now go to sleep. I’ll talk to you in the morning.”

Arianne lay back and thought about the little information she gathered during dinner. She guessed that the ship’s crew was divided into at least two factions, and none of them liked or trusted Lady Colsa. One group believed that their prince was dead and that Colsa was looking for a quiet, shy, young woman who she could control, to pretend that their prince was still alive.

The other group believed that Lady Colsa had imprisoned the young prince and wanted a quiet, shy, young woman she could control to pretend otherwise. Arianne frowned. If either of those theories were correct, she could have serious problems when they reached Alsia. For now, she would play the game until she had more information. Then, she would try to use what she discovered to further her own cause. Obtaining the sailor's support would be difficult, for, while neither side liked Lady Colsa, they didn't particularly trust Arianne either. After all, she was Colsa's choice.

The sailors showed great perception in recognizing that she was not the docile, young woman Lady Colsa would have chosen. However, they didn't realize that she really was exactly what they, and their prince, needed. She still needed to know more about this situation before she could make any intelligent decisions. However, she decided to obtain one bit of information tonight. All during dinner, the question most commonly whispered was, "What, are the guardians doing?" Arianne needed to know exactly who or what those guardians were.

She didn't think the power of her eyes would work on the sailors. They were men of the sea and the sea was the source of her power. She didn't dare try it on Lady Colsa and she had no idea where the other women who had traveled with them were. That left Khat.

Arianne reached over and rang the small silver bell on the table by her bed. In a few moments, Khat entered the room.

"Yes, Princess, how may I serve you?"

Arianne raised her eyes and stared at the young woman. "Khat," she whispered.

At the sight of Arianne's clear, silver eyes, Khat's face went blank, "Yes?" The young woman answered.

"Tell me of the guardians." Arianne commanded.

"The land of Alsia has four guardian spirits: Ocean, plains, forests, and mountains."

"Your people have many gods." Arianne mused.

"The guardians are not gods. They are the spirits of the land. They protect the people and their existence is linked to the health of their prince. As long as the prince lives, the land lives."

Arianne nodded and lowered her gaze. She ignored the nagging feeling that she had not asked Khat the right questions, and that she was missing something important. "Khat, you may brush my hair now."

The young maid stepped forward and started to brush out Arianne's hair. Arianne smiled. All had gone well. Khat would remember nothing of their earlier conversation. "You have beautiful hair, Princess. Legends tell, the Feltan have hair the same color. Legends say that when the Feltan rode the waves, silver hair streaming out behind them, it was the most beautiful sight the gods could show to humans."

"Have you ever seen a Feltan?" Arianne asked.

"No, Princess. Very few have seen the Feltan, and those who do see them, don't talk about it too much."

"Are you a maid at the palace?"

"No, I'm training to be a priestess in the temple." Khat stepped back, "I am finished, Princess. Your hair is all brushed and braided. Can I do anything else for you tonight?"

Arianne stood and started to remove her dress. "Bring me a night robe, then you may leave." After the girl followed her orders, Arianne smiled, "Thank you, Khat."

"You don't need to thank me for doing my duty, Princess Arianne."

"Khat, in Lantia, we believe those who take pride in their labor deserve thanks."

Khat smiled shyly. "Then you are welcome, Princess." The young woman whispered as she closed the door behind her.

Arianne nodded, satisfied, the girl would only remember helping her prepare for bed. She would not recall answering any questions.

Circles within circles, Arianne thought, *how my mother would love this situation. I must sing the song of Lantia's Icina when I reach Alsia, and see if the Icina of that land recognizes it.*

Arianne lay on her bed and let the gentle motion of the ship soothe her. At last, with a smile of pure delight, she pulled the covers up around her ears and went to sleep.

Outside Arianne's cabin Khat shivered in anger. How dare that clumsy, useless princess try to manipulate her? She, Khat was stronger than that stupid Lantian princess, and she was loyal. Why couldn't Lady Colsa see this?

"Oh my Lady," she whispered, "I will make a much better bride for Prince Brian than all these stupid, foreign girls you keep bringing to Alsia."

The Game is the only true test we have of how well our children have learned their lessons of mind control. Every five years, the twelve Houses will send their most promising youths to Carta. These youngsters must then challenge the strongest singers of the people to a game of stealth and deceit. They must shield their minds and hide their true purpose until the game has been played. Those who succeed, remain in Carta for further training. They have the chance to one day become the senior singer of Lantia, or the senior singer's consort. Those who fail will return to their Houses to be trained as House Leaders, or go with the army for further training. This is the Game. This is what will keep our people strong.

Admiral James Royale (Founder, House Royale)

Chapter 3

Arianne stared uneasily at the shadows that flickered in her room. Something called her from a sound sleep and now she was wide awake. She lay still, touching the barriers she had set in her mind earlier tonight, and found no trace of anyone having tampered with them, so neither Lady Colsa nor one of her agents was responsible for her abrupt awakening.

With a shiver, Arianne got up, threw a heavy cloak over her nightclothes, and left her cabin. The passageway that led to the deck looked longer, darker, and narrower than she recalled. Arianne shivered, and pulled the cloak tightly around her body. At the far end of the passageway a small lantern valiantly tried to lighten the surrounding darkness. The shadows it cast danced on the walls and on the stairs leading up. Arianne closed her eyes, took a deep breath, and clutched her cloak even tighter. She was trembling and sick by the time she reached the deck. The sailors she passed stared at her curiously, but did not speak or try to stop her.

She leaned against the railing of the ship and stared out at the horizon, taking deep breaths and trying to relax. The sky was a smooth, black sheet, its surface unbroken by even the tiniest star. Her long, silver hair blew wildly around her head and her silver eyes gleamed faintly as she gripped the rail of the ship tightly.

Why am I so uneasy? What is wrong with me? Is it the sea that makes me feel this way? Suddenly, she understood what she was feeling. *It is fear. I am afraid. What is causing this? Not the sea. I have no fear of the sea. The dark. I fear the dark. I fear the confinement. I have nowhere to run or to hide. I am alone. I fear being alone.*

“Are you all right, Princess?” Harl’s gentle voice seemed one with the noises of the night.

Arianne jumped, startled, this was the second time an Alsian had caught her by surprise. “Do all Alsians move so softly?” She wiped her damp palms on her cloak and turned to face the speaker.

“I did not mean to startle you, but I know that your people are not used to the sea.” The old sailor’s voice reminded her of a gentle wind.

“I was enjoying the solitude and the dark.” She closed her eyes for a moment. Even as she delighted in the ship's gentle motion, she realized that her statement was false.

"Then I am sorry to have disturbed you." Harl moved a few steps away.

The wind blew in circles around Arianne and the sounds of the men and women who worked on the ship seemed far away. Her hands tightened on the ship's rails.

"For a few minutes," she whispered, "I felt as if I were the only living human creature in a vast ocean of silent darkness. Is it always like this at sea?"

Harl stared out at the night sky, "Like what, Princess?"

"So quiet." Arianne paused. When the old man remained silent, she continued, "Harl, why is it so dark?"

"It's night, Princess." Harl's surprise at her question was evident in his voice.

Arianne chuckled. "I know, but in Lantia the nights are never this dark, even away from the lights of our cities." She hoped that her laugh had sounded more convincing to Harl than it did to her.

Harl joined her at the rails. He seemed to find nothing wrong with her explanation. "Clouds are covering the sky, and the lights are far away," he explained. "On land you will always see some light from cities or even small villages, reflected in the sky."

"Oh." She took a deep breath, inhaling the essence of all the life around her, trying to become one with the silence. Then she asked softly, "Harl, Is the sea always this dark at night?"

"No. Some nights the lights put on a show that astounds even old sailors like myself. The sea is beautiful, and always a challenge and a mystery."

"You love the sea, don't you, Harl?"

"That, I do, Princess. I wouldn't be a good Alsian if I didn't. The sea is the mother of all Alsians. My people originally came from the sea, and we still get most of our food from her. The sound of her waves against our beaches soothes and comforts us. I have lived on the sea most of my life, and most likely, I'll die on the sea."

Arianne and Harl paid silent homage to the view before them for a few minutes. Then Harl cleared his throat, "The men have been wondering about you."

"Oh. What do they want to know?" Arianne smiled in the darkness.

I am fine as long as Harl stands here and talks to me. Maybe my unease is caused by the absence of my people. Their mental chatter cannot reach me now, I am alone. Lantians are not bred to be alone.

"They are trying to understand you, Princess. You come from a land where the people hate and despise the oceans, yet you climb on board a ship like you have done it a hundred times before. Rumors call your people demons, but everyone knows that Lady Colsa wanted a young, docile girl." Harl paused, "You appear to be just what Lady Colsa wanted, yet there is a dead woman in the hold of our ship. Add to that the way you walk," Harl paused again, then continued slowly. "That's what make the sailors wonder. You move as if you aren't afraid of anything."

Arianne laughed softly. "Harl, it would surprise to know how many things I fear. However, you should remind your people that rumors tell many stories and that ships are not the only things that have ropes to be climbed." She paused. "I wondered how the Lady Colsa heard of my people."

Harl was silent a long moment before he spoke again, "The last young woman Lady Colsa brought to Alsia for our prince told her to go get a bride from Lantia. 'They will give you just what you need,' she shouted as she boarded the ship her father sent to take her home."

Interesting wording, Arianne thought. *Not what Lady Colsa wanted, but what she needed.*

She turned to Harl, "Who was the girl? How many other candidates has Lady Colsa brought to Alsia so far?"

Harl seemed uncomfortable with the directness of her last two questions. "I really can't say how many other young women, Mistress Colsa brought to Alsia before you," He muttered. "I do remember the last young one though." Harl smiled briefly. "She was a spunky little miss. Her name was Crista. She was from one of Lantia's neighbors. I forget which one." Harl's smile widened, "Fact is, we sailors are curious folk. We talked to the crew of that other ship. They told us about Lantia and the demons that inhabit it."

"Did you warn Lady Colsa?" There was a trace of laughter in Arianne's voice that she couldn't hide.

"No. Captain Khane decided to let her find out for herself." Harl seemed to share her amusement.

"Instead of a demon, she found me. Are you disappointed?" Arianne teased him gently.

Harl cleared his throat. "Well, we don't know. You could be a demon in disguise." He glanced down significantly.

The darkness hid Arianne's grimace. That blasted priestess was causing more problems for her dead, than alive. She decided that now was a good time to change the subject. Arianne leaned on the railing, hanging over the side of the ship. From far away, she heard the winds call her name. They seemed to be saying, "Arianne, Arianne, here, here. Tell, tell."

No, that wasn't quite right, it was...

"Harl, what are you doing? Why should I tell you to beware?" She asked the old man.

"Here, what are you talking about, Princess?"

"In the winds, I hear a warning that I must give to you."

Harl stared at her for a long moment, then he spun around and yelled, "Captain, problems ahead, might be a storm and a bad one." He turned to Arianne and said softly, "Thank you, Princess, for the warning."

"How disappointing, it was only a storm warning." Arianne murmured, "I thought you might have been involved in some deep, dark plot to overthrow the government of your land." She spoke in jest, but the sudden tenseness in Harl's body made her wonder if she hadn't accidentally touched on the truth.

She decided to probe a little deeper. "Do the winds always warn sailors of approaching storms?"

"It does when we have a Sea Dreamer aboard, Princess Arianne. That's what Sea Dreamers do. They tell our people when storms are coming and our fishing fleet where the fish are running."

"Then the winds are warning me only of stormy weather ahead?"

"For the ship, aye," Harl nodded.

"Only for the ship?" Arianne's voice was soft, a gentle whisper in the wind.

Harl's teeth showed white in the darkness. "Don't know about that, Princess, we all have storms in our future. Some of us have more than others. A wise person would always be prepared. Don't you agree?"

Arianne smiled. She would get no more information from Harl tonight. He delivered his warning, the rest was up to her. She stared out over the dark, restless sea, and leaned further out over the railing.

"Don't hang too far over the edge, Princess. If you were to fall in, we'd never find you in this dark," Harl warned ominously as he walked away.

Arianne listened to the many voices of the ocean. Tonight, she sensed more voices than she'd ever heard before. Not only did she hear the familiar playful chuckle of the small waves as they ran up the sides of the ship, but the deep powerful roar that came from the hidden depths.

It was this latter voice she concentrated on now. The sound beat in her head and throbbed in time with her heart. Maybe it was the other way around.

Arianne felt the hypnotic pull urging her to shed her clothes and come into the water, to join and be one with the mighty seas.

Child of a Far Star, Daughter of the People, Sister of the Waves, Speaker in the Wind, join us. Come play with us, the voice murmured seductively.

So many names for one, small demon? Arianne sent the thought downward, and the laughter of the ocean roared in her ears.

"Arianne?" Lady Colsa's voice broke the spell.

Arianne spun around angrily, "No!" She took a deep breath, "I'm sorry, Lady Colsa, my mind was many miles away and you startled me."

"My child, do not let the motion seduce you. You are not prepared to join the ocean waters yet. The depths hold many dangers that you know nothing about. Maybe someday, you can join them and play, but not now."

Arianne nodded. "First, I must learn to swim."

"First, you must learn self-control." Lady Colsa snapped. "Now, the power of the ocean would overwhelm and destroy you."

"No. It wouldn't harm me."

"It wouldn't mean to, but we are humans and the ways of the sea are not ours. Come down below and have a hot drink. You have more power in you than I suspected and I must teach you to control it or it will destroy you." Lady Colsa didn't sound too happy by this discovery.

"You will teach me?" Arianne wondered at the conceit of this woman. Anything Lady Colsa was teaching was nothing Arianne wanted to learn.

Lady Colsa bowed her head, trying to conceal her smug smile. "I will teach you."

Arianne glanced again at the ocean. Its waves were not playful now, but angry, smashing into the sides of the ship, causing it to twist and turn like a soul in torment.

"Come." Lady Colsa repeated, touching Arianne's arm. "It's dangerous to stay here any longer."

"Can't we do anything to help?" Arianne asked, stepping away from Colsa's touch.

"Yes, we can go below and leave the mariners free to do their jobs without having to worry about our safety." Lady Colsa grabbed Arianne's arm and led her to the shadowed warmth of the lounge below the deck.

"Always," Lady Colsa began as she carefully poured two mugs and walked slowly to where Arianne sat. "Always, the deep calls to those of us with the power to hear, we must learn to listen to the surface voice of the waves, and ignore the seductive hypnotism of the depths. This is the hardest lesson we must learn, but the most necessary one." Colsa handed one of the mugs to Arianne and sat next to her.

Arianne watched the shadows race across the wall as the ship rolled with the strengthening winds "Does the time never come when your people converse with the deep?" she asked. Her unease was back and now, it was worse than before.

"Yes. Sometimes listening to voice of Mother Sea is vital. Then, all we can do is hope we are strong enough to sustain the mental link without being destroyed. Before you can do that, you must learn of our goddess, for only she can protect us." Lady Colsa leaned back gracefully and took a small sip of her drink.

"So tell me of your goddess." Arianne hoped this goddess was a spirit of the land and a possible ally. She glanced at the mug that Colsa handed her, it was about half full of a thick, black liquid that swirled in time with the waves outside. Arianne carefully set the cup in a small hole on the low table next to her chair, the cup remained in place but its contents seemed alive and desperate to escape its boundaries.

Lady Colsa smiled at her, "Taste your drink. It is a favorite of my people, but is only good when hot."

Arianne remembered dinner earlier and some other national favorites. She nodded, raised her cup then paused, "You were telling me of the goddess?" She set the cup down again and leaned forward. Her stomach was beginning to mimic the ship's dance.

Colsa nodded her approval of Arianne's eagerness to learn and continued her lecture. "Our Lady has two faces. A circle represents her. Good and evil, life and death, darkness and light, she is the giver of all life..."

Arianne sighed in frustration, swallowed hard to keep her stomach in place, and tuned the rest of the lecture out. This goddess was not an Icina land spirit. The Alsians merely personified the natural order of the universe and given it a name.

I can expect no help from there, unless I can use the beliefs of these people to influence them. That could be dangerous. Religion has a nasty habit of backfiring when tampered with. Oh well, she would keep it in mind.

Arianne turned the mug around, playing with it, fascinated by the strange dance going on around her: The shadows in the room, the drink in the cup and her stomach all seemed to be moving in time to the wild music of wind and waves. Her sense of unease was intensifying with the storm. She had to get out of this room and back to her own. She shook her head and brought Lady Colsa's voice back into focus.

"You must practice constantly. Try to develop a strong link with our goddess. Learn to control your mind and your awareness of the world around you at all times. When the time for a link with the ocean depths comes, you must have no weakness in your concentration."

Arianne forced a smile and nodded. *I do not understand why Lady Colsa brought me here. Why didn't she just send me to me own room? Nothing that she is saying is that important it could not wait until we reached Alsia. What does she want from me?*

Lady Colsa paused. "Princess, I know very little about your people. Though your mother was kind and courteous to me while I was in Lantia, I would like to know why she took so long to make the decision about sending you with me."

"I am her eldest daughter," Arianne murmured.

"Yes, I can understand that. However, most of your neighbors do not value daughters. Among them, girls are only useful as treaty pawns. I found it quite puzzling that it took your people so long to make what was, after all, a very simple decision."

"Lady Colsa, in Lantia every child is precious. Also, we are very cautious people. Lantians do not believe in committing themselves to hasty actions."

Arianne smiled politely. *Now is the time to end this, before Lady Colsa starts asking questions about Lantia that I will not answer, or before I lose my temper.*

"You have given me a lot to think about, Lady Colsa. I thank you for your courtesy in teaching me, but I would like to return to my room now. I don't feel very well." Arianne murmured, rubbing her temples.

The nagging sense of unease, pretending to be someone she was not, and Lady Colsa's chatter had all combined to give her a headache that threatened to take the top of her head off with each howl of the wind outside.

Lady Colsa nodded, "You are a good student, Arianne. I have decided to teach you how to swim. I had thought to wait until we reached Alsia to teach you that skill. We will begin your lessons tomorrow morning if the storm has passed."

“I am happy to have pleased you, and I would be very proud to have you as my tutor,” Arianne lied. She left the lounge and, holding firmly to the brass rails along the passageway wall, slowly made her way back to her cabin.

Lady Colsa picked up Arianne’s untouched drink and her lips tightened as she emptied it in a small bucket that was bolted to the floor near the curtained wall behind her chair.

“Khat, come out from behind the curtains.” Colsa snapped.

“She didn’t drink.” There was the faintest hint of satisfaction in Khat’s voice.

“No, she did not drink. Now that you have stated the obvious, perhaps you will tell me what you are doing here instead of playing lady’s maid to our spoiled princess?” Colsa stared at Khat, then frowned. “What have you been up to, girl?”

“Nothing.” Khat blushed. “It’s just, well, I don’t know why you keep going to look for a bride for Prince Brian. I would wed him and you know that you can trust me.”

A cruel smile crossed Colsa’s face, “Trust you?” She sneered, “Trust the vicious little Khat who fed three of her fellow sisters in the church to the Dark Mother so that they would not stand in her way of promotion.” She paused to savor Khat’s startled gasp, then continued. “Did you think I didn’t know? I did nothing because they were weak. I am upset about Lucia, though. You wasted energy that could have fed the goddess. Did she catch you trying to harm young Arianne?”

Colsa studied Khat for a moment, then nodded. "I see. I applaud your ambition and even your methods. But I warn you: don't play your games with me, or with this princess. She has the blood of the Feltan and I want the power of that blood for the goddess. I want her alive when we reach Alsia."

"Alive and mindless. Do you think she will be so easily caught? The sailors call her a demon. Why don't we just let her drown and I will take your son?"

"That is enough Khat. You will never be my son's bride. I will feed you to the Goddess first. As for young Arianne, well, she will be controlled or I will keep your suggestion about drowning her in mind. After all, accidents at sea do happen. Now, go to your room and let me think."

Lady Colsa frowned as she watched Khat walk out of the lounge, then gave a tiny shrug and left the room. Neither of them noticed the young sailor sitting in the dark corner on the far side of the lounge.

Arianne moved slowly through ship's passageways and when she reached her room, she found a crewman removing the lamps from the wall.

"What are you doing?" She asked leaning against the door.

"We must take all the lamps off the wall, Princess Arianne. If they fall and break during the storm, they will cause a fire."

The young man held out a hand and helped her across the heaving floor to her bed. "See, I brought you a bucket in case you get sick during the storm." He pointed to a small bucket wedged beneath her bed.

Arianne jerked her hand free of his and fell onto her bed, "Go away. I have a headache, I don't need your silly bucket." She snarled.

"Princess, there is no shame in getting sick during this kind of weather. My first trip out, I was so sick that I could not raise my head. Most of the old sailors say it is normal."

Arianne almost smiled. The young man was trying so hard to save her embarrassment. "Thank you for being so thoughtful, now go away." She whispered as she lay back on her bed and pulled the covers up to her chin.

"You didn't drink anything in the lounge did you?" The steward asked, frowning.

Arianne shook her head.

"Well, you are going to be all right then. I saw at dinner that you liked our ship's biscuits so I brought you a few. They will help keep your stomach where it belongs." He stopped at the door, "My name is Oldie, Eldest Sister. Be careful and I'll check up on you later." He shut the door softly behind him.

Arianne frowned. Only old allies of Lantia called the A-Kiyama, Eldest Sister. It was an old term dating back to the first landing. *So, I have an ally on board*, she thought as she felt the ship tossing beneath her.

Deeper, she felt the power of the waves as they smashed into the sides of the vessel. They were still playing, she realized. They had no idea how dangerous their game was to the humans or the fragile bark that carried them. Dangerous games. Arianne shifted uncomfortably, wishing her stomach would stay still long enough for her to form a coherent thought. Just how dangerous was the game her mother had laid out for her to play? Were they underestimating Lady Colsa?

I am afraid, she thought. *I cannot touch the minds of my people. I am all alone and afraid. Is this what my ancestors felt like in the darkness of space, fleeing The Abomination in frail ships?* She frowned. *Where did that thought come from? Why did I equate Lady Colsa with the nightmare of my people?*

A shiver brought goosebumps to her skin and she sat up in the dark room. As she huddled on her narrow bed, she heard the waves calling to her. *Sister, come out and play. Come and dance with us.*

Silly creatures, stop this. You could hurt someone. Arianne sent the stern thoughts winging through the night.

Laughter from the sea. *Do not be afraid, we won't harm you. Come and play. It's only a game. See?* The ship keeled over sharply as the waves struck a vicious blow. Arianne's stomach heaved in sympathy. *Come play, Little Sister.*

No. I won't play with you if you're going to be cruel. I won't even speak to you until you settle down. Arianne snapped.

Silly, Little Sister, you're missing all the fun. The waves gurgled and tossed the ship again as Arianne closed her mind to them.

Before she pulled the covers over her head to shut out the sound of the storm, she sent a message to her mother. Softly, she sang the song of Lantia's Icina, and then sent a whispered thought into the swirling wind. *Tell my mother that trading with the Alsians is dangerous. They travel the sea and listen to the speech of the waves. Tell her Lady Colsa lies. Tell her I am afraid.*

She lay for a moment thinking of her brother while she attempted to control her fear and her stomach. With a small sigh, she rolled over and tried to go back to sleep. Her last waking thought was that her fear was not of the ocean's storm, but of something darker and more threatening.

When Arianne woke the next morning, the sun was shining brightly through the small window in her cabin and all her fears of the night before had vanished. She jumped out of bed with a gasp of delight and peeped out. The sea was a calm, bright, sparkling blue. Tiny waves laughed as they chased each other to the ship, causing a rocking motion that Arianne found pleasant.

A good morning to you, Little Sister, the waves called as they ran past the ship, *Are you going to play with us this morning?*

Yes, Arianne thought back in delight as she rang the bell by her bed. She remembered the last thing Lady Colsa had said to her the night before, *I was so afraid that it did not even register when Colsa promised to teach me how to swim. All for nothing, I don't think Colsa will deliberately do anything to harm me.*

"Is Lady Colsa up yet?" She asked when Khat answered her summons.

"Yes, Princess Arianne, she awaits you in the lounge." The young woman answered flatly.

Arianne hurried through her morning rituals, and when she was dressed, she ran down the passageway to the lounge.

"Here I am," she announced. She hoped that her excitement was in character with the idiot-child Lady Colsa expected.

"So I see." Lady Colsa smiled gently. "Well, Princess, what can we do for you this morning?"

"Please, Lady Colsa, as you are being so kind and giving your time so generously, why don't you call me Arianne?" Arianne paused for breath, and smiled artlessly, "When do I get my first swimming lesson?"

"How about right now?" Lady Colsa asked, laughing.

Colsa led Arianne to the ship's upper deck and handed her a fat, bulky ring with a long line attached. "Before you enter the water, put this about your waist. It will help you stay afloat," she explained. "When you've learned to swim, we will no longer use the ring."

Arianne nodded, "Now what must I do?"

Lady Colsa smiled. She removed her long robe, revealing a short, black shift that showed off her slim legs and graceful arms. "Now, we enter the water."

"Lady, you're almost naked!" Arianne was appalled at Colsa's lack of proper covering.

"Arianne, you noticed!" Colsa laughed teasingly. "Does it offend you?"

"No...yes-s...I don't know. Lady Colsa, some of the sailors are males."

"Ahh, I see. It is not my lack of clothes that makes you blush, but my lack of modesty?"

"Do I have to dress like that as well?" Arianne asked uncomfortably.

"If you do not wish to drown, you will," Colsa snapped. "Too many clothes will weigh you down. Now, I am tired of your chattering. I am a matron and the high priestess of Alsia. You are a maiden and Chosen of Alsia's prince. There is no one on this vessel who may criticize what we do. Remove your outer garments, the short shift you are wearing underneath your tunic should satisfy your modesty and still not hamper your movements in the water."

Colsa walked to the ship's rails and dove smoothly into the water. Arianne, the bulky ring hanging at her waist, dangled her feet over the water as she sat on the rails. Then, following Lady Colsa's shouted instructions, she slid into the welcoming embrace of the ocean while one of the sailors on deck tied the ring's rope to the ship's railing.

"The water is warm," Arianne said in surprise.

Lady Colsa smiled. "Today, yes, but it is not always warm. Come now, let me show you the basics."

For the next two hours, Lady Colsa taught Arianne the fundamentals of water survival. The playful waves joined in the fun, splashing in her face and upsetting Arianne's balance. At times she was floating upside down, her feet waving in the air. When this happened, Lady Colsa would laugh and dive under the surface to flip her young charge right side up. The young princess learned quickly. By the time they climbed back aboard the ship, she could tread water, float, and do a very clumsy swimming stroke.

Arianne was thoughtful as she made her way back to her room. So, Lady Colsa wanted to be in control. She wanted to play teacher and advisor. Arianne's part was to be an avid student, sitting breathlessly at Colsa's feet, never questioning and accepting as truth each word that Colsa uttered. What nonsense! But if it would gain her swimming lessons she craved, for now, she would play the part.

Arianne's love affair with the sea now entered a new phase. Every morning when the weather was calm, Captain Khane dropped the anchor and Lady Colsa took her into the water for a swimming lesson. After four days of lessons, Arianne no longer wore the bulky ring, though young Oldie insisted that she wear the line tied firmly around her waist. He ignored Lady Colsa's frowns and stood on deck, watching them each morning.

Arianne discovered the joy of playing with the smaller inhabitants of the seas, small fishes that hummed and swam around them, nibbling on Arianne's toes and tickling her feet. They had no wonderful songs to sing and no clear thoughts that came as words, but she read their emotions easily.

Arianne enjoyed the times when they joined her swimming lessons, for between them and the small playful waves, they turned the whole exercise into a game. Lady Colsa would float nearby watching as Arianne, her laughter ringing out over the waters, played and tumbled in the waves.

For Arianne, it was an enchanted time and she wanted it to never end. At night, when all was quiet, she stood on the ship's deck and exchanged gossip with the winds. From them, she learned that Rolto had returned home with the campaign in the north ended. The Lantians now had no enemies on the continent where they lived. Rolto was surprised and pleased to find that these new allies had the beginnings of a very strong psi talent and he was considering marrying their princess, a young woman named Crista.

The queen also sent a warning to Arianne. "Something dark and evil is happening in Alsia. We have obtained some very disturbing information from our new allies. Walk with extreme care, my daughter; if you need help, call us. If necessary, call the Feltan. By oath and by blood, they owe you aid."

Arianne pondered that message carefully. With a small shrug, she stored it away for future reference. There was nothing either she or her mother could do right now.

Two nights later, Arianne learned that her parents signed a marriage contract for Helen with a young man from the Merchant House. That bit of news made Arianne smile. She heard that Patria finally got the Home Guard's books straightened, and the supply lines were working smoother than they had in years.

The wind whispered that though the men missed having their commander train beside them, getting their pay on time went a long way in overcoming their disappointment. The Icina of Lantia sent a song of warning, many changes would be coming to the land soon, but she would not specify.

Arianne tried to get more information about her destination. When she questioned the ocean breezes, they laughed and ruffled her hair. The waves chuckled and told her useless gossip.

Finally, one night, she questioned the deep ocean. *Why does so much secrecy surround this land? Why doesn't anyone want to tell me what I'm getting into?*

We do not know exactly what is going on in Alsia at this time. We will not share gossip that may frighten or worry you. Have patience. When the time is right, you will know what to do. We will not influence your choices in any way. You must decide with free will and open mind.

I will sulk and pout. Arianne threatened. *I will not speak to you for a week.*

The ocean voice laughed. *Relax, Daughter of the Stars, and listen to my stories.* The voice was so compelling that Arianne did relax; she joined in the laughter and listened to the stories.

*****

The days of the journey to Alsia passed swiftly. On their eighth day of lessons, Lady Colsa suddenly turned and called out, “Look Arianne, you have visitors.”

The Alsian woman didn’t sound very pleased.

Arianne sputtered and wiped the water from her eyes, “Who, what...where? I don’t see anyone.”

“Right over there,” Lady Colsa answered as the water around them churned with life.

“What are they?” She asked, halfway between fear and delight.

“Have you never met any of the beings who live in the sea?” Colsa asked.

“No. I know fishes live in the sea, but these are not fishes.”

“No child, not fishes. They need air as we do, but they also need water. They are a link between what we of Alsia once were, and what we have become. They are the mischief makers and the clowns of the sea, come to meet to you.”

Arianne laughed in delight as the bright angels of the sea circled and dove around her. She stared in fascination at the two large sea creatures when they finally broke the surface. Their bright red and blue scales sparkled like a handful of carelessly tossed jewels upon the water. She blinked rapidly. The sunlight reflecting off their long, sleek bodies brought tears to her eyes.

As they moved closer, Arianne could see the faces of the creatures. They were wonderfully expressive with large, golden eyes full of laughter and intelligence. Their wide, smiling mouths were full of long sharp teeth. These sea mammals might be the clowns Lady Colsa named them, but they were also dangerous predators.

Arianne watched the antics of the large creatures, then laughed, “How graceful they are.”

“In their own fashion, yes,” Lady Colsa said sourly. “They are noisy, undisciplined creatures, with nothing worthwhile in their heads.”

Arianne reached out with her mind to the large creatures swimming around them and found joy and laughter.

Hello, Sea Sister. Their voices sounded bell-clear in her head. *We are the Olpho. Play with us, and we will sing you a song.*

Arianne laughed. *What sort of song?* She thought back.

Our sort, the Olpho laughed. *Very long, very beautiful, and very boring, to humans at least.*

I know human songs that are very short and exciting. Would you like to hear one?

Oh yes, please. No human has ever sung us a song before. Sing us a human song.

Arianne thought for a moment, then sang in her mind a rollicking, drinking song that was very popular among the soldiers of the Home Guard.

When she was through, the creatures were silent, then a small giggle erupted from one of the Olpho.

Thank you, they thought politely.

You are welcome, Arianne answered. *Didn't you like the song?*

Well, it's good that human songs are so short, for they are very ugly. Here, we'll sing one of ours.

The two Olpho started to sing. Their songs had no words, just clear, sweet notes full of emotion. Their wordless croon held sorrow, joy, love, hate, life, and death. Arianne cried and laughed with them. The sounds entered her brain and sped along the paths of her nerves, drawing her into their world, making her soul a part of theirs.

Suddenly, the Olpho stopped singing. *We must go now, Sea Sister, be cautious. Some day, we will return and sing the rest of our song for you.* With a flip of huge tails they disappeared beneath the water and were gone.

"Lady Colsa, did you hear the song they sang?" Arianne asked cautiously.

She knew the lady was deaf to the Olpho's speech, but she could not conceive of anyone who could remain unmoved by the song of the Olpho.

"No, Arianne. My talents do not lie in that direction. I've no music in my soul; I can hear the noise they make, but I don't recognize it as music. I cannot appreciate its beauty, mimic it, or feel the intense emotions that lie within it, not the way, it seems, that you can.

"I have heard tales that claim, those who can sing in their minds the songs of the Olpho, can call them in time of need. Their songs are a method of identification. Each Olpho has a different song. With enough practice, you may one day get those silly creatures to come when you want them, though why anyone would want those creatures around is something I can't understand." Lady Colsa's lips thinned with anger. "Enough chatter. Let us get back to your swimming practice," she snapped.

The beauty of the Olpho's song didn't leave Arianne. In her mind, she kept trying to reproduce the sounds they had sung. Later, she found herself singing the notes in her mind, changing a bit here and there, putting her own hurts and frustrations into the song, making it a part of herself, joining her experiences to theirs.

That afternoon, Arianne stood on the deck of the ship and let the song of the Olpho once more wander through her mind. Then she sang the new song she created. When she was satisfied, she let the new song drift away. As soft as a breeze, it floated until the Olpho heard it and knew that she was one of theirs.

Greetings, Sea Sister, this is a true human song that you now sing. If ever you need us, send your song to call and we will come. The thought came to Arianne across the miles of open sea and the waves laughed in glee.

They encountered no more storms, and on the evening of the last day, Harl pointed out Alsia to Arianne. She couldn't see much, just the blurred outline of darker green on the horizon.

"Look upon Alsia, My Princess, Alsia of mighty mountains and rivers, the blessed land." Harl smiled down at her.

"I thought your home was the sea, Harl. I'd never have expected you to go all misty about the land," Arianne teased.

"Oh, aye, I'm a man of the sea, but Alsia calls to me strongly, for that land is in my blood almost as strongly as the oceans." He grinned.

"Even old sailors like me must have a safe harbor to rest in."

"What are your people like, Harl?" Arianne asked softly.

Harl smiled proudly. "We are good people, Princess Arianne, hard-working farmers and fishermen. We are proud people, and loyal to our prince."

"Blessed land of Alsia, to have no merchants." Arianne grinned at the old man.

Harl scowled. "The House of the Lords and the Temple of the Bright Lady handles all that." His reply was short.

"Is that the temple Lady Colsa is high priestess of?" Arianne frowned.

Harl shifted, "No."

Arianne waited for him to continue, but Harl said all he was going to about that subject.

"Tell me of your prince, Harl." Arianne broke the uncomfortable silence.

"Prince Brian? Oh, he was a fine, strong boy, took to the water like an Olpho. He would have made a fine sailor. Then, when his father died and Lady Colsa took over his education, he never had time to come and visit with common sailors anymore." Harl shook his head sadly. "He wasn't a weakling, not that boy. He was twice as stubborn as the ocean itself. I can't imagine what his mother told him to keep him away from us." Harl sighed.

Arianne laughed softly. "Mothers have a way of controlling even the most stubborn of their offspring, Harl."

"Well, I suppose you would know how it is done." The old man grinned slyly at her, then returned to his duties.

Arianne stood at the rails of the ship and stared at the smudge of dark green on the horizon. She tried to bring a shape to it in her mind.

Sister, one will come to visit you soon, in secret. After he leaves, we will talk again.

Arianne glanced down at the small Olpho swimming beside the ship. *Another test? Is this Prince Brian so important?* She thought idly.

He is the life of the land. Do you blame us for trying to protect him?

I will protect him, Arianne swore.

Who will protect him from you? the Olpho asked.

Why should he need protection from me? I will do nothing to harm him.

Will you swear to that on the power that joins us? The Olpho demanded of her.

I swear it on the song that is my name, Arianne sang.

The Olpho turned one large golden eye upward to stare at Arianne, then, with a flip of its massive tail, it was gone. Arianne frowned thoughtfully, she had not seen or heard from Colsa since her final swimming lesson yesterday. Khat was sullen and uncommunicative, doing her job then leaving quickly, and Oldie dogged her every step. He stood behind her now, trying to look busy, but not succeeding.

With a sigh, Arianne walked up to him, "Oldie, don't you have something to do?"

"Yes, Eldest Sister, I am doing the job that Captain Khane assigned me."

"Do not call me by that title here." She warned, and Oldie nodded. "Have you told anyone about my people?"

"Captain Khane, a little of the truth. The other sailors, I have told all the myths and half-truths, things that are common knowledge. I would not betray the guardians of my people."

Arianne stared at him for a long moment then nodded. "Say no more. Walk softly, son of my people's friends."

Oldie smiled grimly, "Walk with caution, Princess. You are not surrounded by friends."

We will sing unity to this land's spirits.

We will not betray the lifeforce of this world as we betrayed the life of our home world.

We will hold truth and love in our hearts for all nature.

We will do nothing to harm the balance of this world.

We will protect it unto death.

Lantian Vow of Repentance

Chapter 4

Arianne opened the door to the ship's lounge where, according to Khat, she was supposed to meet Lady Colsa after dinner. She walked slowly into the empty room and stared around thoughtfully.

In another day, I will be leaving this ship and I still have no idea where I am going or what I have to do once I arrive. I will miss this ship that has been home for three weeks, but I will be glad to begin my new life, whatever it brings.

"Tomorrow is the end of our trip. Soon, we will be in Alsia," Lady Colsa's voice broke into Arianne's thoughts. "I'll be happy when this journey is over." This was the first time Arianne had seen Colsa in three days.

"Don't you like sailing, Lady?" Arianne asked as she watched the older woman walk briskly across the room.

"Yes and no. I love the sea. However, it's always good to return home." Colsa poured a hot cup of karm and, with a small sigh, dropped gracefully into a chair. "I miss the tall trees and the mountains. I also miss my family and my friends. I am eager to return to my temple and make sure that all has run smoothly during my absence."

Arianne thought quickly. It would be in character for her to complain about missing someone also.

"I miss my brother, I wish he were home when I left," she said quietly.

"You poor child, this has all been so strange to you, hasn't it? You may wish to stay in the temple for a week or two until you are completely adjusted to the ways of Alsia."

"Why must I stay in the temple? Does your prince have no home?" Arianne frowned.

"It would not be fitting for you to live in the palace before you and my son take your final vows. What would happen to your reputation if you changed your mind and decided to go home?" Lady Colsa objected.

"I won't change my mind. I could not return to Lantia now anyway. After all that I've learned from you, about the sea and everything, there's no way I could live in a society where the sea is forbidden to me."

"Oh Arianne, we Alsians have not been fair to you. What will you do if the land and its inhabitants do not accept you?"

"They have to," Arianne said quietly. "I've told you before, Lady Colsa, you will bring no other candidates for your land, or its people, to inspect. I will not go back to Lantia. I don't belong there anymore."

"Well, we could always send you to train as a priestess in the temple, I suppose." There was more than a touch of spite in Colsa's voice as she added, "They will be glad to have one of your skills among them."

Arianne sat in the nearest chair, a small smile tilted her lips. "No, I will not go to the temple. That is not one of your options. I am Lantian, and while I will respect your people's right to worship their goddess, I do not worship her."

Lady Colsa gave Arianne a startled glance.

It is as if the table suddenly started talking to her, Arianne thought bitterly, *I have let this charade go on much too long.*

"Hear me, Lady Colsa. I will not go to a place where others rule me. You promised me my own home. That is what you will give me. You will need to find no other candidate for your prince. He will take me and be glad of it."

"Suppose you don't want him?" Lady Colsa asked curiously.

"I have signed a contract. My people do not give their word lightly. When we make a promise, we keep it. What do I have to complain about? You have told me that Prince Brian is not fat, ugly, old, or deformed in his mind. Even if he were, I would have no choice. I have given my word."

"Others have reasons to complain." Colsa replied silkily.

Arianne gave a startled look at her companion, "Another secret? What haven't you told me?"

"Many things, My Child," Lady Colsa paused and studied the young woman sitting across from her. "My son can be hard to take at times." She warned.

Arianne shrugged, "So can I, Lady Colsa. You have done your part by bringing me here. The prince and I will solve any other problems. Neither of us has any further choice. I must take him, as he must take me."

Lady Colsa gave a startled laugh, then frowned, "You have a stubborn streak in you, Little Lantian Princess, and you are arrogant. Your mother never mentioned this. I will warn you to be very careful. That arrogant stubbornness could get you into more trouble than you expect." She said as she stood and left the room.

Arianne smiled grimly, *so Lady Colsa has decided to remove her mask. That's a relief, for it means my days of pretending are about to end. Good. I am tired of playing a demure maiden, and I do believe that Lady Colsa has just threatened me. Now, the next move will be mine. I wonder what is wrong with this Alsian prince that makes him unacceptable to some women.* She shrugged, *well as I have said to Lady Colsa, I have no choice. I will have to take this Prince Brian no matter what.* Arianne slouched down in her chair and stared blankly at the far wall, *there is so much I don't know. This is not the Lantian way, to go blindly into battle. Yet, I have no other options.*

Arianne sat alone in the lounge for a long time lost in her thoughts and drinking cup after cup of sweet, hot karm. She knew that sleep wouldn't come easily to her this night. Too many unanswered questions wandered through her mind.

"Princess Arianne, are you well?"

"Captain Khane, I was thinking about all I've learned on this trip." Arianne turned and smiled at the tall man standing in the doorway of the lounge.

"Why aren't you in bed? Tomorrow will be a long day for you." The captain said, walking into the room and sitting next to her.

"What's going to happen tomorrow, besides us reaching Alsia?" Arianne glanced at the captain. Maybe she could get some answers from him.

"Oh, we don't drop our anchor in Pride's Harbor until dark, so it will be the next morning before you meet the temple mistresses, and the court noblemen." Captain Khane poured himself a glass of karm and sat back.

"Then why is tomorrow going to be a busy day, and when do I get to meet your prince?"

"Tomorrow, the nonhuman citizens of Alsia will come to the mouth of the harbor to greet you."

"The nonhuman citizens?" Arianne frowned. No one ever mentioned nonhuman.

"Aye, the Olpho and some of their smaller cousins. Also, some land creatures will swim out to see you. They are all part of our society, and the welfare of Prince Brian affects them even more than it does the human population of Alsia."

"Why can't they wait until the humans come to meet me and just have one big ceremony?"

"The human citizens will not come to greet you until the others have passed judgment, Princess Arianne. If they deem you not fit, then they will not accept you."

"I see." Arianne frowned, "No, I don't see. I don't understand any of this."

Captain Khane frowned, "Didn't Mistress Colsa explain the judging to you?"

Arianne stared blankly at the captain, "She said the land and its inhabitants would judge if I were a fit mate for her son, nothing else. How will the sailors of Alsia judge me?" Arianne asked softly, raising her eyes so the captain saw them for the first time. As she had expected, they did not enchant him, but they did surprise him.

Captain Khane stared at her in surprise, then a slow smile curved his mouth. "They judge you not at all what you appear to be, Princess." He whispered as he set his glass down, and stood up. "Now, I must go back to the running of my ship. Try to get some rest, Princess Arianne. You'll need all your wits about you tomorrow. A word of warning: The power of your eyes will have no effect on either our priestesses, or our sailors, so don't expect to use them to influence Mistress Colsa."

It wasn't until much later that Arianne realized that the captain hadn't answered her question about the prince. She smiled. She would find out tomorrow.

Nonhuman are not so involved in politics as humans. She thought, then laughed aloud. What nonsense. The nonhuman she had met so far could give any Lantian Elder lessons in playing politics. Usually, however, the nonhuman would give a straight answer; the secret lay in asking the right question.

Arianne had no worries about meeting the nonhuman the next day. Her problems always came from humans. Though she had been raised in court, Arianne never mastered the art of diplomacy. If she felt something, she said it. If she wondered about something, she asked. Now, she suspected she should have paid more attention when her mother tried to teach her tact and deceit. With a shrug, Arianne shed that particular worry. It was too late for her to change now, the Alsians would have to take her as she was.

She walked slowly to her cabin and was surprised to find Khat still up, waiting for her. "Why didn't you go to bed?" She asked the young woman.

"Mistress Colsa left orders that I was to wait for you, Princess Arianne. I'm to explain tomorrow's ceremony to you."

Arianne sighed and sat on her bed, "All right, what should I know about tomorrow?"

"The ship will anchor outside the harbor of Kopol. At dusk, we will summon you to the decks to meet the nonhuman. After the greetings, you may have to join them in the water. Lady Colsa wanted me to tell you not to ask them any questions, and to be very careful of what you say to them."

"Why?" Arianne asked.

"I don't know," Khat answered as she started to leave the room.

My move now, Arianne thought with a smile. Khat might not know why Lady Colsa had issued that particular order, but Arianne knew. Lady Colsa had guessed what Arianne was planning to do. The problem was that Arianne was not the docile maiden Colsa thought her to be. *I am not going to let a mildly worded request stop me from doing what I want. I will question the nonhuman tomorrow. Lady Colsa can do nothing to stop me.*

"Wait a moment, Khat, how would this ceremony have gone on if I didn't know how to swim?"

"You would have worn the belt, Princess." Khat said as she softly closed the door behind her.

Arianne stretched out on her bed. She needed more information and knew just where to get it. Closing her eyes, she sang softly to the Olpho.

Their reply came swiftly, *What do you want Sea Sister*?

Company. Arianne answered.

All is well. We will greet you on the morrow.

I'm glad you'll be there. Can you tell me about the prince of the land dwellers now, or do I need to pass more tests?

We may tell you a little now. Tomorrow, you will learn even more. You must learn to be patient, Wind Speaker. What would you like to know of the Sea Brother?

What is he like? Arianne whispered.

Gentle. However, he has lost his song. Though his mind is still one with ours, he no longer sings. Promise us you will teach him to sing again.

Yes, I'll teach him that human song I sang for you. Arianne teased.

Their laughter whispered all around the ship, *Please, Sister, not that.* More than one Olpho voice replied.

Why does so much mystery surround Prince Brian? Each time I ask about him, the humans evade my questions.

The Olpho were silent for a moment, *We don't know the answer to that, Sea Sister. We touch only his mind now. It has been many years since he last swam the depths with us.*

I am to tell you this: The one who calls herself his mother will try to keep it from you. Listen well, Little Sister.

Arianne sat up in her bed. *I am listening, my friends.*

The Sea Brother, upon his father's death, left the waters and went to the caves of learning, where he must remain until a suitable mate is found for him. She must go to him deep in the mountains of Alsia, and lead him from the caves, back into the outer world.

Where are these caves?

Among those who will greet you tomorrow, are land-dwellers. Ask them. They can lead you to our prince. You must hurry, for the time grows short. After a set amount of time it will be too late to bring the Sea Brother into the light. The Olpho warned.

My friends, the Lady Colsa thinks to lock me away in the temple when we reach Alsia. We must think of a way to stop her.

We will speak with the land dwellers. You have sworn to us, Sea Sister. Do not forget your oath.

I have sworn to you and your prince. I will not forget my oath. Arianne smiled smugly. No matter what Lady Colsa said, she was going to ask at least one question tomorrow.

All around her, the sea and its inhabitants chuckled in private glee. They sang softly among themselves without touching Arianne's mind. She was the true Chosen, a proper mate for their Sea Brother. Now, they only had to send a message to the nonhuman land-dwellers.

Arianne, unaware of the plotting going on, curled in her bed and fell asleep with a wicked smile that would have alarmed Lady Colsa.

The next morning, Arianne got up early and ate her breakfast alone. When she was through, she headed for the upper deck of the Alsian's Pride, hoping to see more clearly the island that was to be her home.

Harl was already there. He turned to her with a smile, "Excited, Princess?" He asked.

"Yes. I'm looking forward to the greeting ceremony." Arianne answered calmly, hiding her grin at Harl's surprise.

"I heard you were worried last night, what caused the change?" He watched her closely.

"I was a little worried, but, a good night's sleep can work wonders." Arianne replied. "After all, there's no doubt in my mind that I'm the true Chosen, so what do I have to fear?"

"Are all your doubts gone," Harl asked, "What about your questions concerning the prince?"

Arianne stared out over the calm, green water. From the depths came a warning, *Caution, Daughter, this one seeks to trap you into admitting what we do not wish him to know.*

Arianne turned to Harl, "Soon, I will have the answers to all my questions. I am here now, and that is what truly matters. I will not be leaving Alsia, Harl. I will be your queen for a long time." Arianne smiled.

The old sailor stared at her for a moment, then turned on his heel and left the deck, a frown on his face.

Arianne chuckled and sent her thought out over the water. *My mother would have been proud of me.*

Laughter greeted her statement, *As am I, Sea Sister. I have decided the land-ones will take you to the prince. Be ready to move when they give the word.*

Will you spoil all the ceremonies these Alsians have planned for me? She asked. Her thought was full of laughter.

No. First they have their fun, then we have ours, all right? The ocean echoed with feelings of mischievous joy.

Arianne giggled, *All right*.

"Princess, are you feeling well? Harl thought that you were different this morning."

Arianne tensed as Lady Colsa's voice interrupted her silent conversation with the ocean spirit. "Different, Lady Colsa? How?"

"He said that you were talking and laughing to yourself. You do realize that the ceremony tonight is very important? You must be calm if you hope to make a good impression on the nonhuman. I will pray to the Lady that your prolonged exposure to the sea and its inhabitants have not unbalanced your mind."

Arianne felt Lady Colsa's mind try again to touch her own. She deflected the probe carelessly then glanced at Lady Colsa. The older woman was staring at her, and Arianne smiled at the expression of puzzled surprise on Lady Colsa's face.

"Lady Colsa, I have a perfectly balanced mind." Arianne let a small grin touch her lips. "Please, don't make the mistake of thinking me mad. It's just that I'm looking forward to this evening."

"It will not be easy. The nonhuman will judge you harshly."

"Oh, I don't think so." Arianne murmured.

"What was going on when I arrived?"

"Nothing, I was just enjoying the antics of the Olpho. I am thinking of using some of their songs during the greeting ceremonies." Arianne's grin grew wider. She'd had no idea she could be such a terrific liar.

"Be careful, child. These creatures are up to some mischief. My advice to you is to ignore them. The sea creatures and the land creatures do not usually agree on anything. The land dwellers are not like the playful creatures you have met in the oceans."

Why, she is jealous, Arianne thought. *She hates it because I can sing to the Olpho and she can't. Lady Colsa is trying to find some way to wreck this meeting for me.*

"You will find vicious predators on the land as well as in the sea, my lady, and not all of them are nonhuman," Arianne murmured. "Tell me, Lady Colsa, why did you teach me to swim?"

"I had no choice. The sailors were beginning to whisper that I wanted you to fail your test. The mariner guild holds great power in Alsia. They must be satisfied that I have done everything I can to make you acceptable."

Arianne pushed a silver curl back from her face. "I will succeed." She said quietly.

Colsa snorted. "I've told you before, I had doubts about you and I still do. You're a child. I don't believe you will be a fitting mate for my son."

"Would any woman be fitting?" Arianne asked sardonically. Her silver eyes glinting coldly in the morning light. "You came a long way to find me. You made a bargain with my mother. Do not try to negate that bargain now. Lantians make deadly enemies." She paused, "And we of House Royale make the deadliest enemies of all Lantians."

"You are a stupid child to be threatening me. You are young. What do you know of power?" Colsa laughed harshly, "As for bargains? Well, I asked your mother for a quiet, docile maid, and she gave me a viper."

Arianne grinned at Colsa. "Of all her children, I was the closest to what you wanted. My sister, Helen, would have drowned you two days out of Lantia. Patria would have convinced the sailors to do it for her in three hours."

Lady Colsa, her green eyes cold, stared at Arianne. "You know," She said at last. "I like you. If I had given birth to a daughter, instead of a worthless son, I would want her to be like you. However, as long as my son is unmarried, I rule Alsia and I enjoy ruling very much. Why should I give up the power I now have to a stupid, young, foreign girl and my deformed son?" Lady Colsa asked calmly.

Arianne ignored the last part of Lady Colsa's statement. "You thought that pretending friendship would convince me to do as you ordered, instead of what was in my best interests. That was a mistake." Arianne shrugged carelessly. "Sorry, I am Lantian. We have a strong sense of self-interest, and we always do what is best for us. I believe I will get a better deal from your son than from you."

"You really are a stupid girl," Colsa said coolly. "Let us deal with reality for a moment. You and my son have no chance at all to succeed in challenging me. My son has nothing to offer you." Lady Colsa smiled. "However, you don't need to worry. I won't send you back to Lantia against your wishes. I have quite a bit of influence with the temples in Alsia. I'm sure I can find you a place in one of them." Colsa nodded coldly. "As a matter of fact, I would prefer if you stayed in Alsia. You'll do very well as a lesser priestess."

Arianne ignored the touch of fear that danced up her spine and forced a cool laugh. "Lady Colsa, I will not become a priestess in any of your temples. I will marry your son and I will rule as queen in Alsia. That is where my best interests lie. You will bring no other candidates to Alsia. Your people are stuck with me. Why choose now to tell me your son is deformed? You know that I will be found acceptable to the nonhuman, so now you try this way to get rid of me."

Arianne caught the slight tensing in Lady Colsa's body and smiled bitterly. "So that's it," she murmured. "You hope to place doubts in my mind that the nonhuman will find, then they will refuse me." Arianne shook her head in mock sorrow. "Lady Colsa, you disappoint me. I'm sure that with a little more thought, you could have come up with something better. Well, it won't work. I am afraid, Lady Colsa, that you will not be rid of me so easily."

"Fool!" Lady Colsa spat. "Don't say that I haven't warned you. You have made your choice, now you must live, or die by it."

Arianne smiled ruefully, as Colsa stalked off, *I really am not as brave and fearless as I thought. My knees are shaking and my knuckles are white and aching from gripping the ship's rails so tightly. I am a coward. Oh Mother, what have you gotten me into?*

Was what the Lady said true? She wondered. Well, she would find out when she met Prince Brian. She could not bring herself to ask anyone about his physical appearance. Even if his body was deformed, the Olpho called him Sea Brother and said he was gentle. That would be enough. It was more than she expected initially.

Very good, Cousin. Do not let the old woman place doubt or fear in your heart, for if the land nonhuman find it, they will surely judge you lacking. Remember that outward form isn't important, only what is in the heart. The mental voice was deep and strangely familiar.

"Who?" Arianne asked, glancing down at the water.

Over here. See me now. Greetings, Little Cousin, true princess of the Alsians, and one of the old blood.

"Ahh, what are you?" Arianne breathed in awe as she stared at the swimmer.

"I am Ambrio, one of the Feltan, Cousin." The swimmer tossed his long, silver hair out of his face. He dove beneath the water with a flip of his large, golden tail.

He resurfaced. "See me now as few of your people have seen me for two hundred years." For a long, silent moment, crystal eyes stared deep into silver eyes and a feeling of love and acceptance drifted around Arianne's body. "Be of strong heart, Little Cousin. Farewell."

Arianne blinked then looked again, but not the slightest ripple in the water showed where the legendary Feltan had swum. With a smile, the young Lantian princess turned and walked back to her cabin. She found comfort in the thought that she was not alone in her battle against Lady Colsa.

On the way, she saw Harl watching her, a thoughtful expression on his face. "Harl, what do you know of the Feltan?" Arianne wondered how much he had seen and heard of her meeting.

"Not much, Princess. When they left Lantia two hundred years or more ago, they shunned the society of humans and stayed in the sea from which we all originally came. Why do you ask?"

"Oh, no real reason. It's just that among my people, it is rumored that the royal family interbred with the Feltan. I had an old nurse who called me a throw back to the Old Ones. I would like to meet one."

Harl stared at the horizon for a long moment, "I've seen them in the distance. They were swimming with the Olpho. Some people say that to look into their eyes will bring death to a mortal man." He murmured, then shook himself, "But it's considered good luck by the Alsian sailors to see one of the Feltan in the distance. They usually stay far away from the sea-lanes traveled by humans."

Harl was silent. He pointed to the west, "There, Little Princess, is the blessed land of Alsia."

Arianne turned and stared as the island of Alsia slowly took shape against the horizon. The young woman gasped in surprise and Harl gave her a small grin.

"It's beautiful."

"Aye, that it is, Little Princess."

Arianne looked at the scene before her. The ocean sparkled, reflecting the bright sun. Its colors went from palest white-green to a deep, clear, blue.

The island was a perfect emerald set amid a frame of sapphires. The tree line started almost at the ocean, and grew up the sides of the mountains, where mists swirled, and gave quick glimpses of pure, white snow on the highest peaks.

Over the land, like a canopy, spread the cloudless sky, so clear and bright it hurt her eyes. She blinked, and her silver eyes picked up the colors that radiated from the land and turned a pure, bright green.

Harl looked at her, then quickly looked away, “Feltan bred,” he gasped. “The lass is true Feltan bred.”

Arianne didn’t acknowledge his statement. She stood in shock, staring at the enchanted land before her. Her chest hurt, burned with an emotion that was strange to her, and she knew that she would fight to the death anyone who tried to take her from that island.

“Pure enchantment,” Arianne whispered, and backed away, not wanting to take her eyes from the view before her. At last, she stumbled down the stairs and blindly made her way back to her cabin.

The Feltan came to us from the sea. They were beings full of joy and light. In our darkest hour, they brought us hope, and we loved them. Then came the Great Betrayal and the destruction of our city by the sea. Now, we are alone again. Only our duty to protect those who live on this land, and the surety of our old enemy's return sustains us.

Evan Gemi, Poet
House Gemi

Chapter 5

Arianne stayed in her cabin a short time, then left. She was restless and the small room was suddenly much too confining. She wanted to be on deck, staring at the island of Alsia, but she resisted that temptation. Instead, she went into the ship's lounge, where she sat alone at one of the small tables until it was time for the midday meal.

If anyone spoke to Arianne, she did not hear him. Harl had told the other sailors of his suspicions and of how she spoke with the sea and its creatures. Now the Pride's crew watched her with awe and respect. Lady Colsa, who had no idea what was going on, scowled furiously through the whole meal. Arianne, still deeply under the spell the island cast on her, did not notice. She was not even aware of what she was eating.

"It is time that you start preparations for the Greeting Ceremony." Lady Colsa's cool voice broke into Arianne's dreamy state.

Arianne nodded and stood obediently.

"My Child, remember that a place in the temple awaits you if you decide to accept it. There's nothing to fear in the temple," The older woman smiled smugly.

The young princess said nothing. For the first time in their association, Arianne looked directly at the other woman. She blinked slowly and left. Lady Colsa stepped backward and her eyes flashed with anger and shock at the direct eye contact.

"Those are Feltan eyes," Lady Colsa hissed after Arianne was gone.

Arianne, with the help of a sullen Khat, dressed quickly, then waited impatiently for Captain Khane to escort her to the upper decks of the Alsian's Pride.

*****

In a dimly-lit cave, deep in the mountains of Alsia, a young man lay on piles of brightly-colored cushions thrown carelessly on the cave's floor. He ignored a small table piled high with fresh fruits and the aroma of fresh-baked bread that tried, in vain, to tempt him. Different colored crystals sparkled on thewalls of the cave, and the gentle sound of running water created a peaceful backdrop that belied the scowl on the man's face.

One comes, Sea Brother. The mental message was full of excitement.

Brian sighed and stared at the webs between his fingers. *So, Ambrio, my Feltan friend, my mother has found another useless candidate? Why does she not leave me alone?*

He heard laughter in his mind, *This one is not useless. Your mother has brought one of the demon princesses of Lantia to you.*

She did what? Brian sat up and stared at the wall in astonishment.

Remember the last princess she brought to you?

Crista, she was from some savage little country across the sea. Brian laughed. *I liked her. It was a shame that she wanted to kill all the nonhuman land dwellers for their fur. Do you know what she told me before she left?*

The voice in Brian's mind laughed with him, *She said that she would take you any day. However, she refused to live in the same land as your bitch mother*. Both the Feltan and Prince Brian relived the moment in silence. Then the Feltan continued. *As Crista left, she told your mother to go see the Lantians for a princess. 'They will give you just what you need.' Those were her exact words.*

My mother was arrogant enough to go to Lantia? Is she completely mad?

The Feltan laughed, *If she was not when she left, she is now. The princess she brought back is of Feltan blood. Lady Colsa suggested the temple instead of her deformed son. The Lantian laughed in her face. 'My people have no religion, what good would a temple do me? Lantians worship power, and it is only through the prince that I will get power. I will take Prince Brian.' Your mother is furious.*

Brian sighed, *Are my people going to accept her?*

She is Feltan blood. Ambrio's mind voice was smug. *Add to that the fact that the Lantians have the power to sway the minds of the guardians, and there can be no doubt that they will accept her.*

My friend, she is too late. She would find it impossible to reach me before time runs out. Brian refused to get excited by the prospect of freedom.

She is a trained warrior and she has sworn to us that she will free you. This one will not fail.

Another voice slid into to his mind, *She will teach you to sing again.*

Brian smiled, *Singing is only important if you are an Olpho. The rest of us have names.* He teased.

Sea Sister has a song. The Lantians know the value of true singing and your princess is very good. Brian heard laughter from more than one Olpho mind. *She has many songs. Some are really awful.*

She has promised to teach them all to you. Another Olpho mind chimed in.

You trust her so much? Brian frowned. *She is a Lantian. Who is to say she will not betray us as her people betrayed the Feltan?*

No, Sea Brother, the Lantians did not betray us. Ambrio said sadly. *Feltan greed betrayed both races. If the Lantian gives her word, she will die trying to keep it, then her family will carry on the responsibility of fulfilling her obligations.*

If my mother has her way, this one will die trying to reach me. Brian spat. *Do not try to raise my hopes now. I could not live with the disappointment if she failed.*

This one will not be easy to kill, or to catch. We will arrange for her to leave the ship and have guides waiting to lead her to you. Keep your mind open and stay in touch with the guardians. They will know where she is and how she is doing. Have faith, my young friend.

Brian lay back down and tried to figure out what he was going to do with another ambitious female. *My mother's ambition has placed me in this position. Now, I have to rely on an ambitious, Feltan-bred, Lantian, demon princess to release me.*

At least I don't have to worry about this one fainting at the sight of my scales and fangs like one of Mother's earlier selections. Damn, how I hate being in this position. I am used to solving my own problems. All my life I have been trained to nourish and to protect. Now, I am the one who needs nourishment and protection.

Do not let bitterness control your soul, my brother. The Feltan chided Brian.

Brian laughed bitterly, *You would saddle me with another ambitious woman and then warn me against bitterness*?

She is a match for your mother.

Brian sighed, *I am tired, my friend. I am angry at the guardians of this land. Because of their laws, my mother found a way to control both my father and me. They sat back and did nothing to stop her when she was weak. Now, she is strong and there is nothing they can do. They are helpless.*

The guardians made the law to ensure the continuance of your line. The Feltan said softly.

Yes, I know the reasons behind it. I understand why it is necessary. For centuries, my people have lived by the guardians' laws. Now, it seems, I will die by it. Brian's mental voice was full of sadness.

No! That would defeat their purpose. Ambrio objected. *The law states that before a prince of the blood can become the king of the land; he must be married. If he is not wed by twenty-one, the change begins. If he is not wed by twenty-six, the change ends. The prince can no longer face the light, unless one is found who will accept him as he is. You will not die.*

Brian closed his eyes as despair welled up inside him. *My Feltan friend, you do not realize what power my mother has called up from the darkness. Even the guardians could not preserve my life if the last hour of my twenty-sixth year finds me still unwed.*

That statement shocked the guardians out of their silence and a female voice whispered, *No, she could not have done this without our knowing.*

Brian closed his eyes. When he spoke at last, his mind-voice was bleak. *I am sorry, Guardian. I grieve for me, for my land, and for its inhabitants. The darkness to which my mother prays, will soon cover all Alsia.*

No! The female voice was hard and determined, *We are not so easily defeated. She will not succeed.*

Who will stop her? Brian asked sarcastically, *Your demon Lantian princess? Forgive me if I have serious doubts about her abilities. You are all fools, guardians, Feltan, Olpho, all of you. Why can you not see the truth that I see so clearly? My mother has a powerful ally and she will stop at nothing to rule Alsia and eventually the world.* He laughed bitterly, *You all expect some little princess out of legends to save us, when we cannot save ourselves. Well, I will not expect anything but my own death. Then, when it comes, I will not be unprepared.* With that, he closed his mind to both the Feltan and the guardians.

*****

The breeze molded Arianne's short, white tunic to her body. Stray tendrils from her hair played about her cheeks as she stood at the rail of Alsian's Pride. Her face was solemn. She realized that this was an important step in her future dealings with the Alsians.

Despite her show of confidence to the others, deep inside her mind, a small doubt still nagged at her. With a mental shrug, she pushed it aside again and firmly fixed her eyes on the water. She knew that if she looked at the magic island of Alsia now, she would forget everything but its beauty. This was not the time for her to be under the island's enchantment. She needed a clear mind for the meeting ahead.

Behind her, the crew of the ship stood. Lady Colsa stood coldly by her right hand. Captain Khane, a troubled expression on his weathered face, stood silently on her left.

"They come, Princess." He whispered to her, and Arianne nodded. She widened her eyes in surprise at the variety of life-forms now swimming toward them.

Slowly, the teeming mass took shape, and Arianne realized that at least twenty different species of land creatures were swimming in the water around the ship. Separated by ten feet of calm water, swam an equal number of species of sea creatures. She recognized the Olpho, but she had never seen most of the sea dweller species that swam around the ship.

Arianne stood quietly, waiting and watching. She felt a hundred different minds touching hers, but she kept her shields firmly in place. Now was not the time to open up for these creatures to inspect her, not with Lady Colsa standing by waiting for a chance to pry.

Sing greetings, Little Sea Sister. The voices of the Olpho brushed against the surface of her mind.

Arianne closed her eyes and sang. The waters were still as all the creatures stopped and listened to her song. When she was through, she opened her eyes and stared into the cold gaze of one of the land-dwellers.

So you sing like a sea-creature? Is that supposed to make us feel more kindly toward you? Why should we accept one who sings only of the sea? If you would rule the land, then you must sing for the land and not the sea. It was a challenge.

Arianne smiled softly and quietly sang the song of Lantia's joined Icina. *See*, her song whispered. *Land, sea, plains and mountains have become one. Our joining has brought us great strength and great joy. Even the wild children from the sky, the Lantians, share our song. We are at peace.*

Now is not the time for Alsia to sing that song. A soft voice touched her mind, then drifted away.

What would you have me sing?

The cold eyes stared at her for a moment, then blinked, *Listen, and learn*. It commanded, and all around her the land-dwellers began to sing.

They sang of life and death, and of the sacrifice of some so that others might survive. Predator and prey, they sang. Their song said that some must die for good of all. The strong would survive and the weak would become meat for those that hungered. In this way, all prospered and the children would be strong. Nature made no allowances for the weak or for the uncommitted in her cycle of life.

The sea-dwellers took up the song and produced perfect harmony, for they obeyed the same law. Nature was consistent. Her rules didn't change.

Arianne nodded. She knew and understood this song well; it was also the song of humans. The strong ruled the weak. Land and sea dwellers were sacrificed for food. She smiled. This was a song she could sing, for humans lived by the same rules. Man and beast were one under the laws of the natural world.

Arianne's mind and voice took up the song, and her clear alto blended in with the others. Subtly, she changed the song so that it became a hymn of praise, a celebration of life, a greeting, and a blessing.

As the last note died away, the cold-eyed nonhuman studied Arianne, then nodded his head. *The strong rules. It does not matter if you are human or nonhuman, the song is the same. Daughter of a Far Land, are you strong enough to take and hold the throne of Alsia away from the one beside you*?

Arianne looked into eyes that were not quite so cold now. *With your help, your true king and I will rule this land*. She answered.

We will help you reach our brother, but we will not fight your battles for you. The creature warned.

I can accept that. When the time comes, I'll fight my own battles. Arianne said confidently, *My mother trained me to rule, and rule I will.*

Then we agree to help you. After you have met the humans tomorrow, wait for our call, then join us on the far side of the ship. We will take you to our prince. Come as a babe, uncovered, but bring covering with you wrapped carefully to keep it dry. The voice paused. *Do you trust us?*

I do. Arianne answered firmly. Then added, *And your people, do they trust me?*

All is well. If we didn't trust you, we'd not offer our assistance. We will meet again tomorrow. Later, we will introduce you to those who guard our lands. The ones who even the temple priestesses know nothing about.

Then the cold-eyed one lifted its head and gave a loud howl that rolled across the ocean. The other land creatures echoed his cry, and the sea dwellers leapt in joy. Cheers came from the men on the ship and from the few humans standing on the beach. The nonhuman residents of Alsia had accepted the Lantian princess. At last, the true bride of Prince Brian had been found.

Arianne watched as the swimmers dispersed. When the seas were quiet again, Lady Colsa, her face cold, turned to Arianne, "I suppose you think you're very clever," she hissed. "Know this, foreign child, your ability to carry a tune will not weigh heavily with the humans." She bared her teeth in a parody of a smile, "You still have the meeting with my son to get through."

"My Lady, I thought that I was to join the others in the water?" Arianne ignored the other woman's spite as she watched the nonhuman swim away from the ship.

"It wasn't necessary. They judged you fit by your song." Lady Colsa snapped, turning away and leaving the deck.

With a small frown on her face, Arianne watched her go. She would have to deal with Prince Brian's mother sooner or later, but she hoped that it was much later. Smoke and Fire, so much darkness surrounded Lady Colsa that Arianne became ill each time she tried to touch the woman's mind.

Twice, the sea has brought destruction and pain to us.

The first time, our home world's life force rose from the bottom of the poisoned oceans to destroy us. We fled before its fury. As we had destroyed our world, so its spirit still seeks to destroy us.

The second time was worse. The Feltan, who were our beloved, took the Life and Heart of our people and still we love them. We must turn away from the sea and all who live in its depths. We must protect ourselves and hide lest we be tempted and betrayed again by our sea-bred lovers.

Sara, Senior Singer and House Philo Leader

Chapter 6

"Princess, you should rest now. The humans of Alsia will come to see you at dawn." Captain Khane bowed to Arianne.

Arianne smiled at the man, "I'll be down in a moment, I want to look at Alsia again."

The captain nodded, satisfied by her answer. "Does our fair land call to you, Princess?"

"Does the land call to me?" Arianne laughed aloud. "Captain Khane the land enchants me, overwhelms me, awes me. Never have I seen its equal." Her voice dropped, "Never shall I see its equal. Why did no one tell me what to expect?"

"How could we? Our language has no words that could describe the perfection of our land. If any of us had tried to tell you of this," Captain Khane's hands swept outward as if to embrace the land before them. "Would you have believed us?"

"No. I would have thought it was the conceit of a man for his homeland."

Captain Khane stood silently beside Arianne, then he sighed. "The perfection you see now will soon fade if our prince does not find a true mate. All the magic that is Alsia will wither and die, then we will be just another small island set in a great sea."

"What about the Lady Colsa? Can she do nothing to prevent this?" Arianne turned shocked eyes to the captain.

"Aye, the Mistress Colsa, First Priestess of the Dark Lady's temple, and mother of our prince. She has her ambitions, but she is not of royal blood and she can't renew the magic. We have long known her game, Princess, but all the candidates she chose were wrong. That's why we were so worried when she went to Lantia for you. We knew that she made her choices for her own good, not the good of the land."

The captain grinned, "In choosing you, Princess of Lantia, she made a great error. The gods have foiled her game, but I warn you to be careful. That one is a viper who controls a dark and dangerous power. She will destroy you if you are not cautious."

"She can try, but she will not succeed. The court of Lantia has taught me much about defanging vipers, Captain Khane." Arianne smiled.

She glanced at the captain, was he the ally he seemed, or was he a part of Lady Colsa's plot? She would withhold judgment for now.

"Have you made any plans, Princess?" The captain asked as he escorted Arianne to her cabin.

Arianne shrugged, "Not really, Captain. I'll meet the human delegation tomorrow and after that, who knows? I should have a better feel for what I am dealing with." Not even proven allies needed to know all one's secrets, she decided as she went into her cabin.

Khat was waiting for her, "Would you like a hot drink, Princess? Lady Colsa said that you might be over excited by all that has happened today. A good, hot drink would help you to relax." The young maid offered.

Arianne raised one brow. What was Lady Colsa up to now? She had never told Khat to offer her a drink before, why start now? The young maid stood by the door waiting for an answer.

Arianne stretched and yawned widely, "No, I'm tired enough to sleep without the aid of a drink, Khat. Thank you for your offer."

Khat bowed, "As you will Princess." she said as she left the room.

Arianne stood thoughtfully for a moment, staring around the room, then sighed. Tomorrow was another day, and she'd not worry over it until it came. Now, she must make preparations. Slowly, she folded a pair of trousers and a tunic, then removed a pair of soft boots from her closet. She added a few necessities and laid them in a small pile on her bed, wondering how she could protect them from the water.

After a moment's thought, she smiled and reached into her closet for the large cape that protected her from the rain. If it kept rain out, it should keep out the sea and its dark color would offer some protection from prying eyes once she reached the shore.

She carefully wrapped her belongings in the cape and tied it tightly with one of her belts. She hid the bundle far back in her closet, and wished she had access to a weapon. She would feel more comfortable if she was beginning this journey well armed. Arianne smiled slightly. A good Lantian bow and a quiver full of arrows would be perfect.

Arianne had no illusions about what faced her once she reached land. Lady Colsa could not afford to just sit back and wait. She would chase Arianne all the way to Prince Brian, then she would chase both of them all the way back to the capital.

Again, that was a future problem, and not one she could plan for now. She would be careful, alert, and prepared to use whatever weapon came to hand. Right now, she had a more immediate problem. How was she going to keep Khat from discovering the hidden bundle while the room was empty tomorrow morning?

Arianne lay fully dressed on the bed, her arms folded beneath her head, and stared at the ceiling. She had done all that she could for now. The rest was in the hands of her allies.

"Mother," She whispered into the night, "I am afraid. There is so much that I don't know; so much information that I desperately need and have no means of obtaining. This is not the Lantian way, to go blindly into battle armed only with our hopes. I am afraid and I don't even know what it is that I fear. Right now, I wish I was at home with Rolto and my sisters." Arianne sighed as she closed her eyes and drifted gently off to sleep.

Khat woke her early the next morning, "Princess, it is time for you to dress." She said, shaking Arianne's shoulders.

Arianne rolled over, "In a little while." She mumbled.

"Now, Princess, unless you want to miss the first meal." Khat insisted.

"Okay, okay. Give me a minute. Prepare a bath for me while you wait."

"It has been done, Princess."

Arianne scowled and rubbed her eyes, "Go away, Khat, I've been washing myself since my tenth birthday. I think I can manage this alone."

"Princess, it's not fitting." Khat protested.

"Yes, I know. That's what they told me in Lantia. Still, today I wish to wash my own body. You should know by now, Khat, that I don't always do what is fitting. Go away."

Arianne ignored the hot drink the maid brought in for her and hurried through her morning toilette. With a grim smile, she glanced around the room before she left it. She deliberately made an awful mess, hoping that cleaning up would keep Khat too occupied to snoop.

After the morning meal, Captain Khane handed her a small case, "You must wear the contents for your meeting with the dignitaries of Alsia, Princess." He instructed, ignoring Lady Colsa's frown.

"These are the symbols of your rank in Alsia. Only after the nonhuman have accepted a candidate as the True Chosen can she wear these. You will be the first in two generations to wear the bands."

Arianne glanced at Lady Colsa, and the captain shook his head. "The nonhuman of Alsia never accepted her." he whispered.

Slowly, Arianne opened the lid. Captain Khane reached in and removed two of the objects. "When the humans accept you, they will give you these two." He said holding up a narrow gold circlet for her head and a large signet ring.

"Put on the other objects now." The captain instructed Arianne.

Arianne removed two heavy bands fashioned to be worn high on her arms, and gasped, surprised at the beauty and workmanship of the arm bracelets. One was of pure silver. The Alsians had carved a stately procession of different land creatures. The other was of bright, shining gold, and on it, many sea creatures swam and danced.

She slid the wide bands up her arms until they lay halfway between her elbow and her shoulders. The captain reached over with a strange tool and sealed the clasps.

"You can't remove these bands from your arm now." He told her as he stepped back. "When Brian dies and your firstborn son takes an acceptable mate, the clasps will open. No magic on earth will make them lock for you again. The accepted mate of the ruling prince must always wear these. Do you understand?"

"Yes. I thank you, Captain Khane."

"Don't thank me. It's your right to wear these objects and my duty to give them to you. Come now. We must go to the upper decks and meet the delegates from the court and the temples of Alsia."

Arianne made a striking picture as she stood on the upper deck of Alsian's Pride. Her pure, white tunic and pants were trimmed in emerald green and silver, the Alsian prince's colors. She had polished her black knee-high boots until they shone and had fitted a wide, black belt with a large, silver buckle tightly at her waist to represent Lantian House Royale colors. When the slashed sleeves of her tunic moved, the arm bands glowed brightly in the sunlight.

She deliberately left her hair loose for this ceremony. Now, it danced around her body in the soft breeze blowing off the land. Arianne watched the richly-dressed delegates from Alsia as they came aboard. She glanced down at the large crowd of people watching the ceremony, caught the eye of a young boy in the front row of the crowd and winked at him. The crowd was far enough away that they were not aware of her odd colored eyes. The child stared in surprise until Arianne grinned and winked again.

The boy giggled, "Mommy, the pretty princess winked her eyes at me." he shrieked.

Arianne met the eyes of the child's mother and they shared a smile. Others in the crowd saw the byplay, and the muttering grew louder. Arianne waved and threw a kiss, playing the crowd in the manner of Lantian royalty. The crowd was silent for a moment, then their cheers and shouts split the air.

"It's the true princess come at last." The crowd chanted.

Arianne grinned at them, her face full of mischief, and they responded with laughter and more shouts. She glanced behind her. The captain and crew looked at her proudly.

Lady Colsa and most of the priestesses were frowning; a few of them looked uncomfortable.The noblemen all wore smug expressions.

So, Arianne thought, *dissension exists here as well. The courtiers may not be for me, but then they're not for Lady Colsa either. Colsa also has a problem inside the ranks of the temple. They are not solidly behind her. That's going to make life very difficult for her. I wonder if they would be of any help to me?*

One nobleman interrupted her musings. He stepped forward. A small, middle-aged woman walked beside him. "I'm Lord Orion of the mountains and this is my wife, Athna, through whom I rule. We speak with one voice for the lords of Alsia."

Arianne gave the older man a haughty look, copied from her mother, "I am the Princess Arianne of Lantia. The A-Kiyama, oldest daughter of the royal house and second-in-line to rule after my brother. I am a Singer of Songs, a Sea Dreamer, and a Wind Speaker. The Feltan stand among my ancestors.

"I speak to the voice of the deep oceans. The nonhuman dwellers of both the land and the sea have paid me homage. The tailed Feltan have greeted me as cousin."

A startled gasp came from her listeners.

"She lies." Lady Colsa's voice rang out.

Harl stepped forward, "No, Mistress Colsa, one morning as I stood here on the deck, I saw her conversing with the Feltan. He smiled upon her, and gave her his blessing."

"Why didn't you tell me this Harl?" Lady Colsa snarled.

"Mistress Colsa," the old sailor answered sadly, "My first duty is to the land of Alsia and its prince, not to you."

Captain Khane stepped forward and handed Orion the gold circlet; he and Athna stepped forward and placed the circlet on Arianne's head.

"Welcome to Alsia, Princess Arianne, A-Kiyama of Lantia." Lord Orion stumbled slightly over the strange word, then continued. "We do homage to you as the true chosen of our prince." He said formally, then bent over and kissed her cheeks.

The Lady Athna hugged the young princess and whispered, "Be cautious, youngling, the welcome is not the crowning and our prince not yet king. Until you and Prince Brian have accomplished those objectives, you still stand alone."

Arianne nodded; that was about what she had expected. She then turned to the priestesses. "Well?"

Lady Colsa stepped forward, a large signet ring in her hand. "When you accept this symbol, Princess Arianne, only death will free you from your commitment to our prince. Do you understand this? I suggest you go to the temple and finish the training that you started with me. Then, when you are ready, we'll introduce you to our prince, and he can give you the ring."

Arianne shook her head and held her hand out, "I lost the right to refuse your prince when I stepped aboard the Alsian's Pride. The signet ring, Lady Colsa, give it to me. I have the gift of my ancestors, the Feltan, I can see clearly into the hearts of others.

"It is a gift well-honed by living in the court of Lantia where treachery is an everyday occurrence, and assassins lurk in every shadow. At first, I didn't seek treachery from you, but still I sensed that your purpose was not what you said. Now that I know of your true ambition, I can see clearly how you would threaten me. I know now that I cannot trust you and yours.

"You would place me in your temple in the care of your priestesses and none would hear of me again. I am young, Lady Colsa, and even at times, thoughtless. However, no one has ever accused me of stupidity, and to trust you would be very stupid. Give me the ring, Lady, now."

Lady Colsa looked around her, then slowly handed the signet ring to Arianne. "This contest is not yet over, Princess," she hissed.

Arianne placed the ring on her finger and held her hands up so the watching crowd might see it. Under cover of their cheers, she gave Lady Colsa her answer, "It is over. Retire to your temple, Lady Colsa. Do not interfere with me and mine again. Your authority over this land has ended."

"Idiot child, you know nothing. You have no idea of the powers at my command." Lady Colsa spat.

"As you know nothing of me, or of my people." Arianne answered coldly. "Do not underestimate us." Arianne paused, then smiled a slow, deadly smile.

"I have much to learn about this land, but not from you or any of yours." Arianne continued calmly.

"Will you return to the palace with us?" Lady Athna interrupted.

"No, not yet. I still have another task left to do." Arianne answered as she turned and walked away.

With a bitter smile, Arianne decided that if she pretended to be brave long enough, it would become the truth. At least Khat wasn't in the room waiting for her.

An hour later, she heard a timid knock on her cabin door. "Who is it?"

"Princess, its me, Oldie. The captain wishes to know if you are joining us for dinner, or if you would prefer a tray in your room?"

Arianne thought for a moment. She didn't want to face Lady Colsa again today. "Please can you, not Khat, bring me a tray?"

"I can do that for you," The young man answered. "When you are through eating, place your used dishes outside your cabin door."

Arianne breathed a small sigh of relief and lay back on her bunk, letting her mind drift into one of her people's relaxing trances. When her meal arrived, she ate slowly, savoring each bite of the highly spiced fish stew. She tried to maintain the calmness she gained in the past hour. She washed her face and hands and watched the sky outside the small, round window above her bunk slowly darken. When it was completely dark, she closed the curtains, locked her door, and lit the small lamp bolted on the cabin wall. It was time for her to prepare for the call from her allies. Swiftly, she braided her hair into a long, tight plait, then pinned it to her head and covered it with a woven black cap. Now, no gleam of silver would betray her when she left the ship.

Arianne was tense as she reached far back into her closet. She only relaxed when her hands closed around the hidden bundle. She added the circlet and the signet ring to it, and bound it with her belt. Then, wearing only her undergarments and the armbands, she tied the bundle to her waist with the ends of the belt. She sat on her bed to wait for the summons from the nonhuman land dwellers.

The Great Tower to signal those we love but cannot trust,

The Great Wall to help us protect those we trust but cannot love,

The Great Library to remind us of both.

Singer, sing for your people, keep them strong.

Never let the memory of the past or the certainty of our future die.

We are doomed.

We are mad.

Carta's Lament by Griff, a Lantian Bard

Chapter 7

As she sat on her bed in the dimly lit room, fine tremors rippled through her body. Absently, she rubbed her arms and wondered if she was shivering from excitement or from fear.

What am I getting into? I have sworn to a group of animals, on the honor of my people and my name, to help a strange, young man fight against his own mother. I don't even know if he wants to fight this battle. I don't know anything about him. All that I do know is that Lady Colsa is a very dangerous and powerful woman.

She laughed quietly. *Is Lady Colsa correct in calling me stupid, or am I just arrogant to believe that I can defeat her?* Arianne shook her head. *This is no good. All these doubts will weaken my resolve. I must believe in myself, and my mother's promise to help. With Mother's help, defeating Lady Colsa will be easy.*

Come. The voice whispered into Arianne's mind.

She stood up, took a deep breath to calm her nerves, and smiled. *I am not so brave after all, s*he thought wryly. Carefully, she drew a large, flowing cape around her body. Then, certain that no trace of the bundle around her waist showed, she softly left her room and headed for the upper deck. She passed no one in the corridors. Once she reached the deck, the few crewmembers on watch ignored her.

Arianne wondered briefly where the Lady Colsa might be as she walked to the side of the ship away from the beach. She gave a quick glance around to make sure no one could see her, then dropped her cape, climbed on the rails, and slid into the water.

Captain Khane smiled as he watched the young princess disappear over the side of his ship. The captain stepped out of the darkened pilot room, glanced around, and nodded. He was the only person in the area. He picked up her discarded cape and hid it below deck in his private quarters. He walked to the ship's lounge to find Lady Colsa berating a frightened and embarrassed Harl.

"Mistress Colsa," Captain Khane interrupted, his voice cold, "Harl is one of my men. It is not your place to discipline him. He told me what he saw the day the Feltan visited the Lantian princess. I decided to keep that information from you."

"How dare you make such a decision? Your position as master of the Mariner's Guild does not place you above my laws. Have you forgotten that I am the ruler of this land until my son is fit to take over? You have betrayed me, Captain Khane," Lady Colsa snarled, "I will remember this, and you will pay dearly for it."

"I have forgotten nothing, Mistress Colsa." The captain's voice was calm as he glanced at the gathering of priestesses and noblemen in his ship's lounge, "You may have forgotten, however, that the Mariner's Guild is an independent entity in this land. Anger us and we will take our ships and go elsewhere. Our love for Alsia does not extend to you, and we would find new harbors before we let you force us to do your will." He smiled and asked softly, "Do any of you think your power is great enough to challenge me?"

Khane waited a minute, giving those gathered in the room time to absorb the import of his words, then shook his head and continued. "I thought not. I have never sworn allegiance to any Alsian ruler, though a bond does exist between your son, Prince Brian, and my guild."

Colsa stared at Captain Khane, her face reflecting her deep, frustrated anger. At last, she hissed, "Where is the Lantian bitch princess?"

Captain Khane laughed. "If you had listened to the gossip, Mistress, you would have known about the demon princesses of Lantia. However, you considered yourself above common seaman gossip. So now you must pay for your arrogance. As for the young princess, she went to her room and locked the door behind her. She needs a rest from us and our petty squabbles."

Captain Khane smiled at the people gathered in his ship's lounge and then stepped forward to ring a small bell by the door.

"Drinks, anyone?" He offered, his deep voice rich with quiet satisfaction.

Il Ho a Lantia, the life and heart of Lantia,
The Battle Cry and the lament of our people.
Il Ho a Lantia, the name of the jewel that holds the soul of every Lantian who has died since we fled our home world.
Il Ho a Lantia, the tears of a people.
History of the People
Kenda Larum, Historian, House Larum

Chapter 8

I'm not a very good swimmer. Arianne warned the waiting animals.

That's all right. You can hang on to my tail and hold on tightly. We swim much faster than most humans anyway. The speaker, one of the larger land creatures, belonged to the same species as her cold-eyed inquisitor of the day before.

Arianne grabbed his tail and asked, *Who are you?*

I am Kelv, of the forest, and pack master of the Cantus. The smaller creature swimming on our right is Ulph, of the plains. She's howl-mistress of the Wolvines. On our left is Bunto. He is of the mountains, and burrow-master of the Montro. He knows all the underground passages and all the caves in Alsia.

I thought that more than just your three species were at the greeting yesterday.

We came for you because we are the only species that are comfortable in the water. The others will swim, but only when absolutely necessary. Ulph answered.

Where are we going?

Do you see the area where the land sticks out into the sea? We go around it. Where the forest meets the water, we go ashore. We will rest for a few hours then go on to meet the forest guardian. We will guide you through the forest, across the plains, and into the mountains. Bunto will take you through the caves to where Prince Brian is. After that, you'll be on your own. Kelv explained.

Who will guide us back to the city? Arianne asked.

Kelv snorted, *Prince Brian is of Alsia, why would he need guides?*

The Cantus' tone of voice suggested that Arianne had asked a stupid question.

Arianne blushed and was quiet. *I thought my question was reasonable. After all, I don't know my way around all of Lantia. I would never find my way from the northern border to the palace.*

They swam the rest of the way in silence. It took them almost an hour to reach the section of the shoreline that was their goal. The princess and her three escorts pulled themselves tiredly out of the water, then walked the short distance to where the trees began.

The animals shook themselves vigorously, then Ulph loped away, *Come, Princess, let us rinse the salt from our fur.* She called.

Arianne followed Ulph to a small, freshwater pool and removed the bundle tied to her waist before sliding into the cool water to rinse her body and her hair. Then she unwrapped her bundle and rinsed her cloak. She sat in the clearing, combing her hair and shivering in the cool night air.

She had not brought a towel so Arianne decided that the night wind would have to dry her off. When she was dry, Arianne dressed, braided her hair, wound it around her head and covered it with one of the hoods she had brought with her.

The animals waited patiently for her to finish her toilette, then loped off toward the distant mountains. She followed slowly, carrying her waterproof cloak thrown over one arm. As they walked, Arianne studied the animals. The Cantus, Kelv, was a large, well-muscled creature, with blue fur broken up by dark green stripes. The top of his head reached her shoulders when he stood on all four paws. If Kelv ever stood on his hind legs, he would be taller than most of the men she knew. The Wolvine, Ulph, was solid green and smaller than the Cantus, only half his length or height. Both had the sharp teeth, and powerful jaws that proclaimed them meat eaters.

The Montro, however, was completely different. He had the blunt teeth of a plant-eater. His fur was a solid smoky-gray, and he was long and thin, with four, short, powerfully-clawed feet. He was easily as long as the Wolvine, but only about one-third her height.

As they traveled into the forest, Arianne was aware of other animals joining them on their journey. The others kept out of sight, and when she reached out to touch their minds, she received no response. Her three guides were silent. They walked in front of her, stopping occasionally to make sure she was keeping up. Arianne wished that they would communicate with her. Their silence left her too much time for worrisome thoughts. She bit her lip, realizing that these creatures would have to make the first move. She could not force them to accept her; she would have to wait until they were ready. They traveled for two days, stopping only to sleep. Kelv and Ulph hunted during the night and Arianne and Bunto shared the bounty of the fruit trees that grew in abundance around them.

Deep in the forest, they came to a large clearing. Huge stones surrounded a small pool of black water. Kelv led Arianne to the pool.

Stand here, Princess, he instructed, *This place is the heart of the Alsian forest. Before we go any further, we must introduce you to the forest land and its guardian.*

Then, leaving her alone, he stepped back among the tall, silver-leafed trees.

Arianne took a deep breath and looked around. The trees blocked most of the moon's rays, creating a dappled effect of light and shadow. The air was cool and damp, with the musty smell of decaying matter. Fallen leaves covered the ground and a few smaller plants struggled valiantly to survive in the shadow of their larger brothers.

She glanced into the pool and her own reflection stared back at her. The water was absolutely still. The slight breeze did not cause a single ripple to disturb its surface. Arianne frowned, trying to remember where she had heard of such still, black water before. It was something to do with Lantian history before they came to this world, and it was not pleasant. The arrival of the other forest creatures disturbed her thoughts.

Silently, the forest creatures joined her. Each came up to Arianne, sniffed her hands and then moved away. When the strange ceremony was over, Arianne stood alone in the middle of a circle of animals.

From the creatures around her, came a low humming that slowly grew in intensity until the whole forest echoed the sound. Though she felt no breeze blowing, the branches of the huge trees around the clearing bent toward her. The whispering of their leaves wove through the sound of animals' humming. The water in the pool at her feet churned and boiled then shot straight up in the air, creating a towering pillar of liquid.

Arianne stared in astonishment and a touch of fear, as not one drop escaped from the fountain. The water swirled in the air and formed the shape of a woman. The humming around her grew more intense. The whispering grew louder, and Arianne felt the sounds pass through her body and lodge deep in her mind.

The liquid from the pool, now a solid shape of a tall woman with flowing silver hair and green skin, smiled and reached her hands out to Arianne.

Welcome, Daughter of a Far Land. Alsia's forests greet you. The words tumbled into the young woman's mind, and shimmered in the air before her.

Arianne knew she should do or say something, but she didn't know what. She felt overwhelming relief. Whatever she feared had not happened. She smiled, pulled the concealing hood from her hair, and from deep in her throat, imitated the sounds the animals were making. She stretched her hands until her fingers touched those of the Lady in the pool, and for an instant, she and the Lady were one. The forest and all that dwelt in it became a part of her soul.

"Icina," she whispered, "I bring you greetings from Lantia."

Softly, Arianne sang the song of Lantia, and the Lady of Alsia's forest smiled.

I name you, Friend, Sister, Daughter. The Silver Lady's voice echoed through Arianne's mind, then darkness closed upon her and Arianne knew no more.

When Arianne opened her eyes, she was lying in the clearing. The pool was again just a pool, and only her original three companions were with her. *Did I dream it?*

Kelv, raised his head to stare at her, *What do you think?*

So, are we going to be friends now? Arianne whispered in her head.

We will see. It will be easier now that the Silver Lady, guardian of the forests of Alsia, has called you sister and friend. She has accepted our judgment of you and blessed our journey. The animal shrugged his massive shoulders, *Who can tell what the future may hold for us? Go to sleep now, Princess. Tomorrow, we travel toward the plains.* Kelv rumbled softly.

It was late the next day when the four travelers left the forests and stepped onto the plains of Alsia.

Arianne, her hair once more covered, was glad to be away from the forest. The stale, damp air irritated her nostrils and chilled her body.

We'll spend the night here on the edge of the forest, Kelv said. *Tomorrow, Ulph becomes our guide, for the plains is her domain as the forest is mine. We go to hunt. Do you wish us to bring a part of our kill back here for you to share?* He asked slyly.

Arianne nodded, aware that this was a test the predators were giving her. She was sure she could probably figure out some way to make the meat edible, and a diet of only fruits would not keep her strong for long.

The two large predators loped off into the gathering dusk, and Bunto, the Montro, whispered shyly. *If the princess wishes some roots and fruits, I can gather them for her.*

Arianne smiled. *Thank you, Bunto. I would love to have some fruit.*

The Montro disappeared, a small gray shadow lost in a forest of gray shadows. Arianne sat on the ground and leaned back against a large tree. She watched the orange sun slide behind the purple mountains.

She closed her eyes, and she fell into a dream that was not a dream. In her mind, she saw towering mountains all around her. She saw a dark cave high in the sky and shivered from a cold breeze that brought a touch of frost to the heart of summer.

At the mouth of the cave she saw the outline of a tall, muscular man and knew that this was the prince for whom she searched. She found no welcome, but a challenge in his stance. Arianne strained to see him more clearly...

Princess, see, I've brought the fruits I promised you. Bunto's soft mind-voice woke her. *It's not yet time for mountain dreams. We have many more sunsets before we reach them.*

Arianne blinked and looked at the small creature sitting at her feet. By his side lay three bright, red fruits, wrapped in leaves for easier carrying.

My thanks, Friend. She murmured picking up one of the fruits and taking a bite.

What are these? She asked in surprise. The fruit was soft, juicy, and very sweet. *I've never eaten anything like them.*

They are a delicacy found only in the land of Alsia. My people call them 'Sweet Fruit'. I don't know what the humans name them.

Arianne licked her lips and greedily started in on the second fruit. "Good." She mumbled, her mouth full.

Arianne wiped her chin with the back of her hand and grinned at the thought of Lady Colsa's reaction if she saw her docile, little princess now. She finished the last of the fruit, and was wiping her fingers on the grass when Kelv and Ulph returned. Kelv was carrying a bloody chunk of raw meat in his jaws. He dropped it at Arianne's feet and wandered off, leaving her to stare in shock at his offering.

Arianne had never cooked anything in her life. She didn't even know how to start a fire. When she trained with the Home Guard, the cooks took care of the fires and food, leaving the fighters free to concentrate on their fighting.

She sighed. Well, now was a good time to learn. The young princess walked around gathering dead twigs off the ground, then she set them in a pile and stared at them. She needed a fire, but had no idea how to make the wood, burn. In the back of her mind, she once more saw that shadowy male figure. She didn't need mind touch to let her know that he was mocking her ignorance. She sensed, deep down, that this was another test she must pass.

All right, she told herself sternly, *I know some Lantians eat raw meat. They put lots of seasonings on it first, but I don't know what kind of herbs they use. I don't think I would recognize the herbs needed, but if I can remember enough about the taste and smell of those herbs, Bunto might know what they are.*

Bunto, I need these. In her mind she projected the taste and smell of the herbs that she remembered.

The small, gray creature nodded and scurried off. He soon returned, carrying the spices she had asked for in his mouth. Arianne rubbed the leaves between her hands and then carefully rubbed the spices on the raw meat. When she had covered the meat, she took a tiny bite, and chewed cautiously.

She gagged, this could not be how the spiced meat that came out of her mother's kitchen tasted, she must have forgotten some important ingredient. Arianne swallowed her first bite and took another. She would eat this offering if it took her all night.

The three animals watched her until they grew bored and lay their heads down to sleep. Arianne caught a flash of thought as the animals shared their amusement over her behavior with the meat and spices they had provided for her.

Arianne ate as much of the meat as she could, buried the rest, then sighed. *I am doing a lot of sighing lately*, she thought with a smile. *I need to wash and I need to drink.*

This way. Ulph stood up lazily and motioned Arianne to follow with a swish of her tail.

After Arianne drank and washed, she went back to her tree, and lay down to sleep. Briefly, she wondered if Alsia's prince, and her mate, would visit her again.

Bunto woke her early the next morning with another offering of fruit. After she ate, Arianne washed her hands, then braided and covered her hair.

Bunto, you do not claim either the forest or the plains as your home. How did you know where to look for the plants and the fruits we have shared? She asked as she gathered her pack and prepared to leave.

I live off the bounty of the forests and the plains. In the summer, I come out of the mountains and gather *supplies to last me through the winter. Do not the creatures of your land do the same?* Bunto's nose twitched curiously.

I don't know. My brother, who will rule Lantia, is closer to the wild brothers and sisters than I am. I have never had contact with them. Arianne smiled at the thought of her brother. He would love this land as much as she did.

She did not recall if she'd dreamt last night, but, remembering what she felt earlier, Arianne was glad that she had not left her cloak on the beach. The mountains would be cold and the cloak would come in handy.

Are you ready, Princess? Ulph stretched and yawned. *Let's go, the plains are hot this time of year, and it's best if we travel during the morning and the evening's cool. We'll rest during the hottest part of the day. It will take us seven nights to reach the foothills, and small cousins in Kopol warn that warriors of the temple are already looking for you.*

Kopol? Arianne asked as she stretched her muscles.

Yes, that is the main city in our land. It is also where the main temple of the Dark Lady is.

Dark Lady? Arianne was beginning to feel like an echo, but all of this information was new to her. *I have heard of the Bright Lady, but who is this Dark Lady?*

The Bright Lady is what the humans call the major guardians. The Dark Lady is... Ulph paused.She wrinkled her nose in distaste.

The Dark Lady is something that the mother of our prince created. It stands for everything the true guardians abhor. Bunto finished the explanation.

Arianne was thoughtful as she followed the animals. The Bright Lady was a combination of all the Icina of this land. Alsia had at least three spirits and no one had yet sung the song of joining to them. That would mean the Dark Lady wanted to destroy the land instead of protect it. Why would Lady Colsa make an agreement with an Icina that wished to destroy what Colsa wanted to rule? Arianne shrugged. Right now, it didn't matter, though something deep within warned her that she must know the answer to that question before she met Lady Colsa again.

They moved swiftly across the open ground. The land here was flat and covered with a thick, dark grass that was soft and spongy underfoot.

Do the people of Alsia have farms on these plains? She asked.

Yes, but the farms are farther to the east. Ulph replied. *Sometimes, when the winter is very harsh, and food on the plains is scarce, we raid the farms. We'll not meet any humans on this trip if we're lucky, though. The guardians have given the western plains to the fur brothers and the humans have the eastern ones.*

Don't the humans come this way at all?

Ulph laughed, *Just as we raid their farms in winter, they raid our grounds for meat and fur. The guardians don't interfere, for all must eat and have shelter. During the summer months, we each keep to our own territory. We must stop now, for soon it will be too hot to travel.*

Arianne nodded and wiped the sweat from her eyes. Her body had been telling her that it was too hot to travel for the last three hours. Lantia was north of Alsia, and this kind of heat was unknown in her lands.

The three animals soon found a spot they thought suitable and set about digging a shallow depression in the ground. When they were through, all four travelers lay in it. At first, the freshly dug earth was cool, but as time passed Arianne became very uncomfortable. Her clothes, wet with sweat, stuck to her body. Her head itched and the air was so hot and moist that each breath threatened to drown her. She shifted, trying to find a cool spot in the earth, then stiffened as she saw in her mind the shadowy, mocking figure of the prince of Alsia.

What's wrong, Sister? Ulph murmured sleepily.

He watches and mocks me. Your prince doesn't think I'm strong enough to make this trip.

Are you? Ulph rumbled, amused. *The worst part of this journey is still ahead of us. If you want to quit, let us know now. We could take you to the temple outpost in the guardian lands east of here.*

I'm strong enough. I won't quit.

Then lay still. It makes you even hotter when you wiggle like a cub. Ulph advised. *Think cool thoughts, of moonlit nights, deep rivers, and white snows. It helps.*

Arianne tried to follow Ulph's advice. She tried to imagine the sweat on her body was the result of swimming; that she was laying on a Lantian Beach and not in the middle of a hot, Alsian plain. It worked well enough for her to sleep fitfully during the rest of the day.

When the sun finally set, Ulph stood and shook the dirt from her fur, *Come. Time to move on.*

The air was still hot, but now, a strong breeze was blowing, and after they traveled a while, it started to rain. *Ulph, is it always like this?* Arianne asked.

Yes. Hot, dry days, warm, wet evenings and cool nights. In this way, the plants that grow on the plains receive nourishment.

At first, Arianne enjoyed the rain. It cleaned and cooled her body. She tilted her head back and caught the raindrops in her mouth, quenching her thirst.

All around her, she sensed other animals going about their business, for during the night, the plains of Alsia came alive. Ulph and Kelv disappeared for an hour or so, while Bunto and Arianne walked on. When they returned, Ulph gave Arianne a part of her kill.

The young princess held the bleeding chunk of meat in her hands and shrugged. Her body needed nourishment and while it might make her gag, the raw meat wouldn't kill her. She ate with small, cautious bites while they walked. The pouring rain washed the blood from her hands and face. She sensed the approval of her traveling companions and smiled.

This would definitely convince the enemies of her land that she was a demon princess. Arianne laughed softly. The Princess Royal and A-Kiyama, second-heir to the throne of Lantia, traveling in the rain, accompanied by three wild animals and eating raw meat would surprise no one, except, maybe, the Alsians.

I can see why the other princesses failed. Arianne grinned.

You've not passed yet, Princess. Ulph warned.

I will, Arianne stated quietly.

Ulph was silent, then she murmured, *Yes, I believe you will.*

Toward dawn, the temperature dropped and the rain stopped. Arianne shivered. As she trotted tiredly behind her guides, she unfolded her cape and wrapped it around her shoulders, but the wet material chilled her even more.

Don't worry, when the sun comes up, we'll all dry out very quickly. We've made good time tonight. If we can keep up this speed, we'll reach the foothills before the seven nights allotted us. Ulph glanced over her shoulders at the shivering princess.

We have heard from our small brothers that Lady Colsa has sent her temple warriors out to search for you. She has told them that you are lost, that they must find you and bring you back to the temple. Ulph snickered, *She has also told them that the trip away from your home has unhinged your mind. They are to pay no heed to anything you should say.*

Arianne laughed, *Smoke and Fire, I gave her that idea myself. Do you know where the temple warriors are?*

They are heading for the foothills, hoping to intercept us. We must reach there first, and be gone before the warriors arrive. Right now, they are traveling slowly, thinking that you will slow us.

Soon, they'll know better and speed up their march. Ulph was worried. *Sister, if we must travel by day, could you do it?*

I don't know, but I'll do my best to keep up.

We will see, it might not be necessary, but if it is, we'll try to make it as easy as possible for you.

They traveled far into the heat of the day before the animals again dug a shelter and the companions collapsed in it. Arianne was so exhausted that the heat didn't bother her at first. She quickly fell asleep, only to awaken hours later drenched in sweat.

Come, I know that it is still hot, but we must hurry. The temple warriors now have riding beasts and they know where we are. Ulph's voice said urgently in Arianne's mind.

How did they find out where we are?

The minor guardians, those of the Bright Lady's people who keep the border between our lands and the lands of the humans, told them. Ulph was already moving out.

I thought they were on our side.

They are, but they are sworn to give aid to the temple and must always tell the truth.

That must be very uncomfortable, having to tell the truth all the time. Arianne grinned and the animals gave short barks of laughter.

By dawn of the next day, Arianne was stumbling with exhaustion. She traveled in a daze, her feet moving more through habit than any conscious effort. She had eaten the raw meat given to her by Ulph and drank the rain to quench her thirst, but she'd done it unconsciously.

When the animals stopped again that day, Arianne collapsed in the shelter and didn't move again until Ulph called her urgently, *Hurry, Sister, we must move on. We've done a seven-night journey in five. Dawn will find us in the foothills.*

Will the temple warriors be there? Arianne asked as she stumbled to her aching feet.

Pray not. We must all rest before beginning the trip into the mountains. A safe place for us to rest before we reach the foothills exists, but only if we can reach it before the temple warriors reach us.

Then let's go. Arianne said and forced her tired body into motion.

As she moved numbly along behind her guides, she felt the touch of her prince's mind and smiled. Thinking rude things to him took her mind off how tired she was.

Have you touched her mind, my son? The soft voice of the forest guardian whispered in Brian's mind.

"I have." Brian whispered back.

Well, what do you think?

Does it matter what I think? Just get her here before my birthday. That's all that matters, isn't it?

Son of Alsia, she is a worthy mate for you.

Brian sighed and spoke aloud again, "I know all of you have done the best you could, but I would have liked to choose my own mate."

As your father did? See what trouble that has caused? The voice was sharp.

"Is this one any better?" Brian asked tiredly.

You have watched her. You know the answer to that question as well as we do. The Forest Lady chided.

This one has honor. Even if I repulse her, she will do her best to hide it and to accept me because she has given her word. This is not what I want from a life mate, Guardian.

Beloved of the Land, I think you underestimate the Lantian. Her people are wise in ways Alsians are not. They see past the outer shell to what is inside a being.

Guardian, I am as deformed inside as I am on the outside. Hatred for my mother and all she stands for, consumes me. I seethe with distrust of my lords. I burn with anger against the guardians of my land. Go away and leave me in peace.

My son, she will understand. Shall I tell you a story I just heard about her people? It would help you to understand her a little. Brian found the guardian's voice soothing.

It would at least relieve the boredom. Brian answered.

The Spirit of Lantia told me this today. She is so proud of her people. The guardian paused, *She is also a terrible gossip.*

Guardian, you are telling me a story.

The Lantians are mighty warriors, and they have great powers of the mind.

Isn't that cheating if you have that sort of power and your enemies don't? Brian interrupted.

Hush. The Lantians, before every battle, put on a show of power. They cause winds to blow around them and lightning to flash. Colored lights dance about their heads. Then, when the show is over, they walk very slowly toward their enemies.

At this point the opposing armies always charge, screaming toward the Lantians. Always, they would find themselves facing the opposite direction, charging back toward their own lines.

The Lantians never kill an honorable foe, they only hit them over the head and knock them unconscious. If the enemy tries any dishonorable tactics however, the Lantians slaughter them without mercy.

They are mad. Brian shook his head.

Maybe. I don't know, but listen. Recently, a general from LaPonte decided that instead of having his troops charge the Lantians, he would walk slowly toward them, that he would mimic their tactics.

What happened? Brian grinned. He had an idea about what those madmen from Lantia probably did, but he wanted to see if he was right.

Well, when at last the two armies stood a hand's distance apart, the Lantian officer in charge laughed. All the other Lantians started singing a song in praise of the general's courage and intelligence. They offered him a glass of wine and signed a peace treaty with LaPonte the next day. I hear the young Crista is to be a part of the treaty. The prince of Lantia is taking her as his bride.

Brian nodded. *I thought that's what would happen. Guardian, these Lantians are completely insane, and Crista will be very happy among them. Tell me, how do you think their insanity will help us?*

Not insanity my son, unpredictability, the Lantians try very hard never to do what anyone expects of them. They live by a set of laws that are all their own. That is why we believe the young princess will outwit Lady Colsa. With her on our side, we have at least a chance against your mother.

"Do you know that she calls me, 'Hers'?" Brian whispered.

You are hers, as she is yours. The guardian answered.

"Go away and leave me alone, I must think." Brian cried out as he closed his mind.

He stared at the darkness around him and felt it seep into his soul. With a groan, he reached for his own small ray of light. Brian opened his mind and touched the mind of the young woman who could be his curse as well as his salvation.

He felt first her exhaustion, then her start of recognition when his mind touched hers.

So, my prince, you are still checking on me. How am I doing so far? Are you proud of me, or are you still waiting for me to fail? I won't fail or give up, you know. I am going to reach you, and when I do, I hope you appreciate all the trouble I've been through to reach you. Her thoughts brushed his.

Brian did not answer and she laughed silently at him. *I also hope that you are worth all this pain and exhaustion.* She waited a moment then asked slyly, *Are you going to be this silent always? If so, our marriage will be very boring. I hope you have a good imagination, my prince.*

Brian smiled and gently withdrew. *This Lantian demon has courage and humor.* He laughed aloud, *I have just realized she really is mine, as much as I am hers.*

Lantian Honor

This is all that we are, all that we have been, all that we will be.

Honor is all we have left.

We who are soldiers, who swore to protect a people, who carried their own destruction within them.

We are all that is left and our Honor is all that we have.

Senior Singer Ilona Royale, House Royale

Chapter 9

Just a little farther, Sister. See the stone circle over there? Once we reach it, we'll be safe. Ulph urged Arianne softly, her eyes shining with pride in the young human.

Arianne nodded. She didn't have the energy to speak. She had never been so tired in her life, and all her willpower was focused on keeping her feet moving. If she stumbled now, Arianne knew she wouldn't be able to get back up.

The temple warriors come. Bunto thought frantically at them, *Run for the stone circle, run!*

Deep inside herself, Arianne found the last bit of strength in her exhausted body and ran with stumbling steps toward their goal. Her breath came in harsh, painful gasps and her eyes glazed.

She heard the temple warriors' riding beasts coming closer. Arrows landed around them, making her stop.

Keep moving, Ulph's voice commanded.

No. You three go on ahead, I will hold them until you reach safety.

They will take you back to the temple. Bunto argued.

The three animals stopped about five feet in front of Arianne.

Go on. Arianne urged her companions. *I'm too tired to go any farther, and will only hold you back. I will not endanger any of you. These temple warriors are using arrows. If I was well-rested, this would be no problem. I could protect all of us from the arrows. In the condition I am now, I can barely protect myself. Trust me. Have your friends watch for me. When I am rested, I will escape and try to meet you somewhere.*

See that line of hills to the north? Bunto asked quickly as the furred brothers moved toward the safe place. *Meet us there when you escape.*

Arianne nodded and turned to face the advancing group of temple warriors.

She reached up and freed her hair so the long mass of silver poured down her back. The tendrils reached out toward the warriors, and then curled lovingly back around Arianne's body, beckoning, enticing, daring her enemies to come closer.

When they were about five feet from her, the riding beasts stopped. No amount of urging or beating would make them move any closer to Arianne. Finally, the men dismounted and walked toward her.

"Men of Alsia, what do you want from me?" Arianne asked softly.

"I am Captain Akino. High Priestess Colsa has ordered us to return you to the temple in Kopol immediately."

Arianne laughed and her hair began its advance and retreat dance again. "Why does she send twenty warriors after one small female?"

"In this land, many dangers can take a stranger by surprise. The Lady Colsa sent us to guide and protect you."

"Do you believe that?" Arianne's voice gently mocked the young captain. "I agree with you. Many dangers exist in this land, and for me, the greatest of them is in Kopol." She laughed softly at the puzzled look on the young officer's face. "Never mind. I am hungry and tired. You will supply me with food and a safe place to rest. Then, we will discuss my trip to Kopol."

"I am going to take you back to the temple." The captain stated firmly, then flushed when Arianne laughed again.

"What if I don't want to go with you?"

"Then we will take you by force."

"First, I will rest and eat, then I will explain to you why nobody ever threatens a Lantian."

Arianne walked toward the captain. When she was standing next to him, she stopped, "Well?"

"You will ride with me, Princess." The captain reached out to grab her arm, but she stepped back.

"If you value your life, you will never attempt to touch me." she whispered.

The captain dropped his hand and stepped back from her. As they neared the riding beasts, the animals snorted loudly, then turned and ran. For a moment, there was confusion as the warriors tried and failed to control the panicked beasts.

"What have you done to our animals?"

Arianne shrugged. "Nothing. I have noticed in the past, though, that type of animal has no love for my people. No one knows why."

"Why didn't you warn us?"

Arianne lifted her head and gazed straight into the captain's eyes. With a small gasp, he reached into his tunic and pulled out a small pendant. Long buried racial memories surged, unexpectedly, into Arianne's consciousness, and she took a step backward.

The Abomination is here! Arianne's mind sent that cry out across the land before it retreated into darkness.

*****

At a council meeting in Lantia, the queen cried out. The elders and merchants all closed their eyes and shuddered. The nightmare they had created was now on this world. They had fled and fought it for many centuries, on many different worlds, and now their young princess must face it alone.

Queen Ilona stared blankly across the table at her people and then sighed. "It will come for us and we must be prepared. The Feltan swore to aid us when we first landed on this world. Now, they must honor their oath.

"For centuries we have played, and in the games, we have sharpened our skills. We interbred with the Feltan and gained new skills. Now, we must put all our games aside and focus on defeating this horror before it destroys another world."

"Call the Feltan." The oldest member of the council, Elder Singer Umbert said, his lips tight with distaste.

The queen glanced at the others. Slowly, reluctantly, they each nodded his or her agreement.

"We must recall our armies and warn the countries on our borders." Queen Ilona smiled, "We will give them Lantian word that this horror will not reach their lands until every living creature in Lantia is no more. Call your people together while I go to the towers and summon the Feltan."

Rolto's bride, Princess Crista, spoke for the first time. "Queen Ilona, my people are your neighbors, but we are closer to the land of Alsia than you are. Will this monster that you fear not attack us first?"

"Have your father arrange to bring your people into Lantia. Take them to the northern plains. Not many of our people live there so you will find plenty of unused land below the mountains. Let us hope it will not be necessary, but be prepared."

Ilona walked stiffly out of the Council Chambers and up the many stairs that led to the great crystal towers of the palace of Lantia.

*****

Arianne opened her eyes and stared around her. She was lying on a blanket. Not far away, a group of soldiers talked around a fire. The aroma of roasted meat and fresh bread reached her, making her stomach growl. For a moment, she thought she was back in Lantia on maneuvers with her Home Guards. Then, all that happened in the last hour came rushing back and she closed her eyes.

"Princess, are you awake?" A young soldier leaned over her to ask.

"Get away from me!" Arianne spat. "You follow one who carries the mark of the greatest threat to life of any sort. What are you? No true human would wear that mark."

"Elder Sister," The young man whispered, "It is merely an amulet the Lady Colsa gave the captain for protection. I admit it is not a pretty one, but why should it upset you? Unless, of course, you intended to harm us by using your magic?"

As the soldier spoke, a small tingle made Arianne aware that the being that controlled the amulet was seeking entrance into her mind. Instinctively, Arianne let the Feltan part of her heritage take control of her. She sensed that if this horror found any trace of Lantia in her, it would destroy her completely. As long as she was in its presence, she must be completely Feltan.

She glanced at the young man, "Who are you to call me Elder Sister?"

"I am Cory, and a Belden. Many years ago, my merchant parents settled here. When I grew to manhood, I had no talent for trading, so I became a temple soldier."

"The Belden knows of this land? Why, then, did your people not tell us when we asked?"

"Elder Sister, though we have been friends and allies with your people for many years, still your first law rules us."

Arianne groaned, “Speak not to us of any who live or work upon the sea.” She smiled bitterly, “This whole mess is our fault. If we had not been so stubborn and narrow-minded, we would have stopped this.”

“This amulet that the captain wears; does it represent The Abomination that brought your people to this world in the first place?”

“Yes. Cory, go and speak to your captain. Tell him all that you know of the Lantians, then try to get word back to your people. Tell them to warn my mother.”

“Elder Sister, what about the first law? Will your people listen to me?” Cory objected.

“The first law is void. Tell them I have said so.”

Cory bowed his head, “You have said so, A-Kiyama.”

Arianne tensed, “Do not use that word in the presence of that amulet.” She hissed.

A shadow fell across Cory and Arianne. They glanced up to see Captain Akino standing over them. “You have spent a long time with the princess, Cory. Have you convinced her to travel peacefully with us?”

The young soldier blushed, “The Elder Sister does as she wills, Captain.”

The captain frowned, “Elder Sister? Why do you call her that?”

“We share the northern continent, her people and ours. I have told you many stories about the Lantians. If she says that she will not return to the temple in Kopol,” Cory shrugged. “We will not be able to force her. The land itself will rise and destroy us."

"We are on temple business. The Lady has given us her blessing." The captain snapped.

"The Lady's blessing will do us no good against the Elder Sister."

Arianne thought this a good time to intervene. She didn't want the captain angered.

"I mean you and your men no harm, Captain." Arianne spoke the truth. Her anger was aimed at Lady Colsa, who opened the door through which The Abomination entered this innocent world.

"Captain Akino, may I have something to eat?" Arianne asked. She must reach Prince Brian and alert him to the danger facing his land. Somehow, she had to get the captain to let her continue her journey.

Captain Akino nodded and Cory hurried over to the fire. He soon returned with a small plate of roasted meat and pan-fried bread. As she wiped her plate with the last of the bread, Arianne studied the men around her. They were soldiers, and she had dealt soldiers all her life. She would take a chance that these were honorable men.

"Captain, have you ever heard the term Lantian Honor?" She asked. If the seamen heard of her people, she could hope that the soldiers did as well.

"Yes, Princess. We have had mercenaries from the northern lands who use that as the strongest oath bond they can give. Young Cory tells us that even death does not release a Lantian from his or her vow."

"Then hear me. I am Lantian, and an Elder Sister." She smiled, "Ask Cory what that term means among the people of the northern lands. I would make a deal with you."

"I already know. Now that I think about it, I can remember the many stories the lad has told. Speak, Princess." The captain took her plate from her and set it aside.

"I still have much I must see and do in your land. Let me complete my quest, and in ten days, I will meet you at a place of your choosing, Lantian Honor."

"You want ten days, Princess?" the captain frowned.

"Ten days, at a place of your choosing," Arianne repeated.

"Let me consider your proposal. Why don't you get some rest? I will wake you when I have decided." The captain walked away.

Across the fire, Arianne met Cory's eyes. The young Belden smiled and nodded. He casually walked over to his captain. Arianne closed her eyes. Captain Akino was correct, no matter what decision he made, she would need to get some rest.

"I will accept your bond." The captain's voice woke Arianne from a deep sleep. "We will wait for you one day's journey south of Lady Athna's Manor. A major road runs from the manor to the town of Kopol. We will camp by the road until you arrive. I warn you, though, many others are traveling the land, looking for you."

Arianne nodded, “If they recapture me before I reach you, I will not mention our bargain.”

The captain studied her for a long moment, then nodded. “Go now in peace, young Princess. We will meet again in ten days.”

Arianne smiled and, as silently as a small breeze, she was gone. She stood, her head thrown back, seeking the mountain winds. It was dark and she had no idea what direction she was facing. Slowly, she turned, breathing in deeply, listening for a whisper of sound that would lead her.

However, the Feltan were creatures of the sea, not the land, and as long as she was Feltan, she would find no clues. Arianne cursed her choices. If she used her Lantian powers, that monster from the temple would find her. If she didn’t use her Lantian powers, she would lose hours of traveling time.

With a shrug, she chose a direction and walked until she judged herself an hour away from Captain Akino’s camp. Then she curled up on the ground and slept. She would have to wait until daylight when she could see the mountains before her. She had no skills for reading starlight. Because of their other talents, the Lantians never thought it important to learn how to tell direction by the stars.

Does a madwoman know she is mad?

Can a madman swear to honor?

Could a mad singer sing a song of peace and unity?

Shall a mad nation glory in its insanity?

We, the people of a world known as Lantia, are mad.

Lantia, a world of blue and white, is now gone.

The dust of her people strewn across the multiverse.

Except for us.

The mad ones.

The survivors.

Anonymous Lantian Bard

Chapter 10

"Mother, have you heard anything else from Arianne since she gave warning?"

"Rolto!" Queen Ilona turned to face her son, "You made good time from the frontier. No, I have heard nothing from Arianne. No one has, not even the Icina. It's as though my daughter has disappeared from the face of this world."

"Could she be hiding?" Rolto walked over to the window of the tower and stared into the darkness.

"I hope so. We don't want to be too obvious in our search. If The Abomination does not know who or where she is, then we don't want to betray her." Ilona sighed, "I called the Feltan yesterday. Just before you came in, they answered. They have lifted the ban on our people, and are sending three representatives to us. They should be here by tomorrow."

"Will they be able to help?"

Ilona shrugged and joined her son in staring out of the window.

"Our neighbors have volunteered to help us any way they can." Rolto smiled grimly, "One of our plans worked anyway. They admit that they have been actively searching among their own people for those with mind powers to help in their wars with us."

"They have not been trained." Ilona's voice was tired.

"No, but we can train them, and if the Feltan agree to aid us, the training could go much faster. Mother, we cannot give up. We must believe that Arianne is alive and well. We must be prepared to give her aid when she needs it."

"So many ifs Rolto: If Arianne is alive; if we have time; if the Feltan can help us. I sent my daughter unprepared into this mess. If she dies, it will be my fault."

"Enough, Mother! You could not have prepared her for this. You knew nothing of it. It is not your fault. Now is not the time for negative thoughts. We have too much to do."

"My son, I am so tired." Ilona stared up at Rolto, tears in her eyes.

"I promise, Mother, when this is all over, I will let you rest. Crista and I will relieve you and Father of your duties."

"Crista will do well." The queen smiled.

"Yes, she is one of the Lapontians with mind power."

"Yes, I know. Your father told me. Rolto, what will happen to our people?" The queen leaned her head against her son's chest.

Rolto put his arms around his mother's shoulders and gave her a hug. "The outcome of this encounter is in our hands. I believe the new strategy will work and our people will survive as we always have."

The queen and her heir stood silently in the great tower, comforting each other. Then, with simultaneous sighs, they turned and walked down the stairs.

*****

Have you found her? Prince Brian asked the guardians again.

No. She saw something that has thrown our whole world off balance. Whatever your mother is dealing with is an old enemy of the Lantians. Now, peace exists between the Lantians and their neighbors. The Feltan are gathering off their shores and have offered to give us any help we may need.

The Feltan and the Lantians? Prince Brian laughed shortly, *I find that hard to believe.*

When the people we know as Lantians first came to our world, the Feltan swore them aid. They are now calling the oath in as due.

So, where is the princess? Brian sighed.

The guardian echoed his sigh, *we don't know.*

*****

"They let her get away. Those incompetent idiots."

"Lady Colsa, calm yourself. I am sure the soldiers had good reason for what they did." Khat reached out to touch the older woman, then let her hand drop as Colsa turned.

Deep behind the green of Colsa's eyes danced a thread of black. Khat hated it when the dark one shared Colsa's body. For then, the Lady took great pleasure in petty cruelties, and Khat was usually the one who suffered.

"What would be a good reason for disobeying my orders?" Colsa asked softly. "I'm sure you can think of one, you little traitor."

"Lady Colsa, never. I have never betrayed you."

"Never? Yet you let the little bitch princess walk through your mind and didn't even tell me of it."

"I didn't know." Khat wept, tears of anger and shame. "I did not know what she did."

Colsa laughed cruelly, "Yes, and that is the only reason you are still alive. Don't worry, little one, I will make her pay for that. She will learn that no one tampers with what is mine. Now, leave me. I have plans to make."

*****

At the first hint of dawn, Arianne stood up and faced the hills. She ran toward them, using the ground-eating lope of the Lantian footman. She traveled this way all morning until the heat of the day forced her to stop and rest. She could not keep up this pace for long, Arianne admitted to herself.

She had no water and no food. Another night's travel and she would have to give up the safety of her Feltan heritage and try to reach her allies. She could only hope that she would be far enough away from the temple warriors and their amulets to escape detection by then.

The moment the sun began to set, Arianne started to run. It was almost dawn the next morning when she felt a small furry shape brush against her leg. She glanced down. The uncertain light made it hard for her to recognize the creature, but when it veered off to the east, she followed.

For the next two hours, she ran beside her small guide and, when the sun rose, she found herself in the middle of a large circle of stones. All around her were different animals. She saw Bunto, Ulph, and Kelv pushing through the crowd. Arianne fell to her knees and held her arms open to her friends. With yelps of joy, they rushed to her, knocking her over in their excitement.

Arianne let her Lantian personality take control just in time for Ulph's voice to ring triumphantly in her head. *You made it! Now, Sister, stand here for just a little while. I must call the guardian of the plains.*

Ulph turned and faced a small, raised platform in the middle of the stone-encircled clearing. *Lady of Silver and Green, I, Ulph Howl-Mistress of the Wolvine, bring you the True Chosen of the prince of Alsia. See her.* Ulph stepped back and sat against the stones as Arianne locked her knees and lifted her chin, forcing her trembling body proudly erect.

The air over the platform shimmered and slowly took the shape of a tall woman with silver skin and eyes, and flowing green hair. Deep in Arianne's mind, a voice like the gentle morning breeze over the plains, spoke, *Welcome, Daughter, Sister, Friend. Let all those who follow the law of the guardians know that you are thrice blessed. The seas call you Daughter, the forests call you Sister and the plains call you Friend.*

One by one, the leaders of each species came up to Arianne and sniffed her fingers, then stepped back to join Ulph by the stones. At the end, Arianne once more found herself standing in the middle of a circle of animals facing an aspect of Alsia's Icina.

You've shown strength, endurance and great courage, Child of Lantia. My plains have tested you and have not found you wanting. You are all we ask for in a queen. I give you right of passage and an easy journey when next you travel in my domain. The Lady shimmered and disappeared.

The sky suddenly became dark as hundreds of flying creatures blotted out the sun. They warbled and chirped while circling Arianne.

Hold out your arms, Ulph instructed.

Arianne forced her arms up, level with her shoulders and the winged ones dropped to greet her. They landed gently on her arms and in her hair, singing softly to her all the while. For about five minutes, they hovered around her, diving, soaring, putting on an awesome display of aerial acrobatics. They then separated, each group flying off in a different direction.

You may rest now, Kelv told Arianne. *The creatures of the plains and of the air have seen you and know you to be the True Chosen of our prince.*

Arianne sank gratefully to the ground, "What of the temple warriors who pursue us?" She mumbled.

You are safe here, Sister. They dare not enter this place and they are barred from the mountains. Sleep. We will find you meat, and when you're rested, we'll go on.

Arianne slept. Here in the circle, the air was cool and the sun didn't beat down mercilessly as it did on the open plains. When she awoke, it was midday, and her three companions sat, watching her with solemn eyes. When she looked around, she saw a small chunk of freshly-killed meat, and three pieces of the 'Sweet Fruit' she and Bunto liked so much.

"Thanks," she mumbled as she started to eat.

It was strange what one could learn to tolerate in a week, Arianne thought with a smile. Her stomach no longer rebelled at the raw meat. She didn't think she would ever really enjoy it, but she could eat enough of it to keep her strength and her health.

Come. You can relax in the bathing pool here. Ulph pulled gently at Arianne's clothes.

Arianne lay in the pool. The warm water caressed her aching body and stung the blisters that covered her feet. She stared at the small hole in the toe her left boot and sighed for her vanity, *I wish I had brought a change of clothing with me. How can I meet this Alsian prince dressed in rags?*

Bunto also stared at her shoes and clothes with dismay. *Princess, you'll never survive in the mountains with these coverings.* He turned to Ulph and Kelv, *We must find her something else to wear. Humans don't have fur, and she must have fur to keep warm.*

Ulph and Kelv nodded. Then, after picking up her clothes and worn boots in their mouths, they left the circle. *Where are they going, Bunto?* Arianne asked sleepily.

They go to the guardians of the border.

Is it safe?

They are the companions of the True Chosen. None will hamper them.

What will we do about the temple warriors who are following us?

Bunto barked his amusement, *those humans? They won't even see Kelv and Ulph. They will be safe, but it is right that you worry for them.*

If they'll be safe, then why is it right that I worry?

You are going to be our queen. The welfare of all Alsia's creatures should be your concern. Two days ago, you placed our welfare before your own. It was the correct action for you to take, though we argued with you about it. Do you still have the circlet?

Yes. Arianne stepped out of the pool.

Her skin was beginning to shrivel from soaking too long. She wrapped her cloak, the only piece of clothing she had left, around her body.

Good, from now on wear it and take that disgusting piece of cloth from over your head. All that we meet must see the circlet so they'll know who you are.

I thought that humans were not allowed to enter the mountains. Arianne said lazily as she lay on the warm grass to let the sun bake out the last of her aches.

The guardian of the mountains is not of the Mother. Humans know him not, and so aren't welcome in his domain. However, many wild folk live in the mountain. Bunto explained, *These wild ones are not true humans, even though they go on two legs and wear artificial covering. They are as strong and as savage as the Silver Bear and they are in the Mountain Master's service. The cave where the prince dwells is deep in their territory.*

Hmm. Arianne smiled at Bunto, *You said that I'd meet others that the humans in Kopol knew nothing about. Are these wild folk the ones you spoke of?*

No, Chosen. You've already met two. One was the guardian of the forest, another is the guardian of this place, and the third is the Mountain Master.

The temple priestesses have never met these guardians?

No. They only know that certain places are sacred to the nonhuman of Alsia and they don't welcome humans. The priestesses don't know why.

"I see," Arianne mumbled sleepily.

She curled up and fell into a light sleep, wondering if she would again see the shadowy figure she believed to be the prince of Alsia. She was only half-asleep when Kelv and Ulph returned. Each was carrying a large bundle.

Is she all right? They asked Bunto.

She is well. She is still very tired. We must let her sleep all she wants before going into the mountains.

Time is short. The others reminded him.

I know, but we all need rest, and the remainder of the journey will require all her strength and cunning. Bunto warned.

It can't be any worse than what I've just been through, Arianne interrupted their conversation.

Bunto turned and studied her face carefully, *Not worse, just different and more dangerous.* He explained.

Is that fresh-baked bread I smell? Arianne sat up quickly, sniffing the air.

She decided to ignore Bunto's last statement about the danger of the mountains. She would cope with it when it happened.

Here, Princess, the border guardians have sent you many items. Kelv nudged the two packages closer to her feet.

Arianne tore into the bundles, eager to see what they contained. "Oh, Smoke," she breathed as she spread out the contents of the first package: A silver and gold comb and brush with a small matching mirror; two soft, green towels with small animals painted on it; two pairs of soft, fur lined boots, heavy socks, two pairs of trousers; three long-sleeved tunics, all in rich, dark green velvet. The symbols of her arm bands were embroidered on each tunic sleeve in gold and silver thread; and most precious of all, a long, heavy cape of the finest silver fur, with matching gloves. The cape and gloves were almost the same color as Arianne's hair, and she stared at them for a long moment.

How many creatures gave their lives to furnish the cape and gloves?

One, Chosen, the great Silver Bear of the high mountains, but we did not kill him for his fur. We took this from an animal that had died of natural causes. We would not bring the Chosen of Alsia a cape made of a stolen fur. Bunto explained.

Arianne nodded and turned to the second package. This one contained: freshly baked bread, succulent baked meats, juicy fruit tarts, a rough trail mix of dried fruits and nuts, a package of highly-spiced smoked meats, two flasks of sweet wine, one of milk, and one of hot karm.

"Oh heaven." Arianne sighed. She offered her companions part of the food, and when they declined, she tore off a chunk of the still-warm bread, stuffed it in her mouth, and washed it down with the hot karm. When she had eaten her fill, Arianne washed and dried her hands and dressed in her new finery. The clothes and the new boots fit perfectly. She glanced at the animals with raised eyebrows.

How did they know? She asked, then frowned. *How did they get all of this done so quickly?*

Remember, we took your old clothes with us. We do not pry into the border guardians' secrets, and they do not pry into ours. Maybe someday, after you are queen, they will show you how they managed to supply clothing for you so quickly. Ulph answered.

Bunto snickered, *Maybe there will be no great secret involved, just good, advanced planning.*

The animals exchanged looks full of laughter and Arianne nodded. She turned her attention to her hair, combing and brushing the silvery mass until it shone. She braided and pinned it up, carefully placing the golden circlet securely on her head. She stared at herself in the small mirror and was well pleased with what she saw. She was no beauty, but she wouldn't shame Prince Brian either, she decided.

Arianne packed everything else into one bundle that she strapped on her back and turned to her companions, *When do we leave?*

At first light, Chosen, Bunto answered.

I have already dressed. Why didn't you tell me I'd have to sleep some more? I thought we were in a hurry.

We enjoyed watching you. Remember, Kelv and Ulph must also rest before we go to the mountains, Bunto warned her.

Oh, my friends, I'm sorry. I'm a thoughtless child. Arianne was contrite, *But does that mean I have to sleep in my clothes?* She spoiled it all by asking.

You'd better. We won't have time in the morning for you to go through the whole ritual again. Kelv teased. *Temple warriors are still roaming around outside the circle. When we do move, it must be quickly and silently.*

Arianne frowned, *Are you sure they won't follow us into the mountains?*

Not if they are wise. Bunto said grimly as the four settled down to sleep.

Arianne lay on her back, her arms folded under her head, and closed her eyes. What was Prince Brian doing now? She wondered if he knew that she was coming to him. Did he even care? Lady Colsa had tried to encourage her to refuse the match because Prince Brian was deformed. Now, for the first time, Arianne wondered if Brian would find her acceptable. Everyone acted as if he had no mind of his own. Did they believe he would happily take any female chosen for him? If the figure who haunted her subconscious was the prince of Alsia, he was not one to accept a bride he didn't want.

The princess sighed and rolled over. Of course he'd accept her. He was royalty, and as such, had no choice in the matter of a mate. He would take whoever was best for his country. The thought didn't make Arianne happy. Her parents had a contract marriage, and once the throne was secure, each spouse was free to find entertainment elsewhere.

Of the four children the queen had borne, only Rolto, Patria, and Arianne were certain that the queen's husband was their father. Queen Ilona and her consort each led separate lives. No, Arianne thought, she'd not share her mate. That was the first subject they would discuss. He'd accept her fully or refuse her. For him, as for her, no other choice existed. She ignored the amusement she felt deep in the back of her mind and shifted again.

Lie still, Chosen, or you'll wake the others. Bunto whispered. *What troubles you?*

I'm being watched. Arianne grumbled.

By whom?

I don't know for sure, but I think it's your prince. He walks through my mind as if it were a public road.

Bunto snickered, *It is good that you two have already formed a mind link.*

Arianne snorted quietly, *A mind link implies a two-way street, my little friend. This prince of yours leaves me no privacy, yet he reveals nothing of himself.*

Nothing? Bunto asked her softly.

Well, nothing that is very important. He remains a mocking shadow with a strange sense of humor, a large, well-formed man who watches me constantly.

See, you do know something of him. Our prince is neither a weakling, nor a fool, and he knows his mother well. He'll not show himself to you until he's certain that you are no pawn of hers. Now, try to get some more rest. Tomorrow will come no matter what you do. Worrying will not change the future, and one can't plan until one knows what is happening. Bunto advised as he turned his back to the young princess and went to sleep.

Arianne grinned, stuck out a mental tongue at her watcher, and fell asleep to the sound of rich, masculine laughter rumbling through her mind.

In Alsia, certain of the animals can communicate mentally with gifted humans.

These humans are greatly prized among Alsians.

They are given positions of honor and many are assigned as liaisons between the two segments of Alsian society.

Ludos De Carpri, Royal Guard, Alsia

Chapter 11

The Feltan stared around the council chambers. Nothing had changed in this room in two hundred years, he thought with a smile as he turned his attention to the people sitting around the table. He gave a deep sigh and started to speak. He spoke slowly, for it was very difficult for him, but some of the people in the room did not have the power of mind speech.

"I am Ambrio, Second-Swimmer of the Feltan. Before we can say or do anything else, I must return this to you." Ambrio stepped forward and laid a small, pink jewel on the table before Queen Ilona.

The Lantians in the room stared in stunned silence at the glowing stone.

The queen reached out and touched it gently. "Il Ho a Lantia. You have returned the Life Stone of my people," she breathed. "How did it come to you?"

Ambrio grimaced, "Through deceit and greed, Sister. Know this, however: In all these years, non-Lantian hands have only twice held this stone."

“Explain, Ambrio!” Ilona commanded.

“Ampho the Lost, First-Swimmer of the Feltan, loved the Princess Sara of Lantia, but she wanted nothing to do with him. Ampho decided that if he took your greatest treasure and placed the life of the sea in the stone as a gift to Sara, she would love him.

“The sea mother, when she found out that he would give her greatest secret to humans, destroyed Ampho. Then she banned any contact between your people and the Feltan. That is why we magnified your normal distrust of the sea until even the sound of the word was distasteful to you.

“The sea mother realized that this gem was yours, and that her people had no right to it, so every few generations, she would call one of your people to her. They came to us and were given the secret of our life, and they held this in trust until the time of need should come.”

Ambrio paused, “Be careful how you use it, for it still holds the secret of the sea.”

Ilona nodded, “That is good, for my daughter, too, has been sea-called. First, we must charge the Il Ho a Lantia with our own powers. After that, we will entrust it again into your care. You must make sure that Arianne has the Life Stone in her possession before she faces our enemy.”

“Has she found prince of Alsia yet?” Rolto asked suddenly.

The Feltan shook his head. “She should reach his place of refuge later today or early tomorrow.”

“Why has it taken so long?” Rolto demanded of the Feltan.

Ambrio sighed, “Priestess Colsa controls more than we expected. Even the weather now obeys her. She has made the journey difficult and we fear that the return from the mountains will be harder still.”

Rolto frowned, “Is the woman completely mad to be using that force against her own land?”

“Not now,” Ilona said softly to her son. She turned to the Feltan, “Ambrio, tell us what you have learned.”

“We have found that Lady Colsa controls this being you call The Abomination. She feeds it the life force of those who oppose her too openly. Whatever it is, it is still weak and has not gotten a firm grip on our world. How long Colsa can control this being, we have no idea.”

“Does the Lady Colsa have any idea what she is dealing with?”

The Feltan shrugged, “She must have some idea of its nature. She has been dealing with it for years. Before she married the last king of Alsia, she first opened the door to this creature. We suspect, though, that she didn’t really start using its power regularly until very recently. We are beginning to suspect that she is using it to keep her son from the throne.”

“Why should she want to do that?” Ilona asked with a frown. “She was merely the king’s consort. Her son is the rightful heir.”

“Not all people are like you Lantians. Colsa enjoys power, and she will do anything to keep it.”

"Even destroy her world?"

The Feltan held his hands out, palms facing upward. "I don't know, but I think that she does not believe it will come to that. The priestess is certain that she can control this being."

"The priestess is a fool." Ilona snapped.

Ambrio smiled as the people in the room nooded their agreement.

"I do not understand your people. You are argumentative, arrogant, and treacherous, but not even death can make you betray a promise. You have no idea of the power greed holds in the hearts of other mortals.

"You all hate each other, and each of you will spend hours plotting the downfall of your neighbor. Yet, at the first sign of danger, you would stand at your enemy's back and defend him to the death.

"You claim to worship no gods. Yet each of you pursues knowledge relentlessly and you are always willing to share what you learn with any who ask.

"Now, on a planet where you have found nothing but enemies, you are willing to risk your own existence to defend those enemies."

The Lantians laughed. Queen Ilona glanced around and saw the same questions reflected in the faces of the other non-Lantians in the room.

"We know all about greed and its power. How do you think The Abomination came into being in the first place? As for us hating each other," Ilona frowned. "What makes you think that? We played a game. A game designed to keep our young ones alert and strengthen our powers. We played the same game with our neighbors to strengthen and train them.

"Ambrio, we came to this world a splintered people on the very edge of madness. During the flight from our own world, The Abomination caused the destruction and disappearance of over three-quarters of our race. We don't know what happened to them and we will probably never know. One thing we have always been sure of: We knew that no matter where we fled, The Abomination would eventually find us. When that day came, we were determined to be prepared for it.

"We have nurtured and added the skills we inherited by interbreeding with your people. That still left us with a world full of innocents who would be blind and deaf to the kind of battle this creature would wage. We had to get our neighbors to develop their own protection." Ilona smiled and gestured at the two hundred young people sitting against the wall of the council chamber.

"Those young men and women are the results of our constant war on the neighboring countries. They have the potential to control more mind-energies than we expected. All they need is the proper training.

"We had hoped for more time, but we are pleased with the results." Ilona glanced at the leaders of Lantia's neighbors. "You realize that if we wanted, we could have used our mind powers against you any time, but we never did. We did not want you destroyed. We wanted you strong.

"As for our own games, it was merely a way to hone our skills. Our people know of no better way to prepare for battle than to be constantly in battle."

She turned to the Feltan. "Ambrio, this is our home now, and we will not let this being drive us away from it." Ilona rubbed her brow, "Do you have any word of my daughter?"

Ambrio nodded. "She is safe for the moment. A small troop of temple warriors captured her two days ago. She has made a bargain with them. In ten days, she will surrender herself to them. After that, it is a two-day march to the temple from the place she has agreed to meet the warriors. That gives us roughly twelve days to get everything in place."

Ilona frowned. "So little time?" She straightened her shoulders, "Let us begin now. The newcomers go with the Feltan. They will begin your training. Learn quickly, my children, the fate of your world depends on your strength.

"Lantians, we have some research to do. I will meet all my elders and their heirs in the library. I will give all of you assignments. You have two days to complete them. Come." Ilona swept from the room, leaving madness in her wake as everyone scrambled to follow her orders.

Time to go, Chosen, Bunto's voice in her mind woke Arianne from a deep, refreshing sleep. *Gather your belongings and follow us quietly. It's a long day's journey until we reach the safety of the mountains and a group of temple warriors is now camping outside the circle.*

Arianne opened her eyes. It was the darkest hour of the morning. She sensed the others waiting for her. Quietly, she felt around for her pack.

I have it. Kelv thought, *We must creep through small places, and having this on your back will hamper you.*

Arianne nodded, *All right then, I'm ready.*

Take hold of my tail, Chosen One, and hold on until I tell you differently.

The princess, still on her knees, took hold of Bunto's tail and crawled slowly behind him. A deep rumbling sound that caused the earth to shiver beneath Arianne's knees echoed through the glade as a large stone shifted. The heavy blanket of the earth's silence wrapped tightly around them as they crept down a long, dark tunnel. The air was stale and so dry it made her want to sneeze. She sniffed hard, trying to defeat the tickling in the back of her throat.

"Ouch!" She cried as a sharp stone cut into her knee.

The animals stopped, *Ssh.* Bunto's mind-touch was abrupt.

They were still for a moment, listening for any sounds of activity above them. When the silence remained unbroken, they moved cautiously on. The dark, cramped space was just beginning to close in on her when the tunnel lightened and they reached the other end. Kelv stuck his head out and looked around. *All clear,* he motioned with his head.

The sun was just beginning to peep over the horizon when the four companions at last stepped out of the tunnel. Arianne took a deep breath of the cool air, then glanced quickly around. Not far ahead were the mountains. Back the way they came, the plains stretched endlessly toward the horizon. They stood on a small hill above the temple warriors' camp.

Come quickly. Bunto was their leader now, for he was a creature of the mountains and he owed his allegiance to the master of these mountains.

They moved swiftly, not even stopping to allow Arianne time to tie her pack on. Kelv still carried it firmly in his mouth. They hadn't traveled far when their pursuers discovered them.

They'll not ride their beasts after us. Their vanity is such that they can't imagine a soft, palace-bred princess outrunning them. Ulph glanced over her shoulders at Arianne.

Then let's prove them wrong, Arianne grinned, and stretched her long legs into a steady lope.

You run well, Chosen. Kelv gave her a toothy smile.

I'm Second-Heir. Arianne reminded him. *I can fight with bow and sword as well as my brother Rolto. I can outrun him any day. We breed Lantian warriors for endurance, and I am a trained Lantian warrior.*"

She sensed surprise, both from the animals with her and the presence in her mind.

They stayed just out of arrow range the rest of the day, for though the temple warriors were fine runners, Arianne and her friends were better. She didn't know if those following had orders to kill her or not, but she was not taking the chance by letting them get near enough to try.

It was dark when Bunto slowed, then stopped. *Well enough,* he panted. *You're full of surprises, Warrior Princess.*

Arianne shrugged, *One doesn't give all ones secrets away. Lady Colsa never asked, so we never told her. She asked for a princess, and my mother gave her one.*

Your mother sent you, warrior and Second-Heir, for a reason? Kelv asked. All of Alsia seemed to hold its breath, waiting for her reply.

My mother does nothing without reason, my friends. Arianne's replied.

We think you'll bear close watching, Princess of Lantia. Ulph finally said. *For now, we are allies, but if ever you betray our land and its prince, we will destroy you.*

Arianne laughed silently and said nothing. She touched the presence in her mind and found it thoughtful, but not alarmed.

So, she thought, *you don't scare easily. I like you, my Prince. Are you aware that I am not the threat to your land? Do you know what your mother has called into your world? Do you care?* His silence did not surprise Arianne. She was used to it.

We can rest now, over here. Bunto led them to a small opening about twenty feet up the path.

Arianne retrieved her pack from Kelv, opened it and began to eat. The animals left her alone in the cave. When she was through eating, she lay on the floor and, using her pack as a pillow, fell asleep.

*****

Arianne stretched her arms and legs slowly, checking for any stiffness from the previous day's exertions, she was pleased to find none. She was pleased that she was still in good physical condition, because her mental condition was awful. What in the world had gotten into her last night? Why hadn't she just told the truth? The queen had sent the Second-Heir of Lantia away because her love of the sea threatened the royal house.

The Lantians did not plan to invade Alsia, Lantia had all the territory they wanted. Why should they worry about a little island in the middle of the hated sea? Arianne smiled grimly, even if her mother was mad enough to contemplate such a scheme, she would never convince the soldiers to get on a ship.

Are you awake, Princess of Lantia? Kelv's voice was colder now than it had been on their first meeting.

Stop it, Kelv. I thought the three of you knew me better than to believe I would betray my friends. If you find it so easy to distrust me, then think of the harm Lady Colsa could do among people who don't know me at all. Arianne sat up, and rubbed her eyes.

The animals were silent, then Ulph sighed, *We have been testing you and finding few flaws. It worries us that the Lady Colsa, who has no love for her son, should choose so well. Yet, the very first test that you place before us, we failed. You are correct, Sister, we should know better, for if we can't trust you, then we have wasted this whole journey. We insist on blind trust from you, forgetting that trust goes both ways. For you to trust us, we must first trust you. We are sorry.*

She is right, Kelv grumbled.

No, we were all tired. I deliberately gave the impression that I was my mother's willing agent in Alsia. Hear the truth, then: My people hate and distrust the sea. They would never willingly cross water. For that reason alone, Alsia is safe from the Lantians.

My mother sent me away because of my love for the sea. That strangeness within me threatened the whole family. I wouldn't be welcome back in Lantia, even if I wanted to return. I will tell you the reason that I stay in Alsia. It is because Lantian Honor demands it and not out of love for your prince. I don't know him. Maybe love will grow between us after a time. That is the future, and beyond my control. I will be a faithful wife to your prince, a good mother to our children, and a just queen to all the people of Alsia. What more can I promise?

It is enough. Have you eaten first meal yet, Princess? Bunto asked.

No, are we in a hurry this morning?

Time is short and we still have a good distance to go. Bunto answered.

Will you answer some questions for me while I eat? I don't know very much about your people or your prince. Arianne removed the last of the fresh food from her pack. All that she had left for the trip into the mountains would be the high-energy dried foods the border guardians sent her.

What do you want to know? We will answer any questions that we can for you. Kelv replied.

All right. Why is your prince in these mountains, and why do I have to go to him?

It is the way of the royal house of Alsia. The consort of the ruler must have three powers: sea dreams, mind speech, and heart sight. Each step of your journey has been a test to verify before the major guardians that you have these powers.

Had you been born a child of Alsia, we would have already known you, and this journey would only be a part of tradition. There have been none born in Alsia for many years with the necessary powers. When the time came for our prince to be married, Lady Colsa announced that she would search for one who had the powers.

Now that we know of her deception, we think she may have been the reason no girl-child of power has grown up in Alsia.

Do you think she may have killed any promising candidate? Arianne had a sudden horrifying thought. Could Colsa have fed the children to The Abomination?

Princess, are you all right? Bunto asked.

When Arianne nodded, Kelv looked at her closely, then continued. *You know the heights of her ambition. If she didn't kill the girls, then she had them placed in the temple at very young ages. The training that they received there would render them useless for our purpose.*

Lady Colsa is of the temple. Arianne protested.

Yes, she is, and as such, she was never acceptable to us. The old king loved her when they were children and was determined to have her as mate. We warned him that she would cause great harm to Alsia, but he ignored all advice. We've guarded the young prince carefully, and when his father died, we called him to safety.

Then you hid him in the mountains?

Bunto answered, *Yes and no. It is tradition that our prince awaits his bride in the deep caves. There, all the major guardians could come to witness the joining. The old king didn't follow this tradition; he knew that we wouldn't accept Colsa. He was a fool.* Bunto added spitefully.

He was human, and in love. Arianne said softly, *Lady Colsa said her son was deformed. Is he?*

Certain changes come over the heir to the throne when the king dies. When a mate is found and the joining blessed, the changes are reversed, and we publicly crown the heir king. The longer it takes to find a mate, the more difficult it becomes to reverse the changes. Kelv sighed, *we have no idea if the changes can be reversed for our prince, he has been in the caves so long.*

What about the old king? If his marriage was never blessed then how was his change reversed? Arianne decided she wouldn't ask the nature of those changes, not now. She would wait and see for herself what she had chosen.

Colsa used magic to reverse the change of her husband. Ulph shuddered. *She used a magic that even the temple she ruled forbade. That was what caused the split among the humans. Now, they have two temples and two high priestesses. One priestess rules the temple of the Bright Lady, and the other rules the temple of the Dark Lady.* Ulph wrinkled her nose.

Could she use that same magic to make Brian's change irreversible?

The animals stared at Arianne in shock, then Kelv groaned. *We never considered that. It may be possible, but not while he is in the care of the Mountain Master.*

S*he is his mother.* Ulph objected.

Arianne smiled grimly, *history is full of unnatural mothers; women who murder their own offspring for power. Is there any way that we can prevent her from working evil on Brian once we leave the mountains?*

If we knew the source of her magic, the major guardians could probably protect him. We will have to ask.

Arianne chewed the last of her meal slowly, deep in thought, then asked, *Explain major and minor guardians.*

We have four major guardians. Three of them are faces of the Mother. The fourth major guardian is the Mountain Master. The minor guardians are humans with special powers who guard and protect the borders between the wild ones and the humans. Many rules constrain them, for they must obey both human and non-human laws. We went to the minor guardians for your supplies. Ulph answered.

Major guardians, sea, forest, plains, and mountains, Lady Colsa warned me not to touch the heart of the deep, saying that it was a destructive power.

For Colsa it would be. Kelv grinned. *Don't worry, Chosen, the deep-sea guardian has met you and approved of you. She sent her agents to see you, and listened to, and joined in your song.*

I didn't sing for the plains, do I sing for the mountains?

Bunto barked his amusement, *Don't sing in the mountains. The Mountain Master will bury you in rocks if you try.*

He may very well bury us in rocks anyway. Ulph grumbled, then added, *you were too tired to sing on the plains. It would please our Silver and Green Lady if you sang for her on the return trip.*

Arianne stood up and reached for her pack, *one more question before we leave. Why do you keep saying that time grows short?*

This is the last chance we have to help our prince. On the last hour of his birthday, the changes will become irreversible. You must be at the caves four days from now or the entire journey will have been in vain.

Arianne frowned, so*, that is why the Lady Colsa would have me go to her temple. The longer she could keep me from Brian, the less chance he'd have. Much of her behavior is clear to me now.* She nodded firmly. *Let's go.*

Take the cloak and gloves out and wear them, Chosen. Bunto instructed.

When they left the small cave, Arianne had her bundle firmly tied to her waist and hidden under the flowing, silver cloak. They traveled steadily upward the rest of the day. The going was slow. Arianne found it difficult to keep footing on the loose stones and once, she tumbled almost back to the foot of the path.

I don't understand this, she muttered, *I've run up trails steeper and more dangerous than this one. Why am I having so much trouble now?*

It's one of the Mountain Master's little games. Ulph snorted.

Arianne tightened her lips and pressed on. As they reached the top of the path, Arianne felt her feet start to slide out from under her again. She quickly threw herself forward, and grabbed onto Kelv.

Smoke and Fire. Enough is enough. I'm tired of these juvenile games.

Standing, her hands on her hips, she planted her feet firmly, and called aloud, "Mountain Master, if you object to my being in your domain, then say so. If not, then behave yourself."

Lady, Chosen, no, Bunto whispered, *Don't challenge the Master. You'll anger him.*

Kelv and Ulph snickered.

Arianne glared, *Anger him, will I. Well, I've something to say to your Mountain Master. He is behaving like a six-year-old boy who doesn't want to share his favorite toy. You claim that he is a major guardian. So far, all I've seen is a spoiled brat.*

In reply, a shower of small rocks and pebbles fell from the mountain heights and rained down on their heads. When the shower was over Arianne checked her companions. No one was badly hurt, but all four were bruised, and Arianne was bleeding from a small cut over her eyes.

"Has anyone spanked you lately?" She asked aloud.

Loud laughter boomed out over the mountains, then, an even louder voice asked, "Who trespasses in my domain?"

"You know very well who I am." Arianne snapped. "You're supposed to be a major guardian of Alsia, well then, how about acting like one, and stop these childish antics. Your whole land is being threatened and you're behaving like an undisciplined child."

"Mortal woman, you either have great courage, or have little sense. Don't you know who I am and what powers I can control?"

"Most of the time, I am probably a combination of both, and no, I don't know who you are. I'm not Alsian, and right now, that pleases me. My people wouldn't put up with a god who acts like a child."

"I'm not a god. I'm master of the mountains."

"You're master of nothing until you're master of yourself."

"What do you want, Mortal?"

"Free passage through your mountain for my companions and me."

"You would remove the prince of Alsia from my care, and take him into danger."

"He is to be the ruler of Alsia. Danger is his birthright. Would you have him hide like a weakling up in your heights, while all his land is destroyed?"

"I would have him safe."

"You know what the Lady Colsa has called forth. I have sent the warning. How long would he be safe hidden here?" Arianne paused, "What does your prince want to do? So far everyone but Prince Brian has had a say in his future. Give him a chance to decide for himself. Let me through to him. If he accepts me, then we leave. If he refuses me then..." Arianne paused, "Then we both stay," she finished softly.

The Mountain Master laughed long and loud, "I like you, Little Mortal. You are right. It is time for the young prince to decide for himself what path he would take. Go on to the heights with my blessing."

Well, that takes care of falling rocks and slippery paths. Arianne grinned at her companions. *Is there anything else we have to fear?*

Just the weather, Princess, Bunto breathed, awe showing in his small eyes. *This is the only place for many hours that is level enough to rest on shall we stay here for the night?*

Why are you asking me? You're the leader of this part of the trip, you decide.

As you command, my Princess.

Something new in the tone of Bunto's thoughts caught Arianne's attention. She stared at him, then looked at the others. In all their eyes was the same expression. They looked like the kitchen hounds in Lantia, when anyone showed them the least attention.

Arianne didn't like that expression of animal devotion in the eyes of her friends. *What's wrong with all of you?* She snapped.

You challenged the rights of the Mountain Master and he did not destroy you. Bunto breathed.

Oh Smoke! Look at me. I'm still Arianne. Nothing has changed. I'm the same person I've always been. You are my friends, not my pets, Ooh... Arianne sat suddenly. *I don't need this.* She opened her pack, grabbed a handful of dried fruits, threw it into her mouth, and silently chewed, ignoring the others.

Would you like some 'Sweet Fruit', Chosen? Bunto asked.

No! Arianne snapped.

Now who is behaving like a spoiled brat? Ulph asked. *Until now, you were our traveling companion, one who might be the right mate for our prince. You had passed many tests, and the chances were great that you would be our future queen. Now, we know that you are the one, so we give you the love and respect that is your due. Why does that anger you?*

I want to be your friend.

You can be both. However, give us the right to acknowledge our friend as our queen. Ulph thought fondly to her.

Arianne smiled, Ulph was right. *Thank you. Bunto, I'd love some fruit. I apologize to all of you*

Ulph is correct: I'm behaving like a spoiled child. It's just that I've never had any friends before. Always, I've been second-heir, feared and respected by some, mocked by others, but never loved as just a friend. I'm going to miss that.

Kelv walked over and licked Arianne's face, *We'll be your friends.*

You'll yell at me if I do something wrong, and remain my friends? Arianne asked.

The others laughed, *We will tell you when you err, and still love you as friends.* Bunto dropped the fruits by her feet. *That's what being a friend means.* He added.

Arianne wiped her eyes and sniffed, *Come on, let's go find our prince;* she picked up the fruits to eat as they walked. She reached deep in her mind and found the presence of the one she knew was Prince Brian.

Well, what do you think? she asked silently.

Thank you. The answer came promptly. Arianne stopped in shock, then gave a delighted giggle, he had answered her at last.

Are you my prince?

I guess I am. The presence in her mind answered dryly.

You guess you are? Don't you know who you are?

A feeling of amusement, then, *am I yours?*

Arianne blushed and glanced at her companions. They were unaware that she was in contact with Prince Brian. *Smoke, you dare ask that, after all I've been through to reach you. Why didn't you talk to me earlier?*

If you had been a pawn of my mother's, the less contact we had, the better. After all, my mother could have engineered your whole trip.

Arianne pulled her cape closely around her and shivered. *Why did it take you so long to decide I wasn't a part of your mother's schemes?*

The Mountain Master doesn't maintain communications with the other guardians. The only contact I have with the lowlands comes through occasional visits of the Feltan, though sometimes, one of the major guardians will risk the Mountain Master's anger to speak with me. I didn't even know about you until the guardian of the forest gave you her blessing. You have done well, Princess of Lantia.

I had help. Arianne answered absently, then asked, *Did you know about the other women your mother brought to Alsia?*

Oh yes, Brian laughed, *at first, my mother wanted me to take one of her temple women to mate. When I refused and the change began, she brought in the foreign princesses. She thought that their girlish horror would make me see things her way. It didn't work though. I'd seen what was happening to my country because my father insisted on a temple bride. I was not about to make the same mistake, so I left the palace and came up here.*

Were they pretty?

Who?

The others?

Yes, they were. Why?

I'm not. Arianne paused, giving him space to mention his own looks. All she received was a feeling of deep amusement. He knew what she wanted and had decided not to give it to her. Finally, she went on, *You're lucky that you have the option of refusing a chosen bride. Remember Crista?*

Brian chuckled, *Yes. She was a very dangerous young woman.*

Well, she is to become my sister. Maybe she already is. Of course, if she is as dangerous as you say, then my people are getting exactly what they deserve. Poor Rolto, he had no say at all in the choice of his bride. Arianne whispered sadly.

Rolto? Was he your lover? Brian asked quietly.

No, he's my brother. I've never had a lover. Have you?

Princess, you're not supposed to ask me that.

Call me Arianne. Why shouldn't I ask you about your lovers? You asked about mine. Arianne paused, *Oh Smoke, don't tell me you've never had a lover.*

Why should I tell you anything? Amusement tinged Brian's voice.

I'm glad you find this amusing. I don't. She snapped.

Don't worry. Brian was openly laughing now.

That's easy for you to say... She began, when sharp teeth fastened on her arms and broke her concentration when she was jerked suddenly off balance. *What...* She stammered.

Sister, this isn't a road to dream on. We tried to reach your mind but found it closed to us. Look where you were going. Ulph scolded.

Arianne looked. Her next step would have taken her off the path and down the side of the mountain in a straight drop. She closed her eyes and pulled her body up against the mountain.

Smoke and Fire! I could have been killed. Thanks, my friends.

What were you doing? Bunto demanded.

Having a talk with your prince, Arianne answered, fighting nausea.

Love talk? Kelv teased, *no wonder you almost fell off the cliff.*

Arianne blushed, *No love talk, just conversation.*

Ulph nodded seriously, then glanced at the others, *That's what we thought, love talk.*

Bunto interrupted their teasing, *Come quickly. A strange fog is moving in. We must get off this path before it reaches us. This time, Chosen, keep your attention on your feet.*

They moved upward, until Bunto stopped before a large boulder. *Here, help me move this. Behind this boulder is a cave where we can find shelter.*

Arianne and the others put their shoulders against the large stone and pushed, but nothing happened.

This is ridiculous, Arianne snapped, *where is the Mountain Master when you need him?*

“Hey, Mountain Master,” she yelled aloud. “You like throwing rocks around? Well throw this one.”

“I take no orders from mortals.” The Master shouted back. The volume of his voice made the mountain shiver.

Arianne grinned, “In other words, you can handle the small stuff, but this one is too large for you. All right, I won’t bother you again.”

“Too large! Stand back, puny mortal, while I show you the power of the Mountain Master.”

The four companions pressed against the mountain face as the huge boulder shook, then flew into the air and disappeared down the path. Arianne smothered a laugh.

“Show off.” She teased softly.

“Sneaky female. Now I remember why I have no use for your sex.” The Master grumbled, “Hurry and get off my mountain, before you drive me to violence.” His voice was soft though, and as the animals stared in shock, Arianne let her laughter out. The deep rumble of the Mountain Master’s laughter joined hers.

I like your Mountain Master, Bunto. Arianne grinned. She stood at the mouth of the large cave where they took refuge from the descending fog.

The Master likes you also, Chosen. Bunto replied, watching her closely.

Well, don’t sound so surprised by that. It’s not very flattering to me. I’ll have you know that I’m a very likable person. It’s evident that your Mountain Master has good taste. Arianne sniffed haughtily and the others silently shared her amusement.

She breathed deeply. The air up here was clean and crisp, and she found the patterns the swirling fog made, fascinating. *The beauty of your land constantly surprises me.* She sent the thought at Brian.

I'm glad it pleases you. He answered politely. *You will stay for the beauty of the land.*

Not for the beauty of its prince? After a moment of surprised silence Prince Brian's presence abruptly disappeared from her mind.

She still worried about the 'deformity' Lady Colsa claimed Prince Brian suffered. That was why she made that stupid comment. She tried to disguise it as teasing, but Brian was not fooled. Arianne shifted on the hard floor and closed her eyes tightly. Lady Colsa wrought well when she planted doubts in Arianne's mind about the acceptability of Brian. Arianne frowned. Allowing the doubts to grow was stupid of her.

Why accept Lady Colsa's word, when she knew the woman was a trickster and a liar? If Lady Colsa came to her and said, "It is snowing outside," Arianne would go and check before she believed. Why do less with Brian?

"Smoke and Fire, I am a fool!" Arianne jumped to her feet and walked again to the mouth of the cave.

Chosen, what is wrong? Bunto asked softly.

I have caused pain to one who didn't deserve it. I'm a vain, stupid girl, who is no more fit to be queen of Alsia than... Arianne looked around,

Than this pebble. She snarled, kicking at the small object in question.

Not so, Chosen. Any pain you cause would not be deliberate. You are an honorable child, with a gentle heart. Now stop pacing and try to sleep. If you can't do that, at least stay still so the rest of us can get some rest.

Bunto's advice was easier given than followed, Arianne found, as she lay on the cave's floor. Forcing herself to lie still, Arianne let her mind wander over all that had happened to her in the last three weeks.

I wish I knew what my people plan to do about The Abomination. I know I cannot defeat The Abomination, but maybe, I will be able to buy my people the time they need to prepare a defense. I hate having to face that monstrosity alone. If I have to though, I will call upon all my training, and die protecting the land. This is the Lantian way, and the true meaning of Lantian Honor.

Everything the Lantians did since they first discovered their new home already had a native population, had only one aim: To protect the innocents who inhabited this planet. They must be kept safe from the nightmare that her people created; a horror that followed them and destroyed the other worlds they had chosen; a horror that they must not allow to destroy this world.

Arianne rolled over carefully, trying not to disturb the others. How much should she tell Brian, she wondered, then frowned in disgust at her own thought. The inbred habit of secrecy was hard to overcome. In less than two days, she would meet

Brian and she must have no hesitation in her soul when she accepted him. She brought to mind again the tall, muscular figure she'd seen in her mind.

She grinned in the dark. The body she'd seen was definitely one with which she could live. Honesty forced her to admit that she had no grounds to object to anyone's face. Not as long as she was stuck with her own.

Maybe we would turn out the lights after all, she decided with bitter humor. *A little darkness and my mother's technique might be the only way we could accept each other. So be it, as Bunto would say; tomorrow will come and worrying will not make its decisions any easier.*

She felt better now that she came to a decision about Brian. When she met him again, she would apologize. With that thought, she fell asleep, not hearing the soft whisper that floated through her mind. *I need no apology, my Lady. I wish you would share your deeper worries with me. I would protect you if you would let me.*

They were on their way again before the sun rose the next morning. A sense of urgency now drove them on. By nightfall, they needed to meet Prince Brian. They still had another day's journey into the mountain to reach the place he waited.

The fog of the day before lost them many travel hours, and now, the weather threatened to slow them even more. The winds grew stronger all day, blowing in their faces and slowing their progress. Shortly after midday, it started to snow. At first, light flakes fell, but as Bunto looked up at the heavy, black clouds above them his face grew grim.

In a few hours, it'll be snowing so heavily we won't be able to travel. The rank stench of dark temple magic hangs heavily in the air.

Can't the Master do something about this? Arianne asked.

No, it's out of his domain. The mountains are his, but whatever being Lady Colsa worships can control the air above the mountains.

We're going to need his help again. Arianne said a short while later. *Too much snow is falling. We can't see where we are going. Sooner or later one of us is going to fall off this mountain.*

Bunto agreed, *there's a way, but only the Chosen and I can walk it. We must find shelter for you two while we go on.*

Ulph and Kelv nodded. *We aren't important. She is. You must do whatever is necessary.*

Stay here for a moment. Bunto advised, as he slipped out of sight.

While they waited for him to return, Arianne asked, *Lady Colsa told me her temple worships the goddess. Is that different from the Mother you worship?*

No. She worships a different aspect of the Mother than we do, Ulph answered shortly. *As you reminded us, not all mothers are kind and loving. So it is with our Lady. Not all aspects of her are light. Some are dark beyond belief.*

Bunto returned a short while later, *This way. I've found the place.* They followed him closely for an hour, and all four sighed with relief when he led them into a small cave.

Kelv, Ulph, you stay here. The storm will not last past sunset. When it has passed, go back to the foothills and await the coming of the prince and his Chosen. Bunto ordered. The Cantus and the Wolvine nodded and curled up close together, sharing their warmth.

Bunto turned to Arianne. *Chosen, leave your pack here with the others. They will take care of it for you. Where we are going it will slow you, and you will not need its contents.*

Arianne removed the small package of dried foods from her pack and stuffed it down the front of her tunic. She dropped the pack on the cave's floor and turned to Bunto. *All right, I am ready.*

Bunto nodded and led her deeper into the cave, into a passage where the roof slanted downward at an alarming rate.

Bunto, how much lower does the roof get, Arianne asked.

Much lower, Chosen. You will make this trip on your stomach. I hope you're not afraid of the dark. He added.

What would you do if I said I was?

Offer you my sympathy.

Well, that's more than I expected. I don't think I'm afraid of the dark. Arianne took a deep breath. *I should warn you, however, I have a racial horror of closed-in places.*

My sympathy. Bunto said calmly, *You Lantians are afraid of many things, aren't you? If your fears become too overwhelming, just reach out and take hold of my tail. Maybe that will help.*

Thanks, Arianne said dryly, not bothering defending her people.

She didn't exaggerate when she claimed to have a horror of closed in places, and as the roof got lower Arianne's nervousness grew. At this rate, she thought with black humor as she dropped to her knees, she would be a gibbering idiot by the time they reached Prince Brian's cave.

Oh Smoke, Bunto, squeak at me or something, I can't stand the silence. She moaned softly.

"Squeak, squeak." Bunto said obediently.

That didn't work. Bunto's squeaky voice reminded her of the rodents in Lantia. Why hadn't she noticed his resemblance to those creatures before now? Oh Smoke and Fire, she was trapped in a small dark tunnel with a cursed rodent. Arianne felt a scream rising in her throat. Her conscious mind lost control, and her subconscious was taking over as terror flooded over her.

Stop it! The command came from deep in her mind.

"Brian, help me!" The words came out a scream that left her throat raw, and echoed throughout the tunnel.

"Brian!" she screamed again.

Be quiet, you little fool. Do you want to bring the entire mountain down on your head? Brian's voice sounded sharply in her mind.

"No." Arianne sobbed aloud. "No, help me, please help me. Where are you?"

Not much farther ahead, Arianne, listen to me. Concentrate on my voice. Very soon now, you'll be able to stand up again. After that, it's just a short walk to where I am.

"Come to meet me." Arianne sobbed desperately.

I can't come to you. You must come to me. Easy now, easy, you have done so well up to now. I am just a little farther away. Soon, soon, Brian's voice crooned in her mind.

Arianne's mind locked onto Brian's touch with a strength born of fear. What he said was not important. What mattered was the contact with another human.

"I am not going to make it. Brian I'm not going to make it. I have just discovered that the darkness is as terrifying as the small space. Ahh smoke, when did I become such a coward?" Arianne's voice was rough from crying.

You must make it. I need you. Brian said quietly, and Arianne forced herself to go on.

Brian needed her. That was just the incentive she needed. Duty must always come before one's fears. All Lantian parents taught their children that from the day they were born. She would go on, and she would succeed, because Brian needed her.

When this was over, Arianne would feel shame at her lack of control. Now, in a world bound only by her terror and the low, dark passage, she clung desperately to the touch of Brian's mind. Arianne had no idea how long she wriggled like a small worm down the dark passage. Time had no meaning to her. She didn't feel the small stinging bruises on her elbows and knees. Her body was numb. She didn't even hear the small hysterical sobs that pained her aching throat. Her ears and her mind were closed to everything and everyone but Brian. He was her sanity, her only contact with reality.

When Bunto jerked his tail from her grasp, she screamed. "No, Bunto, don't leave me."

Brian's voice came to her, *Arianne, relax. You're out of the tunnel. When our minds join, the others can't contact you. You're safe now.*

It's still dark. Brian, why is it still dark, if I am out of that tunnel?

Open your eyes. Brian's voice held a hint of laughter.

"Oh." Arianne opened her eyes, then promptly closed them again.

She was surrounded by hundreds of huge, fierce, shaggy beasts. Brian lied to her. She wasn't safe.

Chosen, Chosen. Please answer me, are you all right? Look. We have found friends. Bunto's worried voice came into her mind.

Arianne opened her eyes again, and swallowed. Now that she had her terror under control, she saw that only three strange creatures faced her, not the hundreds she originally feared. There was one large silver bear and two ragged humans. She tried to smile, found that her face didn't work, and quit.

Er, Bunto where are we?

In the front of the Caves of Learning. I must leave you now. The Mountain Master's people will escort you to Prince Brian. Hurry. We don't have much time.

Bunto, why can't you come with me? Arianne didn't want her friend to leave her alone with these, dangerous-looking strangers.

You will be safe. They will not harm you. Kelv, Ulph and I will be waiting for you at the foot of the mountain. Now, you must go with the Master's children.

The Mountain of Learning is a mountain in central Alsia. This is where the heir to the Alsian throne studies under the tutelage of the Mountain Master, Spirit of the Mountains. It is also where the heir awaits the arrival of the chosen mate. Usually, it was just a ceremonial journey, but during the regency of Colsa, High Priestess of the Dark Lady, the trip was no easy ritual, but a grueling journey with the life of our world at stake.

Lady Athna, High Priestess of the Bright Lady

Chapter 12

Arianne nodded and swallowed with difficulty, she pulled herself up on legs still shaky with the remnants of her fear, and followed the mountain people out of the cave.

They walked through passage after passage and cave after cave, all of them lit by a soft green light that shone from the walls. As they went deeper and deeper into the heart of the mountains, each passage was larger than the preceding one, and each cave was more elaborate than the one before.

Arianne reached out to touch the minds of her escort, and found a wall, nothing. These beings had not the power of mind speech, she thought sadly. How very lonely Brian must have been while living here. Deep in her thoughts, she didn't notice the floors growing more uneven until she stumbled and fell, hurting her already bruised hands.

"Ouch. That's it, I can't walk another step, I need something to drink." Arianne croaked through her raw, parched throat.

The others turned and looked at her, then one of the wild humans shuffled off. It soon returned, carrying a small cup filled with liquid. Arianne thought it water and drank swiftly, choking on the sour taste that filled her throat.

"What...?" She stammered after swallowing the liquid.

Her guides stared at her silently, she shrugged. It was wet and gave her the energy to go on. It even killed some of the pain in her throat.

Brian, where are you? How much further do I have to go before I reach you? Arianne asked as she walked down yet another passage, and into a brightly-lit cavern.

She stopped, forgetting the need for haste as she stared at the large chamber before her. The same soft green light that illuminated the other caverns and passages lit it. Only here, the light was brighter, and reflected from walls and ceiling by millions of large, precious stones. The light shimmered and flickered across the chamber. Against one wall was a large sleeping pallet. A table and three chairs sat by another wall, and in the center, was a large pool of water.

Oh, how beautiful! Is this where you've lived all the time you were here?

Yes, it is, and it's likely to be where I'll spend the rest of my life if you don't hurry. Brian's mind touched hers.

Arianne turned and saw her escorts waiting patiently for her on the far side of the cavern. They moved aside and motioned for her to enter the passage ahead of them. Arianne stepped in and then turned to see the mountain folk walk away.

"They can go no further, Chosen. From here on, the trip is yours alone. Just follow the passage. Our prince awaits you at the tunnel's end." The Mountain Master's voice was gentle. "Hurry. You took an awful long time getting here. Now, your time is short. Already the sun drops behind my mountains."

Arianne forced her feet down the passage that stretched darkly before her. No magic light lit this room, and the floor was damp and slippery. She reached out to touch the walls then drew her hands back quickly. The walls were covered with a slimy growth. Her brief touch disturbed the growth, which emitted an obnoxious odor.

Arianne shuddered, wiped her hands on her cloak and quickened her pace. Moving as speedily as was safe, she walked down the long passage. At the far end, she saw a dimly-lit cavern she recognized. It was where she'd first seen the prince of Alsia in her dream that was no dream.

Now, as she neared the mouth of the chamber, she saw him standing there, watching her. That too, was just as she remembered. He was tall and wide through the shoulders, his form almost blocking the entire entrance to the cavern.

He lifted his arms and held his hands out to her. With a small cry Arianne put all her doubts and fears behind her and ran toward the waiting figure, only to slip and fall at the last moment.

"Clumsy little female, aren't you," A deep voice said aloud as Brian reached down and pulled her to feet.

Arianne's giggle was a nervous reaction. "No, I just thought I'd fulfill one of every man's favorite fantasies for you."

"Which one was that?" Brian asked amused.

"You know, the one where he has a woman at his feet."

"No, I don't know that one," Brian chuckled. "Personally, I prefer to have my woman at my side. Come, we have very little time and still we must be wed."

"We are already wed." Arianne stared at him puzzled.

"What do you mean? We have gone through no ceremony."

"Brian, in my land once we sign a betrothal contract and the woman, with all her possessions, enters her mate's home, they are officially wed. The moment I set foot on the Alsian's Pride, I became your legal wife."

Brian threw back his head and laughed. "Your people have fooled my mother all around, haven't they?"

"It wasn't intentional, not at first. I mean, we never even thought that it was different here. All our neighboring countries have the same law. By the time I realized that she didn't know our law. I had already decided it was none of her business."

They stood in the center of the cavern now. Brian turned to Arianne and hugged her. "Welcome, small princess. Alsia greets you."

At his words, the cavern walls shimmered, then hummed and all Alsia's songs whispered through the cave.

"I will not hurt you." He whispered to her as he removed her cloak, and spread it on the soft, moss-covered floor. Then he slowly removed the rest of her clothing, and guided her down to lie on her cloak.

"I have touched your mind, I know you will not harm me." The cave was silent. Then Arianne whispered, "I promised the Olpho I'd teach you to sing."

"Then teach me." Brian murmured.

Arianne shivered as she felt webbed fingers trail over her breasts. "Your hands are cold." She whispered.

"Then warm me." Brian replied as he kissed her.

He lifted his head and rolled away from her, "I cannot do this."

"What is wrong? Have I done something I should not have?"

"No, it is not you, it is me. It is not honorable that you should accept me before you know what I look like."

"I am your wife, your mate for life. You don't know how I look either. Who knows, maybe in the light, neither of us will be pleased. However, we have much in common, and we both care for the land. If we have respect, and trust, then other emotions will follow.

"I respect your sense of honor, but now is not the time to exercise it." Arianne whispered as she pulled him back into her arms and reached into her mind for the technique her mother taught her.

Arianne warmed Brian, then she taught him to sing. At the end, their song flowed through the caves, out into the mountains, over the land, and far out to sea. All the creatures of Alsia heard their song, and as it rose to the heavens, they joined the singing. For a moment, the songs of Alsia were one as the prince and the Chosen of Alsia were one.

Later Arianne giggled, “You lied to me.”

“Never,” Brian answered lazily, “You made assumptions that I didn’t bother correcting.”

Arianne lifted her hands to touch Brian’s face and he jerked his head back. “Brian?”

“Come, Chosen, we have one more ritual that we must observe, then we may leave this place.”

Arianne nodded and stood beside him. Brian took her hands in his and turned to face her.

“Princess Arianne of Lantia, here in the presence of all Alsia’s gods and guardians, I pledge myself to you forever.” So saying, he bent his head and kissed both her cheeks.

“Prince Brian of Alsia, here before all your land’s gods and guardians, I pledge myself to you forever,” Arianne replied, then tugged at his hands until, with a small sound between a laugh and a sigh, he bent his head so that her lips could reach his cheeks.

Arianne kissed both his cheeks, letting her lips linger on his skin, feeling its texture, and breathing in his scent. “Now, I’ll know you, my

Prince," she laughed. "Even if you turn out the lights."

Brian laughed ruefully, "Put your cloak on, My Lady. We spend tonight in my living quarters. In the morning, we will leave the mountains."

Arianne wrapped the cloak around her naked body and snuggled close to Brian as they walked down the dark passage toward the bright chamber. Each of them worried what the other would think when the lights came on.

"Oh Brian, how lovely." Arianne stood at the entrance to the Cavern of Lights and stared at the changes that had happened in the short time she'd been gone.

The Mountain Master's people had been busy. The table was set with plates of shining gold and silver. Steam rose from the hot food waiting for them. A rainbow of different flowers decorated every corner, and the sleeping pallet had been covered with large, silver furs.

"Master, our thanks. It's beautiful. How did you know which flowers would please me?" Arianne whispered.

"I have noticed that all female creatures love the colors and smell of these particular blossoms." He paused briefly, then rumbled, "See, I do have good taste, Little Queen."

"The very best," Arianne replied as she and Brian joined in his laughter.

"Let's eat," Arianne urged Brian, pulling on his hand, "I'm starving."

Brian smiled. When it came to a choice between seeing the face of her new husband and eating, his little queen had her priorities in the right order.

"Would you like a bath first?" He finally asked, letting her pull him into the light.

"No, we can wash later. I've not eaten a decent meal in days."

Brian seated her at the table, and took the chair across from her. For a few minutes Arianne's full attention was focused on filling her plate. When she was through, she reached for her fork, then stopped.

"Would you like me to fill your plate for you?" Arianne lifted her eyes to look at Brian for the first time. "Oh Smoke and Fire," she breathed, and the prince stiffened.

Arianne stared at her prince. "I will have to keep you locked up, or I will surely commit murder." She whispered at last.

Brian's eyebrows lifted in surprise. "What?"

"Your eyes are the most beautiful I've ever seen." She murmured dreamily, then let her gaze drift over the rest of his face.

Brian shifted. Her intense gaze made him uncomfortable. "Well?" He asked when he could stand the suspense no longer.

Arianne grinned impishly, "You'll do." She said, picking up her fork and beginning to eat.

"I'll do, that's all you have to say?" Brian stared at her.

"Fill your plate, and eat." Arianne advised calmly. "After all that has passed between us, do you think I'd let the little matter of a few scales put me off?" With a snort of disgust, Arianne reached across the table, took Brian's plate, filled it and set it back before him.

"Eat. You're going to need all your strength." She paused, "My husband, I knew even before I met you that your body was well formed, that you had courage, a gentle spirit, and a sense of humor.

"When back in the cave of darkness, we shared warmth, and sang together. I was certain that whatever your face looked like wouldn't matter. You are the mate fate has decreed I have." Arianne shrugged, "It could have been worse."

"No maidenly squeals of horror?" Brian was puzzled.

"I am no longer a maid." Arianne smirked. "You solved that problem a little while ago, remember?"

Brian lifted his hands, showing her the webbed fingers, "It doesn't bother you, the thought of these hands on your body?" He opened his mouth to show sharply pointed teeth, barely covered by thin lips. "The thought of being kissed by me doesn't chill you?"

"Nope. It didn't bother me earlier, why should it bother me now?" Arianne helped herself to seconds. "Brian, do you think that I didn't notice the webbing between your fingers when you touched me? When you kissed me, do you think I didn't realize that your mouth wasn't shaped like other men's? It didn't matter then, it doesn't matter now."

Brian watched her across the table, then shook his head. “Tell me, what did you do to me back in the other cave?”

“Nothing.” Arianne helped herself to another serving of the perfectly-cooked vegetables.

“Arianne, I had no intention of making love to you tonight. I wanted to wait until we knew each other better, and you were comfortable with me before consummating our marriage.”

“I know, and I thank you for being so thoughtful. However, it was not necessary.”

“Why?”

Arianne sighed. “For centuries, my people have had arranged marriages. Even before we came to your world, we had to maintain certain mental abilities in our small group. We were created to guard and protect the rest of our population, and the genetic make-up of each child was vital.

“Sometimes, to protect our genetic stability two people who disliked each other had to create a child. To make the process easier, our people developed a technique that would make it easier for them to mate.” Arianne smiled at Brian, “Not perfect, or exciting, just easier.”

“You did this without my permission?” Brian scowled.

“Yes.” Arianne met his eyes, “It was necessary. You would have jeopardized our entire world out of a misplaced sense of honor. I could not let you do that.”

“You took my right to choose away from me.”

"Yes, but I can promise that I will not do it again." Arianne smiled, "It won't be necessary."

"Can I trust your word?" Brian frowned.

"Why don't you touch my mind? I couldn't lie to you then. Brian, I don't lie, well, I do lie, but I'll never lie to you, at least, not about anything important. I need to wash." She dropped her cloak and walked to the pool.

Brian watched her for a moment, trying to work through all the qualifiers she placed on when she would tell him the truth. Finally, he gave up, and, with a chuckle, dropped his own cloak and joined her in the water.

"Here we are wed not even an hour and we've had our first disagreement." Brian said as he pulled her close to him.

"Have you decided to accept what I have done, and take my word that I will not do it again?"

"For now," Brian answered distractedly. He removed the circlet from her head and took down her braids. He stared in fascination at the silver mass that floated on the water's surface.

"You are so very beautiful, My Wife." He murmured stroking her hair.

Arianne smiled, "I am glad I please you, for you please me also."

Brian laughed. "Shall we start over without your magic, my Lady? So that we know exactly what we are doing, and with whom?"

"I knew what I was doing and who I was with earlier. However, I have no objections to doing it again." Arianne whispered as she moved into his arms.

*****

"It is done. Arianne has found Prince Brian and they will start the journey back to Kopol tomorrow." The Feltan stared at Ilona. The queen had dark circles under her eyes. The rest of her people looked no better.

"Queen Ilona, all of you must rest. Nothing further can be done until your daughter reaches the temple of Colsa's goddess. My people have drilled the young foreigners as best we can. The rest is up to them. Now, they must return to their lands and practice what we have placed in their minds."

"The link?" Queen Ilona glanced at the Feltan and smiled. He looked exhausted. The Feltan smiled, "We have established it."

Ilona handed the Feltan the small, pink stone. "We too, are ready. We have given Lantia's Life Stone all that we can give it. My people have already begun the journey into the deep sleep. We will not awaken again until we have destroyed this monster from our past. If we fail, we charge the Feltan with continuing the battle.

Ambrio nodded. "Queen Ilona, if the Lantians fail, we will die protecting the others."

"Have your people planned a way to reach Arianne and tell her what we have planned?" Ilona asked.

Ambrio rubbed his brows, "We must call her to the sea. That will give us a chance to talk to her, and to give her the Stone.

"She promised the temple guards ten days. Five of them are gone already." The Feltan frowned, "We will have very little time."

"You have influence with the Sailors of Alsia. Use it!" Queen Ilona snapped. "I want my daughter fully protected before she faces that horror."

The Feltan bowed, "I wish you to know one important fact, Queen Ilona, you and your daughter are of our blood. We will not fail her, or you."

Queen Ilona sighed, "Forgive me. I know that you will do all in your power to protect Arianne. You were correct. I am tired. We are all tired. We must consult again with the Icina. We will let you know what it has to say. Ambrio, keep us informed of any rumors you should hear."

Ilona touched her son's arm, "Come, we have much to do."

"Has she told the prince about her bargain with the temple guards?" Rolto asked suddenly.

The Feltan, shook his head. "She has told him nothing, yet."

"Why?" Rolto demanded.

Ilona laughed, "You are even more tired than I am if you can ask such a question," she teased and Rolto blushed.

In Alsia, there are two categories of guardians. The major guardians are: The Forest Lady, Mother of the Plains, The Deep Ocean, and The Mountain Master. These four are also called the spirits of the land. The Minor Guardians are all citizens of Alsia with mind speech. These guardians can be human or animal. The minor guardians watch the border between human and non-human territory. Their allegiance is to the land of Alsia.

Lord Orion, Alsian Historian

Chapter 13

"Wake up, Wife." Brian shook Arianne gently.

"Hmm? Is it morning already? I vow we've only just gone to sleep." She mumbled, snuggling deeper beneath the furs.

"It's morning, and we did." Brian grinned.

Arianne peeped at him, a frown on her face, "Stop sounding so smug." She reached out and touched his face. "Brian, your scales are fading."

"Yes, the change is already beginning to reverse itself." He explained, bending lower to kiss her. "Now, get up. We must begin the journey back to Kopol today."

Arianne sighed, "Must we?" She wasn't ready to leave the caves and face the real world so soon.

"We must. The Master's children have brought your clothes from the other cave. When you're dressed and we've eaten, we must leave."

Arianne got up slowly and walked to the pool, "Come bathe with me?"

"Not if we mean to leave here this day." Brian grinned and turned his back on her.

Arianne gave a small laugh and hurried through her bath. When she was dried and dressed, she joined Brian at the table to eat. "Oh good, they brought the packet of dried food. We can use it on the trip down the mountain." She said as she piled her plate full.

Brian watched her eat with amusement, "Is your appetite always this good?"

"Only when I've had plenty of exercise," Arianne replied absently, then blushed at his knowing grin. "Will you stop acting like a..." Her voice trailed off as she stared into laughing sea-green eyes.

"Like a what?" Brian prompted.

Arianne shook her head, "I'll have to remember to avoid your eyes if I ever want to finish a sentence." She grumbled, and Brian laughed aloud.

"Are you finished eating?" He asked. Arianne nodded, and he pushed his chair back, "Let's go."

Holding hands, they walked through the many passages and caves, toward the opening that led outside the mountain. Along the way, Brian and Arianne talked. They exchanged childhood stories and Arianne told him of her journey across the sea. Brian told her of the lonely years he'd spent in the heart of the mountain. He told her how he worried that his mother would, after all, succeed in destroying his land. It was dark when they stepped out onto the mountain path and found Bunto waiting for them. They decided to spend the night where they were and start down the mountain the next morning.

"Do we go directly to Kopol?" Arianne asked, snuggling close to her husband.

"No. We must visit the major guardians, then the lesser, before we can go to Kopol."

"Your mother will not wait for us to come to her. She will come looking for us."

Brian shrugged, "She will not have to come looking for us. Mother knows the route we must take, and since she can't afford to let us reach Kopol unhampered, she will try to stop us before we reach the city. Go to sleep. We will deal with tomorrow as it comes."

Arianne thought that a very short-sighted attitude, but she was too tired to argue with him, so she said nothing, just curled into her husband's embrace and fell asleep.

They traveled quickly, and by nightfall of the next day, they reached the small cave that had sheltered her from the fog. Arianne was thoughtful all day. As they shared her dried rations, and the 'Sweet Fruit' Bunto brought them, she stared quietly at the wall of the cave, a frown on her face.

"Arianne, what's bothering you now?" Brian asked. His voice startled her out of her thoughtful trance.

"Brian, how far from this cave is the home of Lord Orion and Lady Athna?"

"Half-day's travel south of the mountains. Why?"

"Let's go to visit them. They are the speakers for your noblemen. If they know that we are together, getting rid of us in secret will be more difficult for your mother. She will not be able to claim that I failed, or that we both perished in the mountains." Arianne watched as Brian thought about her suggestion. She had three days left to reach the place where Captain Akino would be waiting for her.

Brian chewed thoughtfully. "Yes, we can do that. It also will throw off any pursuit for a few days, and buy us some time. You are wise, My Wife."

"It comes from growing up in Lantia, My Husband."

"Arianne, before you reached me, the guardian of the forest told me a story about your people. She heard it from one of your land's guardians."

"Icina." Arianne interrupted.

"What?"

"Icina. That is what we call the land spirits of our continent."

"Doesn't your land have guardians?" Brian frowned.

"Yes, the Lantians," Arianne laughed at the puzzled look on Brian's face. "Never mind. I will explain another time. Which story did your Icina tell you?"

"She told me how your people behave in battle; how, when one of your enemies turned your people's own tactics against them, the Lantians made peace, and praised the enemy's general. Why do you make war if not to kill the enemy or take their lands?"

Arianne leaned back against the wall, "Brian, we do not need more land, and killing for any reason besides self protection, is abhorrent to us. As I said earlier, we are the guardians of the northern continent.

"When we came to this world, we were fleeing a terrible and relentless enemy, an enemy that we knew would eventually find us. If we had the transportation, we would have left this place when we discovered it already was inhabitanted. However, we no longer had a way to leave, so we decided that since we were responsible for bringing danger to this planet, we were also responsible for teaching its people to defend themselves.

"That is what we have been doing for centuries. It keeps our people alert and trained, as well as giving the original inhabitants the incentive to develop their own mind powers. No one can control the mind of a rational army. You could probably distract a few members, but not all of them. An army that charges its enemy in an emotional frenzy is open game for anyone with the slightest bit of training in mental warfare."

"What about your land spirits, you speak of them as if you only had one?"

"We have three, just as you have here. We sang them a song of unity when we first came to this world. We showed them the power they could have if they became one. Now, the three of them have pooled parts of their essence and they stay in a grove of fruit trees right outside our capital city.

Icina can be used as either singular or plural. It doesn't really matter."

"Do your people worship this Icina?"

Arianne laughed, "You Alsians think too much about religion. No, we do not worship the Icina. They are terrible gossips and wonderful babysitters. The children love them. The old people sit under the tree and talk about the good old days. The queen sits under the tree and discusses politics. The young people sit under the tree and ask for advice on their love lives."

Arianne frowned, then smiled. "Our Icina is everyone's grandmother."

Brian shook his head, "I don't think Alsia's guardians would enjoy that sort of treatment." He mused.

Arianne giggled. "The Mountain Master would love my people, and the children especially would love him. He would never have another moment's rest."

"Girl. I will be a grandfather to no human child." The Mountain Master rumbled across the cave.

"You will be my children's grandfather. Every spring, I will bring them here to keep you company. They will tell you all the wonderful experiences they have had during the year."

The Master's groan of despair shook the mountains and caused a ripple of laughter from Alsia's other two land spirits.

"We must visit your land when this is over. Would you like that?" Brian grinned. He sensed a feeling of harmony in Alsia's air that had been missing for a long time.

"Yes, I would like to see my brother again." Arianne said thoughtfully, as, in perfect accord, they curled up and fell asleep.

Late the next day, they reached the end of the path they'd been following. Arianne turned and looked back at the towering mountains, then smiled.

"Grandfather, I thank you. I'll come back to visit one day soon with the children."

"You're welcome, and don't bother." The Master replied.

"You are an old faker." Arianne laughed.

"Brian, get that female out of my mountains before I bury you both." the Master roared.

Brian and Arianne ran, laughing, the rest of the way, coming to a breathless halt on level ground. They were out of the mountains now, and the plains stretched before them.

Kelv and Ulph loped over to greet them. *Your Highness*, the animals bowed their heads, *the Silver and Green Lady requests that you spend the night in her shelter.*

Arianne glanced at Brian, and he nodded. "We will be pleased to accept her hospitality," he answered formally, as they turned toward the stone circle.

When they entered the circle, the Lady was waiting for them, "My children will greet you this night, king of Lantia. We know that you must journey swiftly, for your mother already plans to move against you. Our brother has joined us for the first time in a millennium to offer his aid. We have sped up the reversal process, so it will only take a week instead of the year it usually does. Together, we will block any magic your mother may bring against you. Once you are in the city, however, we can do nothing to help you."

Brian bowed his head slightly. "Lady, guardian of the plains, my wife and I thank you and accept your offer of aid. On the morrow, we travel to the castle of Orion and Athna, from there, we go to the forest, and then, by sea, to the city of Kopol."

"We will guard you well. Now my people come."

Arianne and Brian stood in the center of the circle and accepted the homage of the creatures that lived on the plains.

"Sister, Friend, Daughter, Grand-Daughter, will you sing for me the first song of your people?" The guardian of the plains asked, when all her children sat in a circle around Brian and Arianne.

"Guardian of Alsia's plains, that is a song I cannot sing. Now that the Feltan and my people have made peace, the day may come when the One Singer will visit Alsia and sing the song of joining for you."

"Who is this One Singer?" The Silver and Green Lady raised an eyebrow.

"That name I will not speak in this place where they worship The Abomination," Arianne replied.

The guardian was speechless. After a long, silent moment, she said softly, "I will speak to the spirits of the northern continent. Then you and I will speak again."

Arianne nodded, and the assembled creatures quietly left the area. When all had gone except the three original companions, they lay at the foot of the Lady's platform and slept.

The next morning, they gathered to have a council of war, *What has my mother been up to in the last four days?* Brian asked Kelv and Ulph.

Colsa has recalled all of the temple warriors. The priestesses who belong to Lady Colsa's Dark Lady are going to the main temple in Kopol. Since we can't get through the temple's defenses, we've no idea what is going on there.

We do know that at least a dozen of Alsia's most powerful noblemen and women, and most of the priestesses of the Bright Lady, have joined Lord Orion in his home for High Summer's Feast. Ulph answered.

Kelv nodded, *the forest Lady has alerted all her children to watch for you, and to give aid if needed. Word has also come to us that Olpho and Feltan swim in the sacred cove where the forest meets the sea. The Feltan and the Lantians are allies again*.

Brian smiled. "It seems your cousins would protect you, Arianne. It's good that the Feltan return to us. I only hope we survive to greet and welcome them."

"We will survive." Arianne said firmly.

"Well, it was a wise decision to visit Orion, anyway. I'd forgotten High Summer celebrations. Enough of our noblemen should be present to name me king even before we reach the city."

"Won't your mother know that as well?" Arianne asked frowning.

"Yes, she may try to stop us from reaching Orion, but once we arrive not even my mother will be foolish enough to challenge Lady Athna in her own home." Brian grinned smugly. "Well, talking won't get us to our destination, and staying here gives my mother more time for planning. We must move swiftly and hope we can keep her off balance."

The five companions left the sacred circle before dawn the next morning and headed east toward Lord Orion's castle. They saw no sign of the temple warriors, though they caught glimpses of the creatures the Lady of the plains sent to escort them. The plains hadn't changed at all, Arianne thought tiredly. It was still as hot and dry as ever.

The closer they got to Orion's home, the hotter the air grew, and a haze shimmered over everything. "It wasn't this hot before." Arianne gasped.

"This is my mother's work. She seeks to slow us." Brian said shortly.

Ulph snorted, *follow me. The heat haze will distort your eyes and lead you off the road you must travel, but it won't bother me. I'm the daughter of the Silver and Green. Colsa's magic does not affect my Lady's children.*

Staying close to Ulph, the others trudged slowly through the blistering heat.

At last, Ulph gave a bark of satisfaction, *there, ahead are the gates you must enter. We can go no further with you. Travel well and swiftly. We will wait for your return in this place.*

Arianne and Brian squinted. Through the haze they saw the faint outline of Orion's gates. They walked for what felt like hours, and still the gates got no closer. Arianne stumbled and fell. Her eyes closed.

"I can go no farther, leave me and get help. I'll wait here for you."

Brian looked at her, and shook his head, "I dare not leave you alone out here. If my mother found you, she could still ruin everything." He had no strength to carry her. "Arianne, you must get up. I can't carry you. It's just a little farther, My Wife. Come try."

"Smoke, Brian, you're a hard man." She whispered through dry, cracked lips, as she forced herself to stand and walk on.

"The gate has to be here," Brian mumbled, holding Arianne's hand and dragging her behind him. "Ahh, here it is. Orion, Athna, please open your gates," he called out as Arianne stumbled and fell again.

When I was a boy, I loved Colsa. All the lads did. She was beautiful. Her voice was music and she walked with the grace of a willow tree in a soft breeze.

When I became a young man, my love for my best friend and leige lord's wife, shamed me and I took to the sea.

When I became an old man, I discovered that I had wasted my love on a monster. The bitter taste of squandered love lingers with me still.

Harl, Alsian Sailor

Chapter 14

"Brian, oh my dear boy, why didn't you send a message that you were coming?" Lady Athna answered as her guards opened the gates. "Oh, your poor princess! Give her to us."

Gentle hands reached out and lifted Arianne as they led Brian into the coolness of Orion and Athna's castle.

*****

Arianne sighed in contentment and opened her eyes. She was in a cool, dark room, richly decorated with hanging tapestries and heavy, wooden furniture. She rolled over, delighting in the feel of the soft, feather bed beneath her.

"Brian," she called.

"Over here, Arianne," he answered as he stepped into view.

"Come to bed," she invited sleepily, throwing the covers back.

Brian laughed and walked over to sit beside her, "We were worried about you. It's been two days since we arrived here, and you've slept the whole time.

"Athna is the high priestess in the temple of the Bright Goddess. She has blocked my mother's magic, so we are safe for a while. My mother is not sure where we are now, but we must leave here soon. I don't want to leave you with Athna, but I may have no choice if you are not well enough to travel."

"I'm fine, a little tired, but another night's rest should solve that problem. When do we have to leave?"

"Tomorrow." Brian frowned briefly, then added with a smile, "It's dinner time. Athna has a celebration planned. Do you feel well enough to come down and eat with the noblemen of my court? If you're not up to it, I can always explain it to them. They know how ill you have been, and would understand if you would prefer to eat alone in our rooms."

Arianne shrugged, then she glanced down at herself. "Brian, how can I meet your noblemen for a celebration dinner when I have nothing to wear?"

Brian grinned at her. "Now, I know you're better. Lady Athna has had her people working for the last twenty-four hours to make you a gown in case you wanted to join them." He stood and stretched out his hands to help her out of bed. "A bath is waiting for you. Hurry, or we'll be late for dinner."

Arianne stared at those hands, then looked at his face. "Brian your webs and scales are almost gone." She took his hands, and stood up.

Brian stared at her, “Aren’t you pleased by the change?”

“Yes. Only now, you’ll be so handsome that all the other women will chase after you, and I’ll have my hands full trying to keep them away.”

“Why should I notice other women when the loveliest lady in two kingdoms is my wife?” Brian asked softly. Arianne beamed happily up at him as she prepared for dinner.

They heard a timid knock on the door, and Brian opened it to admit a plump, young woman. “My Lady Athna has sent me to help the Princess Arianne dress.” She said softly, then stopped, and stared at Arianne. “Oh, Princess, you have such pretty hair. Let me dress it for you?”

Arianne, glanced over her shoulders at the maid and handed her the brush, “Go ahead.”

An hour later, Arianne stood in front of the large mirror in her room, and looked at herself in astonishment. The soft, silky dress clung to her slight figure from the high collar that framed her face, to the full skirt that touched the floor; the long sleeves ended at a point on the back of her hands, and were slashed to allow her armbands to show. The maid had brushed her long hair back from her face, gathered it in a low bun on her neck, then placed the golden circlet on her head.

Arianne smiled. She was well pleased with her appearance. “Well Brian, will I do?”

Before Brian could answer, Lady Athna knocked at entered the room. “Pardon, but Lord Rabon, the Royal Treasurer, is here. He always carries the Crown Jewels with him, especially at this time of year when the young Chosen is wandering through our land." Athna smiled slyly. "He asks, Princess Arianne, that you go through the case and find some jewelry suitable to wear at dinner."

Arianne opened the large case that Athna gave her and turned to Brian. "You know this jewelry, find me a piece that would speak to your people of unity and strength."

Brian frowned and went through the jewelry case twice before he picked up a necklace of heavy, beaten gold, and decorated with five large gems that formed a star in the middle. He showed the necklace to Arianne, then fastened it around her neck.

"What do the stones stand for?" She asked as she touched the necklace gently.

"The deep blue stone at the top of the star represents the sea. The dark green stone on the left is the forest. The white stone on the right is the mountain. The red stone at the right bottom is the plains, and the pinkish stone on the bottom left represents the City of Kopol," he explained, and stood back to admire the picture she made. "By the guardians, My Wife, you're lovely," Brian breathed in admiration, "You will dazzle my noblemen."

Lady Athna studied Arianne for a moment, then smiled. "Prince Brian is correct. Tonight, you will dazzle all who see you. Colsa has chosen very well."

"My mother has chosen better than she expected." Brian replied shortly.

Athna shrugged, then turned to Arianne. "By the way, a young member of the temple guard stopped by two days ago and left a message for you."

Arianne glanced at Athna, "Cory?" She frowned, "What did he want?"

"He said to tell you this, 'Elder Sister, Lady Colsa has ordered Captain Akino's patrol to return to the City of Kopol. We release you from your bargain. If you need my aid, I will be in my parents' home. Lantia has called all her allies to stand by you, and my first loyalty is to the Elder Sister. If you ask, my family and I will be ready to defend you and your king.'" Athna raised one delicate eyebrow. "What connection do you have with the temple guards, Princess Arianne?"

"Cory is a mercenary from the northern lands. His country, Belden, and Lantia have been close allies for centuries." Arianne turned and walked into the bath chamber, leaving Athna and Brian alone.

It was almost five minutes before she heard the door close, signaling Athna's departure. She waited another minute, then joined Brian.

"Arianne, before we go downstairs, would you explain the message you received from Captain Akino to me?"

"Captain Akino captured me before I reached the caves where you were held. I gave him my bond that if he would allow me to finish my journey, I would give myself back into his custody in ten days."

"Who is this Cory? Why does he call you Elder Sister?"

"I have already explained who Cory is. He calls me Elder Sister because that is what I am. I am the eldest daughter, and the second heir of the royal house of Lantia."

Brian frowned, "Were you going to tell me of this bargain?"

"Yes."

"When?" He demanded.

Arianne shrugged, "When we left this place. Brian, your mother has invited a horror that we call The Abomination to your land. It can only be defeated by a Lantian. It is a being that devours all life and creates darkness and despair in the hearts and minds of all it touches. The Abomination is a monster that leaves death and destruction in its path."

"Why can only Lantians destroy it?"

"Because Lantians created it. It is our nightmare. It has haunted us across space and time for centuries. My people have fled before it until we reached this place and decided that here we would stand. We will live or die with this land. You must understand, we did not intend to involve innocents in our battle. However, once we reached this place, we discovered that we could go no further.

"Now, we find that The Abomination is the same creature that your mother worships as her Dark Goddess. My mother had to break two centuries of silence to remind the Feltan of a promise made and a promise broken, all because your mother called this evil, and invited it into her world to satisfy her ambition." Arianne shook her head.

Brian scowled, “You should be able to understand that. You, too, are an ambitious woman.”

Arianne glanced at him in surprise, “Lantians have only one ambition. To be forever rid of this nightmare, so we may live in peace.”

“...And to rule this world.” Brian added.

Arianne laughed. “My mother cannot wait until Rolto’s training is complete so she can step down from being queen. Rolto, being a sly person, studies slowly. He is doing all that he can to delay that dread day.”

“You want to rule by my side, to be a queen.”

“I want to rule by your side, and to be queen. I want to be wife, partner, and mother. I do not want us to end like my parents, who speak only when politics force them. I would kill you if I discovered that once we have secured the throne of Alsia, you took another to your bed. If you deem that ambition, then yes, I am ambitious.” Arianne glared at Brian.

Brian reached out and touched her hair, “Maybe I have misjudged you in this,” he whispered. “Will you accept my word that I will have no other partner in my bed while you live?”

Arianne tensed, “Lantian Honor?”

“Alsian Honor.” Brian smiled.

With a small sigh, she closed her eyes and smiled, “I guess that will do. I can’t start this marriage by doubting my husband’s honor, can I?”

Brian kissed her cheek. "No. It would be most unwise if either of us doubted the honor of the other. Shall we go down and join the others now?"

Arianne smiled and took her husband's arm as they walked down the stairs and into the dining room. When they entered the room, a hush fell over the people in it. Then, everybody applauded loudly. The noblemen came over to them, greeted Arianne, and welcomed their prince back.

Lord Orion let the informal talk go on for an hour before he called them to order. "Lords of Alsia, my wife Athna, High Priestess of the temple of the Bright Lady, will join our prince and his Chosen in the marriage rites of Kopol. Afterward, we will administer the oath of office, then present Prince Brian with the ring of Kopol and the crown of Alsia."

"I thought we were already joined?" Arianne whispered to Brian.

"In the presence of the guardians, we are one. This is a civil ceremony, to satisfy the humans who live in this land. Alsia has two types of citizens, so we must have two types of wedding ceremonies." Brian explained.

"You Alsians make marriage so very difficult. At home, once one of the partners moves into the other's home, they are joined for life." Arianne whispered back.

Once again, Prince Brian of Alsia and Princess Arianne of Lantia gave their pledges to each other, this time before human witnesses.

Lady Athna stepped forward. "I will ask you, Princess Arianne of Lantia, will you forsake your own nation, and swear loyalty only to Alsia, its king, and its people?"

"Lady Athna, I will swear, Lantian Honor, that I will do nothing to harm Alsia, its king or its people." Arianne answered.

Athna frowned. "That's not quite what I asked, Lantian Princess."

"It is the only oath that I can swear at this time. My nation is in jeopardy because of the actions of an Alsian. I am bound by Lantian law and Lantian Honor. I cannot abandon my people now."

Brian held up his hand to stop the muttering among his noblemen. "I will accept my wife's oath. Even the Feltan swear by Lantian Honor." He turned to Arianne. "I hope in the future, you will find yourself able to swear the true oath of fealty."

"I, too, hope for a future where that is possible. However, I will swear no oath that may hamper me in my battle with your mother."

Brian turned to Lady Athna, "Will you accept that?"

Athna's lips tightened, then reluctantly, she nodded, "I will accept that for now. Brian trusts you, but we will be watching you closely. Betray our king and you will surely die. When Brian has been established in the Kopol as king of all Alsia, I will again ask for your oath, wife of our king."

Arianne's eyes turned black with fury, "When we have defeated The Abomination that lives in your land, I will give you my answer."

Lord Orion stepped forward quickly, between Arianne and his wife. "Prince Brian, do you swear to rule Alsia fairly, to protect her from any threat, whether foreign or domestic, and to abide by the rules of our land? Do you also swear to protect the land and its inhabitants, both human and nonhuman, with your life?"

Brian bowed his head, then stared straight at Orion. "Before all the Lords and Ladies of Alsia, I so swear."

"Then accept the ring of Kopol and the crown of Alsia from the hands of Lord Rabon." Orion instructed as Lord Rabon stepped forward and handed Brian the symbols of his position.

"It is done. Now, let us celebrate. We have completed our part, Your Highness, and named you rightful king of our land. The hardest challenge is yet ahead. You must go to Kopol and challenge your mother and her minions for the right to sit on the throne and rule." Lady Athna said, as she led them into dinner.

The meal was festive, with many courses and free-flowing wine. The noblemen offered toasts to the new king and his bride and drank eagerly to their health. Arianne enjoyed the meal, though some of the advice they gave Brian on handling a new wife, made her blush.

In Alsia she saw an informality between the king and his noblemen that her mother would never allow at the Lantian court. The party would have gone on all night if Brian hadn't called a halt around midnight.

"My Lords and Ladies, give me a moment," he called. When silence descended, he went on, "My queen and I leave this place at first light on the morrow. We have many more things to accomplish before we can face my mother in Kopol. We invite you all to the palace in Kopol for Midwinter celebrations, and we thank you for your aid and your support. Now, we must retire."

Lady Athna nodded. "I'll give you protection to the edges of my lands. It's all that I can offer."

"You have given enough, Lady Athna," Brian replied. "You've defied my mother and given us aid and shelter. You have arranged for my noblemen to be here and performed the marriage rites for me. Our debt to you grows by the minute. Already, we have jeopardized your people just by being here. I will ask no further sacrifice from you and yours."

"My king, all the powers of the Bright Lady go with you. Whether you ask for it or not, you will have my protection for as long as I can give it. Let us have no debts between us. Now, go to your rooms and get some rest. I will see you both in the morning before you leave."

Brian and Arianne left the great hall accompanied by the loud laughter and shouted instructions of the now-drunk noblemen.

Upstairs, in their room, Brian looked closely at Arianne. "Are you sure that you're up to this journey?"

"You cannot leave me behind. We must be together or the whole purpose of this journey will be defeated. It will take both of us to stop your mother's plans."

Brian smiled. "I must admit that I'm glad you'll be with me. Rest well, Little Queen. It will be a long time before we spend another night in a bed this soft. I suggest we enjoy it while we have the chance."

Arianne sighed as she snuggled into the soft bed, "I am getting tired of people calling me little." She whispered as she turned into her husband's arms.

The ruler of Alsia commands all magic of the land. The ability to speak with sea and land animals, as well as with all the guardians of the land, is the primary requirement for our ruler. The health of the land of Alsia and the seas around it rests in the hands of the king or queen.

Lord Orion, Alsian Historian

Chapter 15

As Brian and Arianne stepped beyond the protection of Lady Athna's lands, Kelv, Bunto and Ulph joined them. The air was still cool and fresh from the night's rain, and a soft mist covered the plains.

Did all go well in the home of Athna and Orion? Ulph asked.

Arianne shrugged, *I suppose, it went quite well. All the lords of Alsia were there and Brian took his oath to protect the land. You are now looking at the officially acknowledged king of Alsia.*

Then we must travel quickly to the forests, my Lord Brian. The Lady of the Forest and the Lady of the Plains both await your arrival. It is time that you learned the secret of ruling Alsia and keeping the magic alive throughout the land. Kelv thought as the animals fell in step with their two human companions.

Brian nodded and frowned. Despite Arianne's assurances that she was fine, she had a drawn look about her that told him she wasn't as strong as she wanted him to believe.

Arianne has been ill. She is not accustomed to the heat of Alsia's plains, Brian explained to the others. *I worry that she cannot keep up with us.*

"Brian, I'm a Lantian warrior, trained to endure. I'll not slow you." Arianne objected.

Brian sighed, "Lantians treat their women harshly. In Alsia, our women are gentle creatures. No one expects them to endure many hardships."

"Yes. Your mother and Lady Athna are perfect examples of gentle, Alsian womanhood, aren't they?" Arianne snapped, angered at his implied criticism of her people.

"Arianne I didn't mean to anger you..."

"Well, you did." Arianne interrupted him. "Through all of my training in Lantia, nothing has been as difficult as the hardships I've endured since I landed on the coast of Alsia. If I'd been some gentle, Alsian Lady, you'd still be stuck in that smoke-cursed mountain. I'm sorry that my lack of gentleness displeases you, but I am what I am, and you are stuck with me."

"I am proud of you." Brian objected, "But I also worry about you. All that you've said is true, and I wouldn't change you for any of our Alsian ladies. Is it wrong of me to want to pamper and protect you?"

"No," Arianne sighed, "It's not wrong. I'm just not used to others trying to protect me."

"Doesn't your father protect your mother? All men want to keep the women who belong to them safe. That is the masculine way." Brian explained, "Have you never watched your parents? A man protects what he values."

Arianne shook her head. "Brian, I've told you before, I am the product of an arranged royal marriage. My parents were faithful to each other only long enough to secure an heir to the throne. Once they had achieved that goal, they went their own way. I have one sister who is my mother's child. My father has sent his three children to his home in the northern province of Gemi to be raised. This is common practice among the royal houses of the northern lands. In arranged marriages, no love is given, and none is expected." She paused, "It's not the sort of marriage I want."

Brian stared at her puzzled, "Are you saying there are only two heirs to Lantia's throne? What will happen if your brother dies? Do you have to return to rule?"

"I could never rule in Lantia. That's why my mother was so eager to get me out of the country. Patria is my full sister. If she wasn't, Mother, by law, would not have been allowed to name her Second-Heir in my place. Also, remember, that Rolto is married to young Crista, and if she is wise, she will quickly give him an heir."

"What makes it impossible for you to rule in Lantia?"

"Brian, my people hate and fear the sea. They won't even deal with any who sail upon it. I loved the sea, and spent every spare moment down on the beach of Lantia. If my behavior had become common knowledge, it would have caused my family a lot of embarrassment. Some younger Lantians might have tried to challenge Rolto's right to rule our country. Before that happened, my mother sent me away."

"So, when Lady Colsa came to collect a gentle princess, who, she assumed, hated the sea. Your mother used the situation for her own ends and sent you?" Brian mused.

"Yes, my mother has the ability to turn the most unlikely events into what she wants. Lady Colsa never stood a chance. She received what my mother wanted to give, nothing more."

Brian threw back his head and laughed. "I wish I'd been there to see my mother outmaneuvered."

"You don't mind?"

"Why should I? You came to me out of those two women's manipulation. They did us both a favor, don't you agree?"

"Yes." Arianne nodded, "I am well pleased with the outcome."

"So am I, and I promise you that we will have a proper marriage. Neither of us will have any other partners." Brian looked around, *Soon, it will be time to stop for the day and find protection from the heat.*

Prince Brian, may we suggest that we travel well into the day, before stopping. We must put more distance between us and the lands of the humans. Ulph protested.

Brian glanced at Arianne, then agreed. *All right, we travel until it's too hot to go any farther.*

They traveled until the sun was high in the sky, then dug a shelter in the cool earth and lay down. Arianne smiled grimly, at least this time she wasn't dependent on raw meat for nourishment. Lady Athna's kitchen supplied plenty of dried foods for their trip. She chewed slowly as the sun beat down on the plains and sweat ran into her eyes. This was not a gentle land. The weak would quickly perish. Arianne smiled, no matter what Brian said, only the strong would prosper in Alsia. In spite of its harshness, its wild beauty touched a part of her soul. She could grow to love this country.

"Brian?"

"Mm hm?"

"What mind powers do you have?"

"What?" He asked sleepily.

"Your powers? What powers do you control? I know that you can mind-speak. What else can you do?"

Brian sighed and rolled over to face her, "The only minds that I can speak to are yours and the nonhuman. I can hear the sea, but can't achieve joining with it. As king, I'm supposed to be able to command all the magic of Alsia, but since I've just been accepted, I haven't tried that yet. That's why we are on our way to the Sacred Grove. The spirits of the land will teach me what I need to know before we go on to Kopol."

"Then, Lady Colsa lost the power to control Alsia's weather when you became king?"

Brian laughed bitterly, "That's supposed to be the way of it. However, knowing my mother, I wouldn't bet on it. She has touched much that is forbidden in the land, and many of her magic powers are not even of Alsia. Now, it appears that she is willing to destroy Alsia in her efforts to destroy me."

It was not yet dusk when they started walking again. Arianne had rested, but not slept during their stop and she was looking forward to the rain. The next three days passed quietly. When they stopped on the fourth day, Arianne saw the tall trees of the forest as a smudge on the horizon. By tomorrow, with any luck, they would be in the shelter of the trees. She didn't trust the peace they'd encountered so far, and wondered what Lady Colsa was planning.

"Brian, if I was your mother, I'd know you have to go to the forests and would be waiting there for you."

Brian shook his head. "Our greatest danger was when we first left Lady Athna's home. The closer we get to the forest, the less chance there is of running into any of my mother's people. This part of the forest is the last place she would send any of her followers. The Forest Lady is strong here, for the heart of this section belongs only to her. No one, human or nonhuman, enters here without her permission. No, we'll have no problems with my mother until we reach Kopol."

Arianne relaxed a little. She hoped Brian was correct. This was his land and he knew it better than she did, so she would accept his assessment of the situation.

She finally fell asleep and awoke to find herself hot, sticky, and as tired as she'd been when they stopped. Arianne realized she was nearing the limits of her strength. This trip had tested her in many ways. She was proud of the way she had behaved so far. Only two incidents caused her shame to recall.

As they walked in the rain, Arianne turned to Brian, "Tell me of your land."

"What would you know?"

"Everything. Tell me the history of your land and your people."

"It is said, that once our people were like the Feltan. We lived in the sea, but had the power to change our tails into legs whenever we wished to walk on the land. When we decided to live permanently on the land, the sea mother took that power from us. In return, she and the guardians of the land gave us other powers, then they divided the world in half.

"The Feltan were given the north and we were given the south. The guardians promised us that so long as we held the land sacred and obeyed the laws of the guardians, the land would be ours and its magic would stay strong.

"To ensure there was always a ruler of the true blood among the people of Alsia, the guardians decreed that the heir to the throne of Alsia must be wed by his twenty-third birthday. After that time, he would start to change back into what we had been before we lived on the land. If he found no suitable bride by his twenty-sixth year, the change would be complete. He would not be able to stand on the land until a bride was found who would accept him as he was."

“I thought the sea mother took your tail. You had no tail when I met you in the caves.” Arianne frowned.

“We kept our legs. They were gifts from the sea mother, but in every other way, we became what we were in the beginning. That’s why I had a large pool in the cave where I lived.” Brian explained.

Then he continued, “The Feltan and the Alsians lived in peace for many years until the new people came from the sky. Their ways were different from ours, they had no respect for the land, and even less for the sea. From the beginning, these newcomers had a fear of the sea, but still they traveled on it. Alsia was hidden from their eyes, for we didn’t trust them and wanted no contact with them.

“The outward beauty of these new people seduced the Feltan, however, and they forsook the true way of the Mother. They married into your people’s ruling families and gathered riches and power. Soon, they no longer called the Alsians brothers. They forgot the pledge they made with the sea mother to protect the northern half of the world. They betrayed their heritage so they could become one with the strangers.

“The Lady gave the Feltan a choice. They could remain with your people and be destroyed or they could join with her and wander the seas until all broken promises were kept, and all stolen treasures were returned. When the blood of the three races became one, they would be given another home far from the lands of other men.”

"Any child of ours will be of the blood of three races. As for the rest, well, the Feltan can fulfill those conditions any time they choose." Arianne blinked the rain from her eyes.

"Are you accusing the Feltan of stealing a treasure from your people, or of breaking a promise? I find either hard to believe. The Feltan are an honorable people." Brian objected. "If we discover that the Feltan are out in the sacred cove, would you be willing to face them with your accusation?"

"Brian, I make no accusations, the past lies between the Feltan and my people. They know the truth of what happened. I will discuss it with no one else."

"You keep many secrets from me, Wife." Brian frowned.

"Secrets which are not mine to share. Know that as I keep the Feltan secret, so will I keep any secret you should share with me." Arianne touched Brian's arm gently, then continued. "I met a Feltan on my trip out here. Your mother was very upset about that."

"She would be. It would upset her to know that she had a hand in a prophecy made by an aspect of the Mother she doesn't worship. Ironic, isn't it? What should have been her greatest victory could well turn out to be her greatest defeat."

"Your story is not quite right, you know," she murmured.

"What parts of it are wrong?" Brian asked.

"Your assessment of my people. When we came to this world, we were terrified. We were separated from the rest of our people, and in a strange place. The Feltan came to us and offered their friendship and aid. They introduced us to those we call Icina, spirits of the land. We deal well with them. Our children go to the Icina grove to play. They tell stories, and the old women go to share gossip."

Brian stared at her in astonishment. "You were not joking earlier? Your people really do treat the land mother like a grandmother?"

Arianne giggled, "Yes. The Icina of the northern lands is a terrible gossip. She loves hearing all the news of our lives and always gives us good advice."

"Arianne, the land spirits are a part of the goddess." Brian protested.

"We have no gods. The Icina is our best friend. That is much better than being a god. After all, a Lantian would do nothing to harm a friend."

They walked through the midday heat and reached the cool, dark protection of the trees in the early afternoon. The five companions dropped onto the soft grass and lay resting, too tired to move. For a time, they were safe. This was Brian and Arianne's last refuge. When they left here, they would have to face the Lady Colsa in her own stronghold.

They spent a week in the forest of Alsia, gathering their strength and resting. Brian and the Lady of the forest met every day, and she taught him all the secrets of the true magic of Alsia. Arianne didn't attend these meetings. She spent that time getting to know more of the inhabitants of the forest and learning to identify the edible fruits and plants that grew wild in the area.

Each night, she and Brian practiced singing greetings to the land and the sea. Together, they created new songs of love, peace, and goodwill among all the Mother's children. Their songs drifted through the gathering dark and the creatures of land and sea echoed the music back to them.

One night, Brian turned to her, "It's time we finished our journey. The Lady has taught me how to control the magic of Alsia. Now, it is time for us to continue our journey."

"I'll miss it here, the peace and quiet." Arianne said softly.

"We'll come back. If we linger too much longer, even the peace of the forest could be destroyed by my mother's ambition."

Arianne sighed. She knew Brian was right, "When do we leave?"

"Tomorrow." Brian smoothed the leaves from her hair, "I would leave you here if I could."

"Stop trying to protect me, Brian. I'm going with you."

Brian smiled softly, "Sleep then. Tomorrow we spend on the sea, by the second morning we should be in Kopol."

Arianne curled up on the soft grass and snuggled close to her husband. Soon, this adventure would be over and her life would get back to normal. She had to believe that she and Brian would defeat Lady Colsa and The Abomination. She must have no doubts in her mind when they reached Kopol.

Daughter of a Far Land, come to us. The thought whispered across her mind, soft as an evening breeze.

Arianne got up, careful not to disturb Brian, and walked down the path to the forest Lady's Pool. *You called me, Lady?*

My sisters and I have one gift to give you: The power to become one with the land. We have seen much of the future. We will give you and our king all the help in our power to offer.

Are we going to win?

In all of mankind's dealings, two paths are possible. If you and the young Brian are true to yourselves and each other, you may succeed. Remember to trust your mate, no matter what you see or hear.

We do not know each other well enough for that sort of trust to have developed.

You and Brian do not have the luxury of time. You must both move swiftly and know that you can rely upon each other. Now, come closer and touch my hand, the Lady instructed.

As their hands met, Arianne felt a ripple of surprise go through the land, and a masculine voice boomed in their minds. *I too, would give this mortal female a gift.*

Brother, you are welcome. Both the guardians replied, their joy at this contact from their unpredictable brother apparent in their voices.

Arianne stood in the heart of the forest, joined to the guardians of Alsia, and smiled. She felt the power of the forest, the plains, and the mountains move within her. Then, softly and gently, the voice of the deep oceans joined the others. The air shimmered and a bright, blue light that turned the dark of night into day, surrounded Arianne. From across the sea, a beam of pure, white light came and wrapped itself around Arianne. She laughed softly and sang greetings to the Icina of the northern lands.

"I have missed you, Daughter," The white light murmured. "Your people have gone into deep sleep, and I have been lonesome without their chatter. I bring you their strength and their blessings. Tomorrow, the Feltan will give you an item of great power, and you will take the dreams of Lantia into Kopol with you." The northern Icina paused, then added softly, "Your mother has spent many long hours speaking with the sea mother."

"My mother spoke to the sea?"

"When she learned, the safety of her eldest daughter was threatened, the queen of Lantia demanded both the Feltan and the sea mother give you their protection."

"For the land we have sworn to protect." Arianne murmured.

"For her daughter," the northern Icina replied. "Do you not know how much your mother loves you?"

"Welcome, Spirits of the North." The spirits of Alsia sang before Arianne could answer. "Join us, so we may give the children our world strength."

Briefly, all the guardians became one and Arianne saw the true face of the Icina of all living beings.

“Sit, child of the stars, open your mind and your heart that I may judge you.”

“Have you not tested me enough?” Arianne objected, “Ask the Icina of the north lands what is in my heart. They have known me since birth.”

“The spirits of your lands have told many stories about your people, but much still puzzles me. I do not understand the Star Children. Their actions, at times, do not make sense.”

“We are mad.” Arianne said calmly. “The only contact we have with normalcy is our honor and our oath to protect those who cannot protect themselves.”

“Have your people always been mad?”

“Those of us who landed on your world were guardians against The Abomination for generations. Battling its darkness twisted our way of thinking into unexpected paths. We learned that we must be illogical when fighting a creature of absolute logic.”

“This Abomination is the same being Colsa has called to my world?”

“Yes, and I will swear any oath you require. My people will die to protect your world.”

“This I know, for I have seen and heard the plans of your people.” The being paused, “Tell me, child, do the genuinely mad admit to their madness?”

Arianne laughed, “If they are Lantians, they boast of it, take pride in it, glory in it. We are not ordinary madmen.”

The Icina of all life on the planet was silent while it pondered Arianne's words, then a sigh rippled through the light.

"Know the truth then, Mad Star Child. I am the life of this world. All beings native to this world are a part of me. Good and evil, chaos and order, life and death, they all fall under my control.

"See my true essence and do not be deceived by impostors and false faces. All living creatures have a place in the scheme of life. Protect and honor them. Be true to the promises your people have made to me and to mine. All will be well. Betray the land or choose wrongly, and I will turn my face from you. All that you strive to gain will be lost."

A small sliver of the blue-white light wound itself around her, and deep in the heart of her being, it became a part of her.

"Know this, adopted child, before you face the enemy, you must trust our son and he must trust you without question. The slightest doubt in either of your hearts will mean failure and the end of our world. If you are strong, then the part of me that is with you will give aid during your fight."

Before Arianne could say anything more, the light was gone and she stood alone before the Sacred Pool of the forest.

She blinked, then turned and walked back to Brian.

"Where were you? Are you all right?" He murmured sleepily as she snuggled back beside him.

"Yes, Brian, I'm fine, I will tell you all about it tomorrow. Go back to sleep." She answered, closing her eyes and trying to follow her own advice.

The words of the world's Icina haunted her. How could she and Brian develop the kind of trust they would need to defeat The Abomination? She was a woman. The most important woman in Brian's life, his mother, had betrayed him. Arianne sighed. She too had doubts about Brian. No matter what he said, Lady Colsa was his mother.

She finally fell into a shallow, disturbed sleep that left her feeling more tired when she awoke than she was the night before. The next morning, they walked the path to the beach. She wanted Brian with her when she returned to greet the Olpho. It felt like the right thing to do.

Greetings, Sea Dreamer, the waves sang as she stepped onto the sand. *We've missed you. We have many stories to tell.*

Greetings, little ones, Arianne replied, and the waves chuckled*, I too have missed you, and I am eager to hear your stories.*

Not now, the Olpho sang. *Now is time for the two of you to join the deep and travel swiftly. After the danger has passed, then we may tell all our stories and sing all our new songs.*

"What do we do about our clothes?" Arianne asked Brian.

"Leave them here. Friends will meet us at the Port of Kopol, and will supply us with clothes that are fitting for the return king and his queen." Brian answered as he undressed.

"What friends?"

"We have many friends in Kopol, My Wife." Brian stood back and watched as Arianne shed her clothes and walked toward the water.

They swam out to where the Olpho waited in deep water. *The Feltan want to meet you. They wait farther out. We will take you to them. Climb on our backs and hold on tight*, the Olpho sang.

Arianne laughed with joy, her worries temporarily forgotten as the sleek creatures cut swiftly through the water. Seawater sprayed into her face as she hugged the large fin on the Olpho's back tightly and closed her eyes. She loved the land of Alsia, but the sea was where her special joy lay. She wished that she could travel like this forever.

Soon, the Olpho stopped. They lay, floating on the surface of the ocean, until four of the Feltan joined them. Once more, Arianne marveled at the close resemblance between them. Either of the two males could have been her brother, and both the females looked like her.

"Greetings, Cousins," the Feltan said in unison. The largest male came closer, "Daughter of our daughter, we breed true," he said to Arianne.

"Father of my mother, you breed true. My oldest brother, the heir to the throne of Lantia, could be your double." Arianne answered.

The Feltan were silent, "We have missed your people," they said at last.

"Some of my people have missed you." Arianne answered cautiously.

The Feltan laughed, "Not many, we guess. The time has come. The ban on your people has been lifted. No more will they turn their faces from the ocean." The Feltan paused, "Always your people have been uncomfortable with the sea, will you tell me why?"

"I don't know for sure, but I think it might have something to do with our first home. Legends say that The Abomination came from the seas. It was a nightmare that our ancestors had created by flooding the water with poisons. Our whole world was destroyed almost overnight, and still, The Abomination pursues us."

"That was such a long time ago, couldn't they forget?" The Feltan asked sadly.

"It's bred into our genes. Once in a great while, a child like me is born among the Lantians, but not often, and not many. As for The Abomination," Arianne smiled sadly, "It is a good thing we did not forget it, for now it threatens your world."

The swimmers were quiet while the Feltan thought about Arianne's statement, then it turned to Brian. "Brother, the words of the sea mother have come to pass. We will soon leave this world. The oceans are yours, for we will swim here no longer. Learn from our errors and guard well your heritage."

"Brothers, cousins," Brian replied, "I hear your words and will heed them. The sea will miss the Feltan, as will all who sail upon her."

"Must you go now?" Arianne asked.

The Feltan smiled, "Not yet. Before we can leave, we must right old wrongs: Promises made must be kept, and treasures stolen returned. When first your people landed, naked and afraid, we offered them our protection. When your call came to Lantia, the queen sent to us and demanded that we fulfill our bargain.

"Now, we must help your people destroy their nightmare. Know that when you need their strength, your people will be there to give it to you."

"How? I don't think that Lady Colsa is careless enough to leave an opening in her defenses. Once I am in the temple, no one will be able to reach me."

The Feltan laughed, "You will take the strength and the dreams of your people inside the temple with you. We return the stolen treasure."

A small female swam up to Arianne and removed a heavy chain from around her neck. "Elder Sister, our people have gone into deep sleep. When I leave here, I will return to Lantia and dream for you with them."

"Anna." Arianne whispered in surprise. "What are you doing here? Your father said he had arranged a wedding for you in the north."

"I was sea-called, Elder Sister. The sea mother has given all of Lantia's children who swim with the Feltan the choice of leaving with the Feltan or returning to our people."

"My mother's younger brother?"

"He is with your mother. All of us are returning to Lantia. Our people have seen enough strange places. This is the land we have chosen as our own and we will live or die with it. Lantian Honor." Anna smiled and hugged Arianne.

"Lantian Honor, Younger Sister." Arianne answered as she returned the other girl's hug.

Anna handed the heavy chain to Arianne, “Guard this well, Elder Sister, for it is the life of our people returned.”

“How did you get this?” Arianne stared in surprise at the small pink stone that danced on the end of the chain.

“That is a long story and we don’t have the time to tell it now. The Feltan gave it to your mother and our people placed all their deep dreams in it and sent it to you. Take good care of it, and when your need is greatest, we will be with you.”

Arianne looked at the amulet. “I never realized how beautiful it was. In all the stories I have heard about the life of the people, no one ever mentioned that it was so perfect.” She murmured, rubbing her fingers over the smooth, worn surface of the tiny stone.

“That is because it has more than beauty. Remember, it holds all the dreams, all the memories, and all the power of our people. Now, it also holds all the small powers that remain to Feltan. The Icina of the sea has given the Life Stone a part of her most treasured secret.

“You will be able to swim and live in the sea as the Feltan do, to change your body, and to meld with the deep at will. The power to read men’s hearts, you have already, but this shell will make that talent stronger.

“Use the stone wisely, Elder Sister, and learn to control the magic it contains. We must leave you now; I, too, return to Lantia, and the Feltan patrol the waters of this world; for their vow to protect the north still binds them. Once this is over, they will be free. Il Ho a Lantia."

"Il Ho a Lantia!" Arianne held the Life Stone tightly in her hands and, as she gave the battle cry of her people, she felt the power stir in the Stone.

Anna watched as Arianne freed the small stone from the chain and pressed it to her throat. She held it there for a second, and when she moved her hand, the stone had disappeared.

"Dream safely, Elder Sister." Anna whispered.

"Dream true, Younger Sister." Arianne responded and watched as Anna swam away to join the Feltan.

With a flip of their massive tails, the Feltan dove beneath the water's surface and were gone. Arianne felt tears run down her cheeks. She lifted a hand to wipe them away and Brian saw.

"Arianne, don't cry for them. This is the fulfillment of a long-awaited promise. They no longer have any ties to this world and they are lonesome. The sea mother will send them to a world where they are needed."

Arianne gave a watery smile, "I weep for my people as well as the Feltan. When we have defeated this monstrosity, what reason shall we have for existing?"

"This world will always have those weaker than you who need protecting, and your people will now have the responsibility that was the Feltans'."

When Arianne gave Brian a puzzled look, he explained, "Now, you must protect the northern lands."

Arianne smiled and sent that thought to the small stone hidden beneath her skin. "My people will survive as long as that need exists," she whispered, then glanced at Brian. "You will miss the Feltan, won't you?"

Brian nodded, "For many years, they have been my only friends. Speaking to them kept me sane in the caves. I will miss them."

"I am sorry you are losing your friends. You can be friends with the Lantians who have lived with the Feltan. They will be there for you if you wish."

Brian smiled. "When this is over, I look forward to visiting your country."

Arianne grinned back at him, "You will enjoy meeting my people."

"Arianne, what was the stone that young Feltan gave you?" Brian asked after a while. "Or is that another secret that you must keep?"

"It is the Life of our people." Arianne frowned at the trace of bitterness in Brian's voice. They were both going to have a lot of work developing trust in each other.

"I heard that, but then you both started speaking in a strange language. What exactly does the stone do?"

"It holds the life and knowledge of all Lantians who have died. It also holds the power of my people when we go into deep sleep. The Elder

Singer uses the stone as a focus, drawing strength from it as needed."

"The Feltan stole this stone from your people?"

Arianne shrugged, "Whatever happened is finished. They have returned the Life Stone."

"What happened to all those people who died while the Life Stone was in Feltan hands?" Brian asked.

"Their heirs accepted their power and knowledge in their own minds. Now that the Feltan have returned the stone, the first thing my people probably did was discharge all those extra memories into it."

Brian shook his head, "No wonder your people are mad." He looked even more puzzled when Arianne burst into laughter.

They floated on the sea's surface for a long, silent moment, then the Olpho turned and swam toward the port of Kopol.

The Mariners' Guild is an independent organization that has no formal ties to the rulers of Alsia. Usually, the leader of the guild was named captain of the ruler's ship, Alsian's Pride. However, this was courtesy and tradition, not law.

Captain Khane, Mariners' Guild Master

Chapter 16

It was dark when the Olpho at last reached the Alsian's Pride. Brian and Arianne slid quietly off the large creatures' backs and into the cool water of the harbor.

What now? Arianne mind-spoke to Brian.

Follow me, he thought back, *and be careful.*

With that warning, he swam swiftly toward the ship that was riding gently at its anchor, and climbed the rope ladder hanging down the side. Arianne followed, and was on the ship's deck before she recognized it was Alsian's Pride. Captain Khane stepped out of the shadows on the deck and beckoned to them. Silently, the three figures moved across the ship and down the hatchway to the lower levels.

No one spoke until Captain Khane opened the door to a small cabin. "A bath and clothes are waiting for you inside. I'll be back with something for you to eat," he whispered as he slid back into the darkness and disappeared.

Arianne and Brian bathed and dressed quickly, then sat on the bed in the room to wait for Captain Khane's return. A soft knock on the door signaled the captain's return. Brian opened the door and Captain Khane entered carrying a covered basket in his arms.

"Nothing fancy," he said as he laid the food out on the small table. "I didn't want to risk alerting the crew to your presence." He shook his head. "Normally, I would trust my crew with my life. Still, only the Bright Lady knows how many of my crew Mistress Colsa managed to corrupt during the time she spent aboard my ship."

"Is Harl on board?" Arianne stopped eating long enough to ask.

The captain nodded, "He sleeps. Do you trust him?"

"Yes, he is an honest man. He will do what is best for Alsia." Arianne said thoughtfully.

"Harl is Colsa's man." The captain protested.

"No, Captain, Harl is the sea's man. Colsa could never control him. We can trust him."

"All right, I'll take your word on it. I have to admit I will enjoy knowing that I can trust at least one person on the ship." Captain Khane stood up. "Well, I'll leave you two alone for now. When you finish eating, put everything back into the basket and place it outside your door. Get some sleep. I'll see you in the morning." He closed the door behind him as he left the room.

"This Harl, why do you trust him?" Brian asked after a moment's silence. "I remember him from my childhood. He was a little in love with my mother."

"I think he still is, but he won't do anything that is harmful to Alsia. He realizes that your mother isn't the right person for the job, and he'll not support her." Arianne was certain of what she said.

"All right," Brian nodded, "We'll go with that for now."

"You don't really trust me, do you?" Arianne tilted her head to one side and studied him carefully.

Brian returned her stare, "I trust you. I don't believe that you're a part of my mother's game. She will use you against me if she can," he warned.

"Brian, last night, the Icina of this world told me that before we leave this ship, we must find a way to remove any doubts we have of each other from our hearts. We must believe in each other no matter what we think we hear or see. I have no idea what your mother is up to. I am certain that her first move will be to divide us."

Brian sighed and pushed his plate away. "What you say is true. However, it's hard for me to fully trust any woman when my earliest memories are of my mother's betrayal of my father, my land and me."

"Brian, I have the same problem with you. Colsa is your mother. I am still a stranger to you. No matter what she has done in the past, always a small part of you will hope for her love and approval." Arianne whispered and opened her mind to him. She hid nothing, left no barriers between them.

See, she thought at him, *I am your mate. I'll do nothing that would harm you. Anyone who says differently lies.*

Brian traveled the paths of her memories and her thoughts; he learned what this woman, whom he called his wife, was like. He saw her strengths and her weaknesses, and saw that she was completely committed to him and his land. Still, doubt lingered on the edge of his mind.

"Will you open your mind to me?" Arianne asked softly.

Brian hesitated for a moment, then reluctantly lowered his mind's shields.

Arianne touched his mind and saw his doubts. *Brian, I can't say I love you, but I respect and admire you. I'm not your mother, or my own, for that matter. Their ways are not mine. No human can truly see the future. Perhaps the day will come when we will have true love between us. Until then, can we not be satisfied with what we have?*

My mother claimed she loved my father and yet she betrayed him. Brian's thought was heavy with bitterness.

Arianne smiled. *Brian, you may not have my love, but you do have my complete loyalty. That I swear by both my word as a warrior, and my Lantian Honor.*

Brian relaxed and he withdrew from her mind, "Word of a warrior I can accept, my fierce Lantian ally." He said aloud, and they looked at each other in perfect accord for a moment.

After they had eaten their fill, Arianne and Brian packed the soiled dishes and leftovers in the basket and placed it outside their cabin door. Arianne turned to Brian, a look of mischief on her pointed face, "How close allies are we, my Lord?"

Brian laughed and reached for her, "As close as you want, my royal hussy," he replied as they tumbled onto the bed.

Much later, Arianne ran her fingers through his hair and sighed with contentment, "I like the way you ratify treaties, King of Alsia. I'll have to watch you carefully in the future," she murmured sleepily.

"Only this treaty, My Lady, there will be no other like ours," Brian answered as he tucked the covers around them and they both fell into a deep, dreamless sleep.

Early the next morning, Captain Khane woke them by knocking and calling through the door. "Time to get up. Your breakfast is out here. A change of clothing for each of you is in the closet and I have a supply of weapons in the ship's armory. When you are ready, join me in the lounge."

Arianne opened her eyes and stared at Brian for a long, serious moment before she smiled at him. "Good morning, my Lord," she said softly, touching his cheek. "Captain Khane is an honest and worthy man. We're lucky to have one like him on our side."

"I'll make him admiral of the fleet when this is over." Brian grinned and kissed her gently. "Good morning, Lady. Are you ready for this day and what it will bring?"

Arianne jumped out of bed and retrieved their breakfast, "Not really. I wish we had more time to know each other." She shrugged, not embarrassed by her nakedness, "Come and eat

Brian." She paused, "Will there be a weapon for me?"

"If we can't find something suitable in the armory, we'll borrow one from the king's guard." Brian joined Arianne at the table and they ate in silence.

When they were through, they dressed and walked down the ship's passages to the lounge, where the captain was waiting for them. Neither of them was surprised to see Harl sitting with the captain.

"What now?" Brian asked as he and Arianne sat.

"Now, the time for secrecy is past. The Mistress Colsa knows that you are close to Kopol. As long as you're on the ship, the Lady of the Deep shields you from detection. The moment you step on land, your mother will know where you are." The captain glanced at Harl, then shrugged. "We have sent rumors among the people of your return, and Loudos, the ex-leader of the old king's guard, will escort you to the palace."

"Can we trust this Loudos?" Arianne asked.

Harl nodded. "When the old king died, Loudos and his guardsmen retired to the country after refusing to serve Lady Colsa. He and Colsa hate each other, and always have. The only reason Loudos stayed as long as he did was his loyalty to the throne of Alsia. We can trust him."

"Harl, why do you betray my mother? You love her, and yet you seek to destroy her?" Brian leaned forward as he asked.

"I loved your mother, boy, but I don't like or respect what she has become. Ambition has warped her mind and she is destroying herself and our country. If two people don't respect each other, then their love will not survive."

Harl looked at the two young people sitting across from him and smiled through the tears coursing down his grizzled cheeks. "Long ago, your mother was the most beautiful woman in the kingdom. All the young men loved her then, but she had eyes only for your father. Trouble was, once he let her manipulate him, she no longer respected him. Her love died, and in the empty place it left, ambition grew. That's why we are all in this mess today. Your father was a gentle man, but he had no inner strength in him. A king needs to be strong as well as gentle."

Arianne smiled and glanced at Brian, pride in her gaze. "Then Alsia is a lucky country, for it is getting a king that is both gentle and strong."

Harl stared at them both, then smiled. "We'll see, we'll see," he answered. "You're both so young and so sure of yourselves. I hope you're right, Queen Arianne." He stood up. "Loudos and the guard should be arriving any minute now. I'll go topside and wait for him."

The others were silent as they watched the old man leave the room.

"Poor Harl. I feel sorry for him." Arianne murmured.

"I don't think he wants or needs that, Arianne. He has come to terms with himself, and that's more than most people ever do." Brian answered thoughtfully, and Captain Khane nodded in agreement.

While they waited for the royal guard to arrive, Brian and Arianne went to the ship's weapon's storeroom. Brian chose a long, curved blade with wickedly sharp edges and raised his eyebrows in surprise when he saw Arianne's choice.

"Knives, my Lady? That's an assassin's weapon, not a suitable choice for an honorable warrior."

Arianne laughed, "I have never heard of an honorable weapon, Brian. Weapons are used when honor no longer reigns. In true battle, Lantians fight by no rules but their own." She paused as she carefully hid the knives on her body, then leaned over and kissed Brian. "Now that I think on it, in true battle, we Lantians have no rules."

Three hours later, the massive green man walked into the lounge. His face and arms were scarred with badly-healed wounds. When he spoke, his voice was harsh in the quiet room.

"King Brian, I've come to escort you and your lady to the castle. My men are waiting for us on the pier."

"Loudos, it's good to see you." Brian walked forward and touched the older man's shoulder.

Arianne watched closely and noticed that Loudos hadn't looked at Brian since he walked into the room.

"Loudos, is something wrong? You've not looked at your king once since you entered the room. Why?" She smiled and walked to the men, deliberately wrapping her arms around Brian's waist.

Loudos' scarred face revealed his surprise and, involuntarily, he looked at Brian's face. He looked away quickly, then looked back. "You look just like you always did. Lady Colsa said that you were horribly deformed and not fit to rule the land." A shamed expression crossed his face, "I should have known better than to listen to that temple witch, but we didn't see you, and she said you were hiding because..."

Loudos fell to his knees, bowing his head, "My King, forgive me, I should have been by your side to protect you. Instead, I let the poison that Colsa spread, infect me with dark despair." His harsh voice broke on the words.

"Loudos, old friend and teacher," Brian reached down and helped the man to his feet. "Don't blame yourself for believing my mother. I know how well she can deceive. I've lived my whole life watching her, and still, she can twist my thinking. She tells only the truth, but in such a way that we see what she wants us to, not what is real."

Arianne sighed and stepped back, filing Brian's last statement away in her mind. "Has she circulated this story among all of Kopol?" She asked Loudos.

"All Kopol and all Alsia. The people hide in their houses not knowing what to expect and they curse their overlords for giving them a monster as king."

“Fools, three times fools!” Arianne spat. “Lady Colsa has a lot to answer for when we meet again.”

“Don’t blame the people, my Lady.” Loudos said quietly, “And don’t be in too much of a hurry to face Lady Colsa again. She hates you with an intensity that is almost madness.” He warned.

Arianne smiled grimly. “We will meet, though. There is nothing anyone can do to stop it. The fates have decreed it. She has dealt with one who is an old enemy of my people. Now, she must pay for disturbing the peace of Lantia.”

The men stared at Arianne, then each other. Loudos nodded his head. “I am pleased with your wife, my King. She is not one of the sniveling females that Colsa usually presented to us.” Loudos turned to Arianne. “How did Mistress Colsa choose you as candidate this year?” he asked, a crooked smile on his face.

“She had no choice at all,” Arianne grinned. “She asked for a princess and that’s what she received. I do think she should have studied the ways of my people more closely than she did.”

“She had no choice. Lantia was the only kingdom left that hadn’t heard of her games.” Captain Khane explained.

Arianne looked thoughtful for a moment then she laughed, “I wonder. My mother is the Elder Singer of our people. No one has ever been a successful game player against our House since she came to power. I cannot see Lady Colsa being able to hide everything from my mother. My mother could not have known what the power behind Colsa was, nevertheless, she had to have seen some of Colsa's plans. It just suited my mother's purposes to go along with the pretense. If she thought that it was just a case of parental greed, she would not have worried, for she knew that I could take care of myself."

Loudos turned toward the door, "Your escort waits."

Arianne hugged Captain Khane and Harl, "Goodbye for now, my friends," she whispered, then followed Brian and Loudos off the ship and onto the piers, where twelve heavily-armed men sitting on large, evil-smelling, riding beasts waited for them.

Arianne sighed, "We have a problem, Loudos. Your beasts will not tolerate me on their backs. They will not even allow me near them."

Brian walked over to one of the beasts and touched its head. The animal shook its massive body and stepped back. Brian followed, again touching the animal's head. Finally, the great beast gave an almost human sounding sigh and stood, quivering, its massive head hung low to the ground.

"This one has consented to carry you, my Queen." Brian said as he stepped back from the animal.

Arianne reached out to touch the beast's mind, and felt its terror. "Why do you fear my people so? We have done nothing to harm any of your kind." She whispered soothingly to the animal.

All she received in return was a distrustful glare, though the beast's terror of her. With a sigh, Arianne mounted its back and hung on grimly as they began the journey through the city's streets toward the palace.

Very few people were on the streets and they darted frightened glances at the riders, then stared in shock as they saw the face of their king. Soon, the word passed through the city. Nothing was wrong with the king's face. He was as handsome as ever. As they neared the castle, more people showed up. The small crowd was silent. They knew Lady Colsa's powers and refused to cheer for a king who might not live long enough to protect them from her fury.

The silence of the crowd made Arianne nervous. Her concentration wavered, and was taken by surprise at Lady Colsa's next move . One moment, she was watching the crowd, the next, she was in the middle of a fight between the royal guard and the temple warriors. She spared a moment to regret not wearing a sword, then forced her beast forward, trying to reach Brian's side. As she reached him, she saw a flash of light, felt a quick pain in her head, then fell into darkness.

In silence, we find hope; in darkness, friends; and in sleep, we find peace.

Dream deep.

Dream true.

Il Ho A Lantia.

Lantian Blessing

Chapter 17

When Arianne regained consciousness, she was lying on a hard, cold surface. Her hands were tightly tied behind her. Arianne opened her eyes, then wished she hadn't. She was in complete darkness. Clumsily, because of her tied hands, she stood. Her head ached from the blow she received and her muscles were stiff from lying on the cold floor. She had to rest twice before she succeeded in getting to her feet.

Shakily, she walked around the room. Three steps forward, she hit the wall hard enough to drive her back to her knees. Arianne kept her shoulder in contact with the wall and crawled along it. Searching for a door or anything else that might help her orient herself, she strained her eyes, peering into the darkness.

The room was tiny. If she lay on her back and stretched out her legs, she could touch the walls on either side of her. Arianne shivered and swallowed hard, twice, trying to control her fear. A small moan escaped her, and the sound echoed eerily in the room. She reached out with her mind and tried to contact Brian. Instead of Brian, she encountered a wall of darkness that separated her from all outside contact. She battered the dark wall uselessly for what felt like hours before it moved sluggishly.

It was then that she sensed the life force behind that wall, something large and dangerous. It became aware of her. She threw up her own barriers, closed her eyes, and lay shivering on the cold floor while dark tendrils of fear, distrust, and hate probed lazily at her mind; a tentative, 'I'm busy with something else and will get to you later,' type of contact. Arianne sensed that she would not be able to resist a full strength probe.

Slowly, the dark force retreated. She intrigued it. Now, Arianne would have to be very careful what she did, for it would be watching her. She took a deep, sobbing breath, and forced herself to lie still. She thought, briefly, of the Life Stone pulsing at her throat, then dismissed the idea. Now was not the time to call on her people. First, she must vanquish her fears. If she failed, any hope her people had of defeating their ages-old enemy would disappear.

Arianne tried to relax. She breathed deeply, concentrating on each breath. She would not think about where she was; she would not think about the darkness that surrounded her, or about the small room Lady Colsa had locked her in. Was she locked in? She never found a doorway, so she had no idea if it was locked or not. It would be like Colsa to leave the door unlocked and give her a false sense of freedom. She whimpered. The sound stiffened Arianne's resolve. She was not a coward; she would not let her fear of dark, enclosed spaces cause her to betray everything she loved.

She let the silence around her seep into her mind, let her body absorb it, and slowly began to relax. She was still afraid, but it was no longer the senseless fear she experienced earlier. Cautiously, she extended her mind, staying within the boundaries of the immediate area, seeking any living creature that shared this place with her. At last, she found two small minds. The touch of them reminded her of Bunto. She explored further and recoiled.

The minds she touched belonged to two small rodents hidden in the walls of her prison. Again, she battled her emotions into submission. With a shudde, she forced herself to again touch the small minds.

Greetings, little ones, she thought at them.

She received the impressions of stunned silence, then of surprise and curiosity. Now, she could hear their little feet scratching on the floor as they scampered closer. Arianne buried the fear and distaste as she felt their tiny, cold noses sniffing her tightly-bound hands.

"Help me," she whispered, sending a picture of tiny teeth biting through ropes, to their minds.

They did not answer her, but two sets of sharp teeth started chewing on her restraints. Though it seemed like hours, it didn't take long for them to gnaw through the rope. Arianne sat up cautiously, rubbing her wrists to restore circulation. A quick check of her body reassured her that those who took her prisoner did not discover her weapons. Lady Colsa had underestimated her once again. Arianne frowned. That carelessness did not seem right. Was Lady Colsa so secure in her alliance with The Abomination that she no longer feared opposition of any kind? She shook her head, then winced as the motion brought a fresh spasm of pain to her abused skull. It was more likely, that this was Colsa's way of telling Arianne that in the coming battle, weapons of steel would be useless.

My thanks. Do you know where we are?

Two noses wriggled then pictures flooded her mind. These creatures did not mind-speak in words, but their curiosity took them to every corner of this place. She didn't think that she was in the castle. One final picture flashed into her mind and she smiled grimly. She was in the temple of the Dark Goddess. Lady Colsa, in her arrogance, brought Arianne to the heart of her domain. She would make sure that Lady Colsa regretted this action for a long time.

Arianne lay back on the cold, hard floor. She needed to rest and gather her strength. Now that she had her emotions under control, she placed her strongest mental barriers around the room and went into the dream trance of her people. Cautiously, she slid her mind into the Life Stone and immediately found herself surrounded by the love of her family.

Arianne, my daughter, you have done well. Your father and I are so proud of you. Ilona whispered.

I have been a coward. Arianne replied.

She felt the touch of her father's mind, *No. You have been afraid, but you were never a coward. You have done well.*

In a place were time did not pass, Arianne rested in the arms of her family and her people, then her mother sighed. *I do not know what will happen to our people after this battle, or even if we will still exist as a nation. We may all be destroyed, for if we fail here, we die, and this world dies with us. I cannot tell you what to do. You must decide. You are only one who will know when it is time to fight. Remember that we are with you.*

Our people must not die, for the Icina of our world needs us to help the nations of the northern continent to reach their full potential. We have allies who will help us. We will succeed. Arianne told her mother, then, leaving a small part of her mind still joined to minds of her people, she prepared to play her part when Lady Colsa sent for her.

With her eyes closed, Arianne feigned sleep when she heard the sound of booted feet coming toward her. The door to the room opened and she was roughly jerked to her feet. Arianne kept her body relaxed and gave a small groan.

"Well, well, the little princess who would be queen has managed to get her hands untied." A soft voice purred.

Arianne was surprised. She recognized Khat's voice.

"Did you think Lady Colsa would not discover you had tampered with my mind on the ship? Thanks to you, I am forever forbidden a place in the inner circle. For the rest of my life, I will be just a lowly priestess. I will enjoy watching you pay for what you did to me." Khat hissed in Arianne's ears.

"Shall we retie her hands?" A male voice asked. Khat laughed.

"No, leave her hands untied, the Lady Colsa can handle her. Besides, she is in no shape to cause any trouble."

Those sent to get her laughed harshly as they dragged her from the room and down a long, damp corridor. Far in the back of her mind, Arianne heard the soft patter of little feet following and allowed herself a brief smile. Her small allies stayed with her. They might not be very strong, but they would be able to carry messages. Yes, the little ones could be very helpful in the future.

The Feltan were beautiful amphibians, with silver hair and crystal eyes. They had strong mental abilities and were the guardians of the nothern hemisphere of our world. Named true children of the sea and cousins of the Alsians, they were the first to greet the Lantians in friendship. At the reign of King Brian and Queen Arianne, they disappeared from our waters.

Harl, Alsian Sailor

Chapter 18

When her captors let go of her, Arianne let her body fall convincingly. She lay huddled on the floor until a daintily shod foot prodded her in the side.

"Stop playing games. I know exactly how long it takes to regain consciousness from the blow you received."

Arianne groaned and opened her eyes; Colsa nodded, and smiled grimly.

"Stand her on her feet." Lady Colsa instructed the guards.

Rough hands pulled Arianne to her feet, held her for a moment, then let go. Arianne felt her knees tremble and swore to herself she wasn't going fall on her face, not now. She locked her knees and lifted her chin defiantly. This was her battle; she'd better be strong enough for whatever came. She would have help, if Brian was still alive, and if she could find a way to let him know where she was... She smiled grimly. It would be best if she concentrated on what was happening now, and left the future to take care of itself.

"So, my foolish child," Lady Colsa purred, "Where are all your fine words now? Are you waiting for my son to come to your rescue? You can't believe my son would defend you against me? I'm his mother. We may have our differences, but he'll never forget who I am." Lady Colsa laughed.

Arianne ignored Colsa and took the time to inspect her surroundings. She was in a large room decorated with the most tasteless, violent and bizarre artwork she had ever seen. Before her, a golden chair sat in the middle of a raised platform, behind the chair was a golden altar. Standing between her and the door was Khat and three temple soldiers. She didn't recognize any of the men and breathed a sigh of relief that none of Captain Akino's people were here.

"Interesting place you have here, who did your decorating?" Arianne asked, not bothering to suppress her shudder as she glanced at a particularly grim painting of mass dismemberment.

Colsa followed Arianne's gaze to the picture and smiled coldly, "It serves a purpose. I have some pieces that are much more entertaining than these. However, they are for private viewing only." Lady Colsa laughed softly, "Maybe, if you are very cooperative, I won't have to show them to you."

Arianne shrugged. Her face reflected both her disgust and her disdain.

"So, we will not add art critic to the list of your skills." Colsa raised an eyebrow and smiled coldly. "I talked to some of Lantia's neighbors." She paused, watching Arianne closely. "Did you know that some of your neighbors worked for me?"

Arianne thought of Cory and his family and her lips tightened. Colsa saw and laughed cruelly, “You Lantians are much too soft-hearted, wasting your emotions on lesser beings. According to them, I’ve brought the daughter of witches and shape-changers into my realm.”

“You have been busy these last few days, haven’t you?” Arianne mimicked Colsa’s smile. She would not let Colsa make her angry.

Lady Colsa gave a snort of disgust, “This is no game we are playing, Lantian. Answer me. Is what I’ve been told about your people true?”

“Some of Lantia’s neighbors fear her greatly. Men will always create monsters to excuse their cowardice. The others are friends who will say whatever my mother tells them.” Arianne grinned, “Each man sees his own truth in this life.”

Colsa scowled, “Little girl, you don’t seem to appreciate the position you are in. Let me explain. If you cooperate with me, I might let you live. If you don’t, I will tear the information I need from your mind and your death will be slow and painful. Either way, I will have my answers. So, now, let’s start again. Are you a witch?”

“Not compared to you. You are much more of a witch than I am.” Arianne answered.

“Don’t be insolent, Girl.” Lady Colsa stepped forward and slapped Arianne hard enough to knock her back to her knees.

Colsa stood over Arianne waiting as the girl pushed herself to her feet. “Now, tell me, is it true what your country’s neighbors say?”

“Truth...”

"Girl, I'm warning you, I don't want to hear any more of your philosophy." Colsa interrupted. "Just answer the question. Even someone as stupid as you, should be able to manage a simple yes or no."

"My people don't believe in magic." Arianne tilted her head to one side. "Why is my answer so important? What do you fear from Lantia?"

"Can I trust you, girl, or are you lying to me?" Lady Colsa muttered staring at Arianne through narrowed eyes.

Arianne shrugged, "That's your decision. Look, are we going to stand here and shout at each other or can we pretend that we are civilized people?"

Lady Colsa scowled. "What are you up to?"

"Nothing. Why don't we sit and discuss this situation over a glass of hot karm? You ask me what you want to know about Lantia, and..." Though Arianne's mouth smiled, her eyes remained cold, "Maybe I'll answer you."

Lady Colsa nodded, "Oh, you are still so smug, so sure of your superiority. That comes from dealing with savages. I am not one of your mind-blind neighbors. You have no idea what awaits you. You will soon discover that the power I represent is not to be taken lightly."

Colsa paused while one of her people brought a chair for Arianne. After Arianne sat, Colsa walked over to the golden throne and threw herself carelessly into it.

"You'll tell me what I want to know, Lantian. You'll beg to give me information I didn't even ask about."

"As your people would say, the future is in the Mother's hands." Arianne said softly.

"Yes, it is, and here in Kopol, it is my aspect of the Mother that reins supreme." Lady Colsa's voice was as soft.

She frowned at Arianne. "What do you know about the Mother? She's not one of Lantia's gods."

Khat, a venomous look on her face, handed Arianne a glass of karm. Arianne smiled calmly at the girl as she took the glass from her.

She gave Lady Colsa an artless glance, "Should I trust this drink?"

Lady Colsa laughed, "That's your decision."

Arianne nodded and set the glass down at her feet.

"Yes, so it is," she murmured as she leaned back in her chair.

She studied Colsa's face for a moment, then continued, "Lantia recognizes no gods as her own. Though, of course, we do acknowledge the rights of others to worship as they please. It makes no difference to us whether they call upon the Mother or anyone else. We go our way and do as we wish."

"The Lantians are an arrogant people, but we intend to teach them a much-needed lesson in humility." Lady Colsa glared at Arianne.

Arianne laughed, "We? Who will help you to give us this lesson? Your Dark Goddess?" She shook her head. “I think not. Let me give you a few words of advice: Leave my people alone.”

“Tell me about your people.” It was a demand.

Arianne frowned thoughtfully, “We love beauty, good books, poems about love, soothing music, and playing complicated games.”

“Girl, you try my patience. You know what I want, now tell me.”

“Lady Colsa, you’ve lost Alsia through your own stupidity. Don’t compound matters by trying to take Lantia. Your magic will have no power over my people, and your games won’t work. The youngest Lantian child would brush you and the puny power you control off the face of this planet. Stay away from Lantia. That’s a warning for your own good. You don’t know my people. I do.” Arianne said calmly. “I will give you another warning: This Dark One you worship is not of Alsia. Do not be fooled into thinking that you can control it. We of Lantia have known your so-called god for many centuries. It is an old enemy of ours. When it is ready, it will turn on you and destroy your world.”

Lady Colsa took a sip of her drink and smiled. “Do you think to scare me? It won’t work. I know my Lady’s dark face, and could not possibly be fooled by an alien power. As for your people, I learned a lot about Lantia while I was there. I saw the soft, worthless lives your people live. They will be easy to defeat.”

"As you say." Arianne returned the smile and leaned back in her chair. "So, you're planning to run away from Alsia?"

"No, Alsia is mine. Do you think that the people would accept my monster son as king?" Lady Colsa laughed, "You might have succeeded in bringing him down from the mountains. You made a mistake when you brought him to Kopol. This is where the common people live. They are not used to seeing the change. They will find him frightening, and I will remain in power."

Arianne hid her surprise. So Lady Colsa hadn't yet seen Brian, and he was free and alive. That took care of one source of worry. She crossed her legs at the knees and said nothing.

"Do you think my son will risk his life for you? You little idiot, you have served your purpose. He doesn't need you anymore." Lady Colsa watched Arianne's face carefully. When she saw no change, she stood up abruptly and motioned to the guards.

"I waste my time, take her back to her cell. In a day or two, we'll see if she is still this stubborn."

Arianne sat in one corner of her cell, her back against the wall, and thought about what Lady Colsa said. She could ignore the woman's threat to invade Lantia. However, Colsa's statement about the common people not being used to seeing the change puzzled her. Something teased the back of her mind and she frowned for a moment. On the trip down from the mountain, Brian changed, but not very quickly. When they reached Lady Athna's home, he still had traces of the scales that covered his body when she first saw him. His face still hadn't completely regained its human shape, and the webs between his fingers were not gone. The Lords of Alsia showed no horror at seeing him. She didn't find it strange at the time, for she never saw Brian as anything but a man that she liked and respected.

Now, events she'd noticed, but not paid any attention to, came back to her. Of course, Brian's appearance did not surprise the lords. The heir to each House probably went through the same change before he could take control of his heritage. However, the commoners probably never saw the lords during the change. She also noticed slight differences in the coloration between commoners and lords. Was it possible that two different races lived in Alsia?

Then there was Loudos. With his scarred face, he could be a member of the nobility whose change was interrupted. The question was, how? Arianne wanted that information. It might give her a clue to what Colsa was planning. Colsa didn't know that Brian regained his human features. Arianne had a feeling that it would be best if the lady never found out.

"Smoke, I wish I had more information on this culture." Arianne said aloud as she closed her eyes.

She needed to get a message out of the temple so Brian would know where she was and what was happening. Something or someone in here blocked all her efforts to reach him by mind-touch. That left the small ones...

She reached out her mind to theirs, *Go to the king and tell him where I am.* She thought at them.

???

Pictures, they needed pictures. She didn't know what the palace was like, so if she couldn't send them there, then where? She smiled, and in her mind, she showed the Alsian Pride, and Captain Khane sitting in the lounge.

Go there go to this man. She instructed.

...The answering thought sent the picture back to her, and she heard the sound of tiny feet scampering off into the distance.

Arianne withdrew deep into herself. She had no idea how long she'd have to wait, and she didn't think Colsa would be in any hurry to feed her. She must conserve her strength. Folding her legs under her, Arianne went into the dreaming trance of the Lantian. Her people could stay in this position for days and use very little energy. When they woke, their bodies would be refreshed. While they were in the trance, they did not get hungry or thirsty.

*****

"I don't understand what she wanted with the girl. Unless...do you think it possible that Colsa doesn't know Brian's change is complete?" Harl asked Captain Khane as they relaxed in the lounge of the Alsian's Pride.

"It's possible, but the main reason could also be revenge. Colsa might feel that she has to destroy the young queen for outplaying her in this game." Captain Khane frowned, "Colsa may have taken on more than she knows how to handle. I believe the young queen is a lot more powerful than anyone suspects."

"I pray you are right." Harl sighed, then glanced up as another man entered the lounge.

"Loudos, how's the king holding up?"

"He's doing well, Harl. We're tearing the city apart trying to find out where Colsa's people are holding the queen. So far, we've had no luck."

"There's no question of where she is. For Mother's sake man, check the temple." Harl jumped to his feet.

"We can't. It's locked up tight as virgin. King Brian can't even touch his lady's mind. He's worried that she may be dead." Loudos poured himself a glass of karm and sat.

"That temple looks empty. They grabbed the queen and left the city, that's what I think."

"Then why can't the king touch Arianne's mind? No, that makes no sense. Colsa wouldn't dare leave the protection of her temple. That's where they are, I tell you. It's the only place in Alsia where Colsa can hold the queen.

"I won't believe the young Sea Dreamer is dead. Not yet. But I have a feeling that we don't have a lot of time. We need to find her, and soon." Harl sat back down, and the three men stared worriedly at each other.

They turned their heads toward a series of small squeaks. On the low table before them were two small mice, their noses twitching, their small voices squeaking urgently. The men shouted and the mice scampered off. When the men returned to their seats, the mice climbed back up on the table and resumed their squeaking. With a terse oath, Captain Khane grabbed a book to throw at them, but Harl grabbed his arm.

"Captain, have you ever seen mice this bold?" he asked softly, his eyes on the tiny creatures.

"No, and when I'm through with them, these won't be bold any more either," Captain Khane scowled.

"Don't. I think these mice are special. They have a reason for being here. Look at them, Captain."

Loudos peered closely at the two rodents, then nodded. "I think Harl might be right. Those two little creatures are trying very hard to tell us something."

Khane stared at the other two, "You think they bring a message from the queen?"

Harl nodded, "She has the touch with the wild creatures. I think it's possible that they come from her." He stood up and placed his hands down on the table next to the mice. "Come, little ones. We need to take you to one who will understand your speech."

The mice fearlessly ran onto his hands, and the other two men followed him to the deck of the ship. "We have to take them to the castle. One of the king's nonhuman companions is a distant cousin to these little ones. He'll be able to understand what they are trying to tell us."

They walked through the dark streets of Kopol. When they reached the palace, Harl asked one of the servants to take them where the king's companions rested.

The servant shook his head, "They are all with the king right now. I have orders not to disturb them."

"What do we do now?" Captain Khane asked.

"We wait." Harl turned to the servant, "We need to speak with the Montro as soon as you can bring him to us. It is urgent."

"Now what? We still cannot touch the minds of the animals."

"No, but the king can, and if the Montro agrees with us, we will take these small brothers to the king."

"Why don't we just take these little ones to him right now, instead of waiting for the Montro?" Loudos asked.

Harl shrugged, "Suppose we're wrong. What if these mice are just mice, and only a little bolder than the others?"

The other two men glanced at each other. The captain shrugged, then said, "Let's go to the Montro."

*****

Brian glanced up as the doors to his private chambers flew open. Bunto, of the Montro scampered in, followed by Captain Khane, Loudos and Harl who carried two small rodents in his hands.

"Your Highness, we think we've found where Arianne is." Harl gasped.

"Where...how?" Brian jumped to his feet and reached for his sword.

"We received these two little visitors earlier. We brought them here so the Montro could help us speak with them. Then he got all excited, was bouncing around, so we followed him to you." Loudos gave a garbled explanation.

Brian glanced at the mice then at Bunto. *Well, my friend, do they come from my queen?* His mind touched Bunto's.

Yes, she is in the temple. They know many ways in, but I don't know if any are large enough for men to travel.

Find one. Brian commanded.

Tell the man to place the small brothers down. They are not comfortable in his hand. Bunto instructed, and waited until Brian relayed the message to Harl.

Once the mice were on the floor, they ran over to Bunto and squeaked urgently. Bunto nodded, then turned to Brian. *They think they might be able to find a way in large enough for humans. When you are ready to leave, they will lead us to it.*

"Bunto confirms what you suspected, Harl. My mother is holding Arianne in the temple of the Dark Lady. The small brothers will show us a way in."

"Your Highness, you're wounded. Stay here. We'll bring her back for you." Loudos objected.

Brian winced as he pulled on his boots. The shallow cut along his ribs that he received in the fighting last night, was sore.

He glared at the other three men, "I'm going after her. You get the guards. Khane, I need some of the Mariner's Guild: Fighting men, men you can trust. Hurry."

Captain Khane bowed, "As you wish, my Lord." He backed out of the room.

Loudos frowned, "Your Highness, why are you sending for those thugs from the Mariner's Guild when you have the services of the king's guards? Why don't you use my men?"

"Your men are mainly for ceremonial use. They have not practiced as a group since shortly after my father died. Tonight, I need the sort of fighters that Captain Khane can provide."

"You blame us for the queen's capture." Loudos said flatly.

"I blame myself." Brian's answer was just as flat and he turned away to reach for his sword.

Harl watched the young king, then sighed, "Your Highness, is this wise? What will we do if you fall again into your mother's hands? Listen to Loudos. You stay here and let us go after the girl. Creating a situation where your mother could trap both you and the queen, would be stupid."

"Harl, Arianne and I swore a warrior's oath to each other. I must go after her. I have no choice. I need to believe that the fighting men of the guild and Loudos's guards are more competent than the temple warriors. You can stay here if you wish, but I'm going to get my queen. I will not let my mother rob me of my pride and self-respect. If I stay here, I've proven myself less than a man and no fit ruler for this land."

Harl nodded slowly, a worried look on his seamed face. “You are right. Alsia needs a good, strong king to repair the damage your mother has caused. Yet, I have a nagging fear deep inside me that no good will come of what you are planning this night.”

“Don’t wish us ill-luck.” Brian snapped. “We cannot avoid the coming battle. I don’t want to. We must stop my mother. All we can do now is to pray for a quick victory.”

Brian ran his fingers through his thick, green hair. “Harl, try to understand, I must defeat my mother and the darkness that she has brought to our world. Today, I am the champion of Alsia. If I fail, our whole world dies.”

Harl shook his head stubbornly. “That’s where you are wrong, boy. It makes no difference which side wins this battle; Alsia will lose. We need both aspects of the Mother in our land.” Harl warned.

“Harl, the darkness that my mother worships in her temple, is not of Alsia. It is a foreign creature that she called to her aid long ago. If we do not defeat it now, it will break away from her control and destroy this land.”

“Are you sure about that? You are taking the word of the little Lantian princess, and she knows nothing about our gods.” Harl protested.

When he saw the angry look on Brian’s face, he sighed. “I like the girl, but her people have no gods. She would not understand that the dark and the light are just two faces of our Goddess. Brian, you can’t destroy one without harming the other.”

Brian nodded. “Harl, even if my mother’s god was a true face of Alsia, I would still have to face her. I must bring the light back into the temple and the city of Kopol. We must restore the balance, Harl. That is the purpose for which I was born.”

“What happens if you get yourself killed? Who rules? Will Alsia be once more without a king?”

“If I die in this attempt, then Lord Orion rules with Athna, Mistress of the Light Mother, at his side. Nothing is lost and nothing is gained in this life. Where you have balance, you have harmony.”

“Damn it, Boy! I don’t want philosophy from you. I don’t care about all that rubbish. All I want is for your father’s son to rule this land. So far as I’m concerned, that’s the balance and harmony that Alsia needs.” Harl shouted.

Brian smiled sadly as he turned away. “If that is the harmony and the balance my land needs, then that is what the Goddess will arrange. I’m not so sure that you’re right, though. I am, after all, my mother’s son, and the darkness that controls her also taints me.”

Brian left the room with Harl trailing behind him. He heard the old sailor muttering under his breath, “Damn fool boy, talking nonsense. You are more your father’s son than you ever were your mother’s.”

In the courtyard of the royal castle, Brian found Loudos, Khane and three dozen well-armed mariners waiting for him.

Captain Khane stepped forward, “Your Highness, if you want to wait until tomorrow, I could bring you a much larger force. As it is, I had to take the guards off all the warehouses and ships just to get these few men."

Loudos shook his head, "I don't think we'll need more men if we can surprise the temple guards."

"I cannot wait until tomorrow, Khane. Arianne was alive when she sent the small brothers to us. However, we don't know how long it took them to reach the ship. I will not leave her to my mother's not-so-tender mercy any longer than I must."

They picked thirty of the best fighters and sent the other six back to their duties.

As they left the palace grounds, Bunto slipped quietly up to Brian. *I will go to the entrance of tunnels with you. I cannot go any farther, for the fur brothers and sisters are forbidden to fight humankind. Let me give you one last warning: The small brothers say you must not step in the thick, smelly water, for large, ugly things that eat meat live there.*

Brian and his party followed Bunto through the dark quiet streets of Kopol. They passed houses and shops tightly shuttered against the evils of the night. Eventually, they reached the waterfront where Brian was surprised to find the bars and inns also closed. When they reached the outskirts of Kopol, Bunto led them down to the beach and along the shore. None of them noticed the small shadow that followed them for a few miles before disappearing into an empty building.

*****

Arianne awoke suddenly from her trance. She felt as if a hot iron poker was being driven into her mind. With a small mental cry, she realized that Colsa, using the power of The Abomination, was invading her mind. It was not yet time to show her strength. Arianne wanted The Abomination itself to invade her mind before making a move.

She threw up barriers in her mind, and when they fell before that relentless heat, Arianne shut it down. She moved her consciousness deeper and deeper and still, Lady Colsa pursued her. Arianne poured her spirit, and all that she was, into the Life Stone. Her hands fell limply to her sides, and the stone flared bright pink, then disappeared back into her skin.

Immediately, her mother's voice flooded into her consciousness. *Wait, daughter, be patient. Soon, The Abomination will tire of Colsa's bumbling and take over the attack on your mind. Until then, rest and relax. You are safe here with us.*

"Where did she go?" Arianne heard Lady Colsa's voice cry. She was aware of everything that went on outside her body.

Colsa stared down at the inert body of the young queen. "I know she isn't dead. What did she do? How could she hide from me?"

The guards stepped back. "No one can resist the Dark Mother." Lady Colsa glanced at her people and sneered. "Fools! She is just a girl. By accident, she avoided my probe, but I will find her. When I do, I will drain her mind of all the information I need, then destroy her.

"Do you hear me? I am Colsa, High Priestess of the Dark Mother! No one may defy me and live. Bring her to the inner-sanctum. Let us see if she can evade the Dark Lady in the heart of her temple."

Lady Colsa turned and stalked out of the damp cell.

"Here, lay her on the altar and leave us. I'll call you when I'm through." Lady Colsa instructed, ignoring the look of relief on her guards' faces as they quickly left the room.

Colsa leaned over Arianne's still body, "What are you? Who are you to control so much power, while still so young? I should never have brought you to my land. Now that you are here, I must either control you or destroy you." Colsa frowned, "I should have been more suspicious when I saw how much you resembled the Feltan. Did your mother witch me? Was that why I ignored the possibility that you might have Feltan powers?" Colsa shook her head, "No, your mother has no such power and I would have known if she tried such a trick."

Lady Colsa stepped back from the altar, and stared at Arianne, "Let me warn you, Witch Child," she hissed. "Not even the Feltan can resist the powers of the one I worship. I will destroy you and my foolish son. When I am once again the undisputed ruler of Alsia, I will destroy your people."

The Lantians, listening to Colsa's tirade through their mind-meld with Arianne, laughed at the arrogance of the woman.

Now, My Daughter, Ilona whispered, *Move slowly to the edge of your consciousness. When Colsa finds you, we will show you what to do.*

Arianne obeyed her mother's command, and let her mind drift gently upward.

Colsa, her forehead creased with the effort she was making, suddenly smiled with triumph. "Now I have you," she cried as she found the faint traces of Arianne's thoughts.

Lady Colsa looked up sharply as a young guardsman opened the door to the inner-sanctum and broke her concentration. She snarled at the young guardsman, "What do you want? I told you, I don't want to be disturbed."

The young man stepped back to stand in the doorway, and shifted from one foot to the other.

"Well, don't just stand in one place like an idiot." Colsa snapped, "Why have you disturbed me? And I warn you, it better be important."

"We have just received word from our agent in the city that your son is on his way to the temple." The guard stammered.

"You disturbed me for that! Let him come. I am sure you and the other guards can make sure that he doesn't reach this room. Kill him if necessary. It no longer matters."

The guard bowed his head, "As you wish, Priestess." He turned away and closed the door behind him.

Lady Colsa drew a deep breath and clenched her fists. "I am surrounded by incompetent fools and traitors," she spat. "That stupid creature had to interrupt me just as I was about to find you." She hissed into Arianne's ear. "Now I have to start my search anew." Lady Colsa frowned. "What did you do to my son? How did you give him the courage to enter my temple? Not that it matters, I will let the Temple Guards take care of the young fool and I will concentrate on you."

Deep in the heart of the Life Stone, Arianne heard every word that Colsa said. She smiled. So, Colsa was being threatened on two fronts and her guards were worried. Good.

*****

Loudos stared at the round, dark opening, "Oh Goddess, it's the bloody, stinking sewer."

Brian nodded grimly, "Be careful in here. Bunto says creatures that will eat our flesh are swimming around down here."

Captain Khane sighed, "Why am I not surprised by that?"

Bunto's cold nose touched Brian's hand, *You will not be in these foul tunnels for long. Travel swiftly, King of Alsia. Time grows short. Your queen is in danger. May the guardians protect you.* Then, he faded into the darkness.

"Tie a piece of cloth over your nose and mouth." Harl told them. "This is an underground river that runs under the temple, so the smell shouldn't be too bad. The priests and priestesses use it to dispose of their waste. I had forgotten that my grandfather told me about it a long time ago."

"Do you have any idea how deep it is?" Brian asked as the men fumbled around for spare cloth to use.

Harl shrugged. “We have had two dry years in a row, so the water level should be low right now.”

The frantic squeaking of the mice from the mouth of the sewer, urged them to make haste.

Brian signaled it was time to move. They lit their lamps and began the short trip to the lower levels of the dark temple. Harl was correct: The sluggish river only reached their knees. Remembering Bunto’s warning about what might live in the dirty river, Brian and his men elected to wade through the narrow strip of thick mud running along each side, rather than risk the water.

They had not gone far when they came upon skeletons half buried in the mire. Brian and Loudos bent down to look more closely, then Brian straightened with a low growl. There were more than a dozen sets of bones, and most of them were children.

“My mother does not deserve to live.” Brian’s voice shook with anger.

“At least now we know what happened to the Sea Dreamers born among our people the last twenty years.” Captain Khane said bitterly as he gently touched a tiny skull on the muddy ground.

“When this is over, we will retrieve these bodies and give them a decent burial. I swear this. I also swear that my mother will pay for what she has done.” Brian stood, and walked grimly toward the lower level of the temple.

The men followed him, stepping carefully to avoid the collection of tiny bones strewn about in the mud, until they reached a set of poorly-maintained wooden stairs going up to the cellars of Colsa's temple. Cautiously, they went up the stairs, one at a time, until the entire group stood in the cellars. After silently removing the cloths off their faces, they searched for a way into the upper levels. Each of them suddenly felt a sense of urgency, as if some unknown force was urging them to hurry. One of the men waved his lamp signaling that he found the way up, and, as they reached the stairs, they were driven to their knees as a wave of terror swept over them.

*****

The Lantian minds deep in the heart of the Life Stone warned Arianne that soon, The Abomination itself would begin to probe her mind. When that happened, they would find out if the centuries they spent in research and training was worth anything at all.

Not yet, Arianne thought to herself, *I must wait a little longer.*

Lady Colsa's mind moved closer as she continued her search, until it was near enough for Arianne's consciousness to touch it if she wanted. Arianne held her mind still. She did not allow the slightest quiver to betray its position. Lady Colsa's mind passed over hers, stopped, then returned.

Arianne felt a chill of fear, which she quickly buried, as the other woman's evil laughter pierced her soul.

"So, Little Princess, I have found you and I will not let you escape from me a second time."

Colsa's thoughts reached out to enfold Arianne's mind. Arianne waited. Then, as Colsa's spirit confidently wrapped around hers, she twisted away and laughed silently at Colsa's growl of frustration. Out of the darkness of Colsa's mind, arose the horror for which Arianne and her people were waiting. The creature was impatient, frustrated by Colsa's inefficient attempts to bring Arianne's mind to it. The Abomination was hungry and sensed that this elusive mind was a source of great power. Greedy, dark tendrils reached out eagerly. The dark force wanted this mind, which was greater than any it had fed on since Colsa summoned it to this world.

Worship me, it sang sweetly. *I will give to you all that this one sought. I will give you power, wealth, eternal youth and beauty. Make me a part of your soul, and I will give you this world to rule.*

You have nothing that I want. Arianne answered.

Hate. The darkness whispered. *I will give you revenge against your enemies. You are so much stronger than this one. Look, I will destroy her for you.*

Arianne watched as shapes formed in the dark. She watched Colsa's body and spirit being tormented, tortured, torn apart by the darkness upon which she called.

Stop! Arianne's spirit cried. *I have no enemies and I reject hate. All living things deserve love and forgiveness, even this one whom you would torture and destroy. Colsa, mother of my mate, I forgive you all the wrongs done to me and to your son.*

Yes, our daughter speaks the truth. The whisper of sound came from the Life Stone and flowed into the heart of the darkness. A river of love and compassion rushed from the Lantian people to the nightmare that had followed them for centuries. *We do not hate Lady Colsa. We do not approve of her actions, and we weep for her people, but we will not see her destroyed.*

The darkness quivered and drew back from the emotions that the Lantians sent toward it. Arianne and her people pursued it.

Old enemy, dealing with this one has made you weak. You never tried to bargain with mortals before. They whispered. *Do you not remember us? Has it been so long that you have forgotten the people who created you? Will it bring you pleasure to know that we have never forgotten you? Ahh old friend/enemy, you know we have no need for the power or for the riches that you would offer.*

The dark being paused, then pulsed with fury, *I did not recognize you, I thought you were all dead.* It whispered, *your touch has changed. You no longer fear me. Now that I have found you, I will destroy you as I destroyed the rest of your people.*

Acceptance of its statement flowed from the Life Stone. *You have ruined our home world and followed us across endless miles of space. We were bred to fight you, but you tricked us and destroyed those we were to have protected. You have driven us insane.* The Lantian mind answered. *Now we offer you all that we have left. Take our love,* they whispered to the dark, *for you are the last link with our lost world. Feel our compassion, they sighed, Come, let us heal the damage we have done to you.*

Share our sorrow, they wept. *What we did was wrong, we have caused you pain, forgive us.*

The darkness writhed, trying to flee. Always, its victims faced it with horror, anger, and despair. It drew strength from those emotions. Now, the Lantians were depriving it of its main source of power. In its fear, The Abomination turned on Colsa and drew strength from her terror and pain as it slowly and cruelly tore her body to bits. The Lantian mind wept, not with horror, but with sorrow for the loss of a life.

The Abomination was not satisfied. It wanted more. The sustenance it gained from Colsa's death was not enough to protect it from the Lantians. Desperately, it searched for another source of strength. It found a large group of temple guardsmen and tore their bodies apart. The screams from the temple echoed through the silent night. Animals in the city howled and the humans covered their heads and cowered in their homes. The guardsmen screamed again, and the tormented sound opened the ground and brought rain from the heavens.

The pure blue-white light of the World Spirit flowed into the room. *Stop!* The light blocked the darkness so it could no longer reach outside. *We can no longer allow you to destroy our people at will.*

The World Spirit wrapped itself gently around the tortured being and whispered soothingly. *Come, join us and live in harmony with all nature. Be one with us. We will give you a new home where you will never again have to suffer pain or anger. We offer you peace, serenity, love, and acceptance.*

The Lantians and the land invited it, *Come to us, be one with us.*

With a scream of anger, The Abomination attacked the Lantian mind. The Lantians offered no defense. As they drew the dark into themselves, hundreds of individual Lantians died. Their life's essence cried out. Then, their memories and their power settled into the Life Stone, bolstering the strength of those who still lived.

The light of the World Spirit joined the Lantian mind. Together, they dispelled the darkness and tried once more to soothe the tormented being it concealed. In the temple, walls trembled and lights flickered. The surviving temple guards looked around in fear. The men at the foot of the cellar stairs struggled shakily to their feet.

"We must go on," Brian gasped. "My mother is doing something terrible and we must stop her. If we don't, she will destroy the whole city."

Beads of perspiration ran down their faces as they fought their way up the stairs through air thick as honey, and stepped into the main hall of the temple.

"I don't know what's causing the screams, but we'll never find out until we deal with these." Harl answered.

The temple guards, their swords drawn, rushed to deny Brian and his men entrance to the room where Colsa held the young queen. The fight for the temple was short and bloody. The temple guardsmen fought as if possessed and none surrendered. The floor was slippery with the blood of the wounded and dead when the last guard was finally dispatched. Now, the temple was strangely silent.

The sound of rain echoed loudly in Brian's ears as he and his men stared, their shock showing plainly on their faces, at the carnage around them. Of the thirty men Brian brought, only ten still lived, and only three could stand without help.

"Open the windows and the doors to the outside." Brian ordered as he staggered toward the rear of the room.

"Where are you going, my Lord?" Loudos, one of the uninjured survivors asked.

"To look for my queen," Brian's voice was weary.

"I'll come with you, Your Highness." Loudos volunteered. Brian nodded and they began searching for any trace of Arianne.

Bunto, who came running into the temple as soon as the doors were opened, brushed against Brian's legs. "This way. The small brothers have found our queen."

Brian spun on his heels and ran behind the Montro. When he opened the door to the temple's inner sanctum, he stopped in horror.

Arianne, her eyes closed, lay on the altar. She was so still that, for an instant, Brian thought she was dead, but then he noticed the slight rise and fall of her chest and breathed a sigh of relief. At the foot of the altar lay his mother's head. Blood seeped from one side of her mouth. Her eyes were open wide. The expression in them told something so terrifying that horror alone would have killed her.

"Sacred Lady." Loudos breathed as he glanced around the room.

Brian followed his eyes and swallowed hard. Blood dripped from the walls, which were gouged and chipped as if torn by hundreds of sharp claws. The Abomination had flung pieces of his mother's body carelessly around the room, and the scent of old, decaying flesh filled the inner sanctum.

Keeping his eyes on Arianne's still body, Brian dashed into the room and, ignoring the pain in his side, picked her up. Then, slamming the door tightly behind him, fled that place. He and Loudos moved to the others.

"Out, all of you. Let's get out of here." Brian said hoarsely.

Quickly, they helped each other to leave the temple, only stopping when they stood outside in the clean, refreshing rain falling gently on Kopol.

We are friends with our neighbors. The Feltan are no more and in a few hundred years, the Lantian and Alsian people will be gone. Our powers and our deeds will pass like a gentle breeze into the stories of myths and legends. New dangers will appear and new heroes will overcome. This is good. This is life as it should be.

Arianne, Singer and Queen

Chapter 19

Arianne lay unconscious for three days. She had locked her mind in the deep sleep of her people. The Lantians worked hard trying to salvage something of the being that stalked them for so many thousands of years, over so much distance.

In the end, the Dark One chose death instead of life in harmony with those it could not forgive. The sorrow of that battle left a deep scar on the spirits of her people. Arianne remained with her people for those three days, mourning the deaths of so many friends and family members. She immersed herself in the memories of the first Lantians to arrive on the world she knew as home. She learned of their fears and their disorientation when they found themselves stranded on an inhabited world. They showed her their desperate gratitude to the Feltan and their unmeasured sorrow over the betrayal of their trust by those same Feltan. At last, she said tearful farewell to them, as they, no longer needed, left the Life Stone, making way for others more recently deceased.

Mother, where will they go? Arianne asked.

They will join the Lantian Icina, Ilona's smile was evident in her voice. *We will still be able to speak with them whenever we wish.*

*****

Brian summoned healers from all over Alsia. They told him they could do nothing. Any healing must come from within. He must give Arianne a strong reason to want to regain the outer world, so he sat beside her the whole time she was unconscious. He held her hand and called to her mind with his, until eventually, she answered his summons. Arianne bid her people a temporary farewell, for she knew now that they would have many visits between them in the future.

"What should we do with it?" Brian asked as he and Arianne stood outside the temple of the Dark Mother two days after she regained consciousness.

They attended the funeral service for the fifty bodies, adults and children, that were found under the temple. Once the funeral was over, King Brian and Queen Arianne walked toward the palace.

"Leave it. The priestesses have returned, and they have few warriors left alive. Without your mother to lead them, they will cause no major problems. If you turn them away from here and they go underground, then we have no control over the mischief they could create."

"I would like to have this place destroyed," Brian sighed. "Leveled to the ground, and trees planted where the temple once stood."

Arianne leaned against Brian, "No, we must maintain balance. On the other edge of town is a clearing. Give it to Lady Athna to build a temple dedicated to the fair aspect of the Mother. Someday, another like your mother will rise and rule in this temple. Followers of the light must be near enough to exert some influence."

"The eternal circle, I would break it."

"That is not for mortal man to do, My King."

This was the first time Arianne had been out in the two weeks following the battle in the temple.

She shivered. Though she advised Brian against razing the building, she was uncomfortable in the area. She would never be at ease around this temple and its grounds. Rubbing her arms, she turned her back to the building and looked out over the sea.

"So many of my people died here," she murmured. "Anna, the uncle I never knew, my sister Patria, my father, and hundreds more."

Arianne touched her throat, where the Life Stone rested.

"I must return this to my mother so the families of those who died can say their farewells."

"We must talk about it, Little One." Brian said softly.

"I know, but not yet, and not here." Arianne walked away, leaving Brian to follow.

"Tonight, after our first public appearance in Kopol, I've asked Captain Khane to ready a small boat for us. I think it will do us both good to leave the city for a short time." Brian caught up with her and took her hand.

Arianne gave him a grateful smile, "Can we go to the forest?"

“If that’s what you want.” Brian gave her a quick hug and they walked back toward the royal castle.

“Do you know where the priestesses were hiding during the battle?” Arianne asked after a while.

“No. The next morning, they appeared and started cleaning the temple. They buried their dead, sent the bodies of my men back to the palace in a wagon, and cared for their own injured warriors.

“Loudos dealt with the young priestess who came to the palace with the bodies of our people. I would have told her to get her people and leave Kopol forever, but no one told me of their activities until later.”

“You have an advisor with a great deal of wisdom in Loudos. You’re lucky in your people. They are loyal.”

“Some of them are, anyway. Loudos, Khane, and most of Alsia’s lords,” Brian shrugged. “We won’t always agree, but they will let me know very loudly if they think I’m wrong.”

“Will the lords be at the ceremony tonight?”

“No, this is just for the leading merchants of Kopol and the Guild Masters. They will come to look me over and make sure that I recognize their special interests.” Brian grinned at her. “I’m glad you’re better. For a couple of days, I thought that I’d have to go through this ceremony without you at my side.”

“I thought that Kopol had no merchant class.”

"We have merchants. One of the noble houses or the temples charters them, they pay a small fee to their charter holders, and the rest of the money they make is theirs; except for taxes, of course." Brian grinned.

Arianne smiled at him as they entered the palace grounds, and, still holding hands, made their way up to their room. Harl told her that the first three days after the battle at the temple were rough on Brian. He didn't move from her side, and his kindness touched her deeply. Later that night, Arianne stood silently beside Brian and watched the people of Kopol as they came to swear their allegiance. She felt no contempt for them. One must do whatever is necessary to stay alive, and the citizens here survived. Still, she wondered how many of those taking oaths now would remain loyal if the Dark Mother should rise again.

Now that they knew their king was no monster, the fat merchants of Kopol were happy to acknowledge him. How long, Arianne wondered cynically, before they would be cursing his name. She mentally shrugged. The cursing would probably start first tax time. Such was the way with kings and their subjects. Still, she would watch and listen closely. Too much corruption had flourished in Kopol for it all to disappear in a week, or even in a year.

"Ready?" Brian whispered as the last of the leading merchants left the palace.

"Yes." Arianne smiled up at him.

The ocean was calm. A small breeze whispered over it, touched their cheeks, and moved on. "I'm glad you thought of this. Kopol was beginning to get me down."

Brian nodded as he steered the small boat, "It's not a happy town. I hope that will change in the years to come."

Arianne leaned back, trailing her hands in the water and watching the stars. "They won't thank you for any changes you might make. The people of Kopol are proud of their city. I doubt they'll see any reason to change it."

Brian stared thoughtfully ahead, "You could be right. The merchants seemed very unhappy with several small improvements I mentioned this afternoon."

"Tell me you didn't mention the new temple to them."

Brian turned to her in surprise, "Of course I told them. They have the right to know what is happening to their city."

"What was their reaction?"

"Well, they didn't act too happy about it, but they'll come around."

Arianne grinned, "I wouldn't bet on it, my Prince. They probably think that one temple in their city is more than enough. When you raise their taxes to pay for the new temple, they are going to have lots of complaints."

Brian's answering smile was full of mischief. "I fear you are right," he said in mock sorrow.

The sun was an orange ball on the horizon when they finally beached the boat in the sacred cove and walked into the forest. Arianne found the pool she had bathed in that first day and lay beside it with a sigh of contentment. She turned and smiled at Brian as she reached up and touched the spot on her throat where the Life Stone nestled.

"Ready to talk about what happened to you in the temple?" he asked, brushing her hair back from her face.

"Not really," she broke off a blade of grass and chewed on it thoughtfully. "I don't remember very much. How did you find me?"

"The small rodents you sent to Captain Khane told Bunto. They led us into a hidden entrance. What happened between you and my mother?"

"She wanted to attack Lantia, at least that's what she said."

Arianne rolled over onto her stomach. "Brian, I think your mother must have been mad. Lantia was no threat to her. She acted as if she believed, because I had taken Alsia from her, she had to take Lantia from me."

"I'm sorry."

"Why? It was not your fault and you were not in a position to do anything. My people can take very good care of themselves. I knew you would come for me if you were still alive. All I had to concentrate on was surviving the fight with your mother and The Abomination until you reached me." She paused as the implications of that trust settled in both of them. "As for The Abomination, we tried to save it, really we did. We were responsible for its existence. We would have made it a part of us. We would have loved and healed it."

Arianne sighed, “The darkness had been with it too long. Rather than accept the light, it chose to destroy itself. My people will grieve its passing for a long time.”

“It was your enemy.” Brian objected.

“Not at first, not until the actions of my people forced it to become dark.”

“That was a long time ago.”

Arianne smiled sadly, “Both Lantians and their enemies have long memories.” After a while, Arianne asked, “Brian, are there two separate races in Alsia? I mean, are the noble families a different race from the others?”

“No.Why do you ask?”

“Well, something your mother said about the common people not being used to the change started me thinking. Then, when I remembered how the Lords at Athna’s accepted you without a second look, I just wondered if that was the reason.”

“In the beginning, when we came from the sea, the sea mother gave each family a leader. To make sure that the right person would always be the heir, she put a mark on the true heirs. We’ve never made a secret of it. Since none of the ruling families live in Kopol, it’s possible that the people here aren’t familiar with the change.”

“Is Loudos a member of a ruling family?”

Brian looked puzzled, “Yes he is. Why?”

“What happened to stop his change?”

Brian sighed, “It’s an old story, his mate died of a fever before his change was complete. He left his family and joined my father’s guard.”

"So that is one of the reasons Colsa went after me. She did not know that your change had been completed. If I died, she could still rule Alsia."

"I hadn't thought of that, I should have, we were lucky things turned out so well. I underestimated my mother's ruthlessness at every turn. What made you think two separate races lived on Alsia?"

"The difference in coloration."

Brian laughed, "Arianne, are all Lantians alike? No two trees are identical, nor are any two fishes the same, yet are they not all trees and fishes?" He placed his arm next to hers, green-brown and bronze. "Are we not both humans?"

Arianne smiled sheepishly, "I thought I might have found the reason for your mother's behavior. If she wasn't of the nobility, then a lot of them would have been very upset when she married your father."

Brian shrugged and lay next to Arianne, "Our kings marry sea dreamers, no matter where we find them, so that's not why my mother went bad. She was born with darkness in her soul, as was I."

"We are all born with darkness in us. It's up to us to make sure the dark does not overwhelm the light. You will always find people who go willingly into the dark's embrace."

"So, you have avoided answering my question once again." Brian whispered as he pulled Arianne close to him.

"Brian, I really don't remember all that much. I remember your mother probing, searching for my mind, and I remember retreating deeper and deeper into myself. Then, I think my spirit, seeking sanctuary, entered the stone. Once there, I became a part of the whole Lantian mind. The Icina of this world was there as well.

"I waited there, not for your mother, but for The Abomination to appear. When your mother found me, I twisted away from her..."

Arianne frowned. "Brian, the sadness and the horror will stay with me for as long as I live. I felt so much compassion for the dark that even the memory hurts. The Abomination kept showing me pictures of it destroying your mother, and my people and I cried out for it to stop. Then I became completely one with the Lantian mind, and can remember no more. I vaguely remember hearing screams and praying they were not mine.

"Then I had a sense of aloneness, an overwhelming terror, and an awful smell." Arianne shuddered. "Smoke. I still wake up at nights with that stink in my nose. What was it?"

"I don't know. I do know that the one my mother worshipped, destroyed her in the end." Brian's eyes were bleak. "I'm sorry you had to suffer through all that, Little One."

"I am not little, and I didn't suffer that much. Besides, as I keep telling you, none of this was your fault. If we are going to assign guilt, then it belongs to my people, for we created The Abomination."

They were both silent as they let the pain and the bitterness pass.

Arianne leaned her head on Brian's shoulder and asked softly. "Was there anything else you wished to discuss, my King?"

Brian smiled down at her. "Well, now that we're the rightfully crowned king and queen, we owe our subjects an heir. Don't you agree? Over the next few weeks, we should give serious thought to that matter."

"I thought we already had." Arianne blushed.

Brian gave a shout of laughter. "No, we were just making sure you knew all the basics. From now on, though, we'll work very hard at creating an heir."

Arianne turned away, "And after we have given your land an heir, then what?"

"Arianne, you are my mate for life. No one else will be the mother of my children. Not all marriages are like your family's. I promise not to turn to another woman as long as you are alive."

Brian paused, then smiled, "Word of a warrior." He added.

Arianne laughed as she slid her arms around his neck, "Word of a warrior, My King?" She asked.

When he nodded, she relaxed.

"I accept. After all, one should never question a warrior's integrity, especially not when the warrior is a mighty one, like my husband."

"Arianne."

"Mm hm?"

"Shut up."

The glade was silent then. Even the small night animals held their breath. A soft green mist descended on the island as the magic returned, and for the time being, peace reigned in the land of Alsia.

Aruda Hanna Wilson comes from a culture strong in the oral tradition of story telling, and brings that experience to her writing and tells ripping good stories.

Mrs. Hanna-Wilson was born aboard a U.S. Coast Guard cutter in international waters to Bahamian parents. She was raised on a small island in the Bahamas and married an American sailor. Forty years and three children later, she has decided there is no such thing as normal. Because of her life experiences, she brings a unique view of the worlds she creates into her stories.

"Normal," she states, "Is a word used to describe a non-existent status."

She is an award-winning short story writer who graduated from the Writer's Digest Short School of Short Story and Novel Writing.

After her husband retired from the Navy, they moved to Pensacola, where they have lived for the last twenty years. During that time, she has worked part time for a major department store, a grocery store, and as a paper carrier before she finally settled into writing full time and being surrogate "Mum" for young adults from Florida to Texas.

www.ingramcontent.com/pod-product-compliance
Lightning Source LLC
LaVergne TN
LVHW020528100826
845148LV00010B/1381